CHASING LIBERATION

Also by Doc Ephraim Bates

Chasing Black Ice
Chasing Revenge

CHASING LIBERATION

Boom!!...Killers.

SERIES BOOK #3

Doc Ephraim Bates

Golden Alley Press
Emmaus, Pennsylvania

Golden Alley Press
37 South 6th Street
Emmaus, Pennsylvania 18049

www.goldenalleypress.com

Golden Alley Press books may be purchased for educational, business, or sales promotional use. For information please contact the publisher.

Printed in the United States of America

Chasing Liberation: Boom!!...Killers. series book #3 / Doc Ephraim Bates.

ISBN 978-1-7320276-7-1 print
ISBN 978-1-7320276-8-8 ebook

Back cover photograph of the author ©Starr Belle Photography

Cover design by Michael Sayre

10 9 8 7 6 5 4 3 2 1

To the memory of my brother Bobby

Damsel in Distress

Not terribly long ago – just about eighteen months or so – Kinley Devereaux and Harper Rowe were highly-esteemed and highly-requested government wetwork agents. The two men had carried out copious assignments that had either directly or indirectly stopped potential coups, possible wars, and likely terrorist attacks. The results of their efforts were as immeasurable as a mother's love for her children. Nonetheless, due to the nature of their work, their heroics remained as anonymous as the assassins themselves. Still, to the select few that were "in the know," Harper and Kinley were like rock stars.

But that was some six seasons ago.

Six seasons that, at times, seemed more like six years.

For Kinley Devereaux, the last eighteen months of his life had become an infinitesimal struggle for some semblance of existence. Presumed dead by most, he lived underground and off the grid as he bounced from city to city, country to country, and continent to continent while working as a shadow assassin to whoever could contract his services through the necessary channels. When he was not doing wetwork jobs, he was busy tracking and keeping a watchful eye on his friend, Harper Rowe.

Harper Rowe, who for the last year and a half had also been keeping his movements frequent and unpredictable as he traversed the globe performing various acts of assassination and kindness to whoever might find their way into his always welcoming world. However, unlike Kinley Devereaux, Harper was not presumed dead by anyone. Harper Rowe was just a wanted man.

And not just any wanted man.

No. He was the *most* wanted man. At least, that's what it said on most of the "WANTED" lists that hung in almost every state and federal building throughout the United States of America.

Harper Rowe was wanted for questioning in connection with the assassination of the former United States Secretary of Defense, Paul Michaels. A high-ranking government official had been shot dead in a very public forum, and someone needed to be held accountable. Since Harper Rowe was the one that every eyewitness had identified as the man talking to the Defense Secretary at the time of the shooting, that meant Harper Rowe was the closest thing they had to a suspect or, at least, a person of interest.

Seemingly endless government officials in innumerable interviews had consistently said, "Harper Rowe is not a suspect. We just need to ask him about the events of that day. But with his constant avoidance of cooperation with this investigation, it does make him look more and more culpable for having had some kind of hand in the shooting death of Secretary Michaels."

Harper was not stupid. He knew the game, and he knew all too well the nature of the interrogation that he would be given even if he were to voluntarily turn himself in. It would not be pretty, and it would not end until he told them what he knew, or there was just nothing left of him to interrogate – or torture – anymore.

With that being the case, it would seem that the wanted man would have been keeping an extremely low profile all this time – out of sight, out of trouble. Yet such was not always the case with Harper Rowe. From time to time and in very random yet very public spots around the globe, he would make almost farcical appearances. He wanted to get the attention of his pursuers. As he liked to put it, "I don't show my face so that they'll know where I am. I show my face so I'll know where they are."

So, for the last eighteen months this was the life for Harper Rowe and Kinley Devereaux: cloak and dagger, hide and seek, living in obscurity, and no place to call home. Oddly enough, though, it was not the assassination of the U.S. Secretary of Defense that had actually set in motion the downward spiral that had taken over these two men's lives. In fact, the assassination of Paul Michaels was more like the exclamation point at the end of a very loud, forty-eight hour-long exclamatory sentence.

The true genesis of Kinley and Harper's extended dilemma lay with one person and one person alone: Tara Madison.

Alias: Black Ice.

Some might argue that the official beginning to the duo's tribulations was when Harper went snooping around the cordoned off area of Doug Hopkins' mansion when it was clear that the area was not to be snooped around.

That's a bit of a technicality.

If Black Ice had not been burglarizing the upstairs safe of the Hopkins' residence, then Kinley and Harper would never have caught her in the act, chased her, accidently killed a bunch of government agents, let her get away, tracked her down in Mexico City, met the amazing and ebullient Laurie Chase, got shot at, lied to, double crossed, used, betrayed, shot at some more...none of that would have ever happened. Harper would eventually try to explain it to Kinley by comparing the situation to when Eve went to the Tree of Knowledge in the Garden of Eden. Of course she had been warned not to eat from it, but she would have been fine – if not for that snake.

From the moment that Tara Madison – Kinley and Harper's personal Garden of Eden serpent – had entered their lives, nothing had been the same.

However, one of the bright spots that came out of that whole fiasco was the flight that the two men had taken from D.C.to Mexico City. On it, Harper Rowe had begun a relationship with the woman that had served as their flight attendant, Taralyn Tharp. It was the first time that Harper Rowe had ever met her, and as far as Kinley Devereaux knew, it was also the last. For as much as the elder of the duo had tried to keep tabs on his sometimes-partner, always-friend, he was finding out that Harper had been able to sneak a few things past him – one of which was his continued relationship with Taralyn Tharp.

It was an abrupt revelation. Kinley was taken aback, not so much by the news that Harper had, indeed, had further contact with the beautiful Taralyn. No, the real shock to Devereaux's system was that, now, a year and a half later, he found himself sitting just two tables away from her at a nondescript café in Rio de Janeiro in the wee morning hours of January 3rd, listening to Harper Rowe telling him that Taralyn needed their help.

The two men went back and forth at each other about this particular situation for some time. Harper tried to get Kin to calm down. Naturally, Kin was concerned by the fact that Taralyn was employed by the United States government – the same United States government that currently had Harper at the top of its "Most Wanted" list, and the same United States government that had dispatched a faction of agents to the Rio area that very night in hopes of apprehending the fugitive.

"And what, so far, have you gathered about what she wants? Also, are you sure she wants both of us and not just you?" Devereaux asked curtly.

"Yeah, I'm sure. She needs us," Harp confirmed, "and she needs us to help her with an extraction."

"An extraction? From where to where?"

"From Prague to...parts unknown, at this point."

"Czechia?"

"Yeppers."

"Bit of a hop, skip, and a jump from here, isn't it?" Kin seemed concerned by this, which, in turn, concerned Harper.

"Yeah, cab fare might be a little steep."

"Any idea on the danger factor?"

"Somewhere between a little more dangerous than crossing the road and slightly less dangerous than peeing on an electric fence."

"I don't know, man," Kinley said with some trepidation. He began to look around the place anxiously. "Where the heck is the help staff around this joint, anyway?"

"We're just gonna listen, bud," Harper reminded him. "That's it. If either one of us doesn't like what she has going on, we're Donesville on the whole thing."

"I get that. I do."

"So, what's the hang-up, chief?"

"It's just...I mean, you do understand that Kelly Campbell is trying to clear your – our – name, and you bring me a woman that I don't really know, and she's looking to put us in play with a situation that we don't really know that much about, and in a place that certainly doesn't give us any sort of a home field advantage either."

"A girl that looks like that and has the job that she does and has the connections that she has – come on, bud – she could have had her pick of people to assist her on this, but she came to us. I figure I want to at least hear what she has to say. Don't you?"

At that moment, the waitress came by and set two glasses of ice water in front of the men and asked in her native tongue, "May I take your order?"

"You speak Portuguese. Tell this waitress that I want the greasiest, fattiest, worstest for your heart cheeseburger they've got in stock." Dev was still apprehensive. "And then tell your little heathen friend that...I'll listen."

Harper smiled up at the waitress and said, "*Um hambúrguer de queijo grande para meu amigo.*"

"*Muito bom e para o senhor?*"

"*Tenho a feijoada, por favor*," Harper responded, ordering a traditional Brazilian dish of beef, black beans and rice, and a coentro sauce.

The waitress nodded, smiled, and walked away as she jotted down Harper's order on her little waitress notebook.

"Did you get me the burger?"

"No, I got you the cheeseburger with extra fat and extra grease."

"What did you order?" Kinley asked.

"The house special."

"So...what are you thinking?"

"I'm hoping that they don't get chintzy with the sauce. It's good stuff."

"No, not that," Kinley said, a bit irritated. "You want to invite your friend over here while we eat, or do you want to take our food over to where she is? I mean, it seems kinda rude to make her sit over there by herself while we eat."

"Might be kinda rude to eat in front of her, though, don't ya think?"

Kinley shrugged. "Look, I don't care what you do. I'm just tellin' ya right now that when my food gets here, I'm going to eat it. I'm dangerously hungry, and sometimes when I get this way my royal manners take a hike, and my primal instincts for red meat take over. That's my position on the matter. The ball's in your court now."

"I'll go get her," Harper informed his friend, then stood up and retrieved Taralyn back to the table. She gave a strained smile as she timidly approached and extended her hand toward Kinley. He could see about six different signs that told him this woman was scared to death. He courteously stood and shook her hand. "Taralyn," he greeted her as congenially as he could.

"Mr. Devereaux," she responded, some of the tension leaving her face.

Harper pulled a third chair up to the café table, and the slender woman took a seat. He resumed his position across the table from his partner, to Taralyn's right. "How was your flight in?" he asked her.

"Oh gosh, so very long. I took a sedative to help me sleep, but it didn't really seem to kick in until I landed here in Rio."

"So, you're a little sleepy?"

"Oh, I'm fine. I'm sure it's helping to keep my nerves from—" She stopped in mid-sentence as if she was catching herself before she let out some deep, dark secret. The tension suddenly returned to her face and swept over her entire body. Harper put his hand on her shoulder in an attempt to assuage her fears. Even Kinley – who was never the touchy/feely type – felt the need to reach out and grab her hand reassuringly.

"You're among friends here," he said. "You don't have to be so afraid."

"But I am," she replied, her gaze fixed firmly on the table in front of her. "And I've seen and done a lot of things before and never got scared, but this—."

"Then tell us why we're here, sweetheart, and let us help you," Devereaux said in a comforting voice.

"Because we can help you," Harper assured.

The shaken women took a few seconds to gather herself. Kinley produced a handkerchief and handed it to her. She dabbed around her eyes, made a quick pass under her nose, took a few deep breaths, and handed the satin cloth back to Kin.

"Thank you," she said. She started telling the story of how her best friend in the whole world, Eliska Lukasik, had suddenly called her from Prague about two weeks ago. She said that she needed help, and she did not know who else to go to because she was afraid. Taralyn told Kinley and Harper how she dropped everything and flew straight to her friend to find out what was wrong, and how upon arriving in Prague, Eliska told her about a young mother and her little daughter, Anezka and Jana Bucek, that had seen way too much of a horrible situation.

According to Eliska Lukasik, the mother and daughter had both been privy to a sex trafficking operation that was going on at a local children's home. Taralyn thought at first that she could handle the situation. Take the mother and daughter, give them a makeover to change their appearance, and then get them out of town to someplace safe.

However, something was not as it seemed. What should have been a simple snatch-and-grab relocation had turned into something much more dangerous. Seemingly, somebody that was involved in the sex ring had some major stroke in the Prague community because the city went from its typical distinction of being open and friendly to going on complete shutdown in just a matter of hours.

"They initiated a manhunt like they were going after some sort of savage serial killer who had been on the loose for weeks, when in reality it's just some innocent, helpless, scared woman and her precious, little daughter. I'm telling you right now," Taralyn looked back and forth between the two men as her voice hit a serious tone that equaled that of a nun under oath, "I don't know what they will do to them if they catch them. That's why I came to you two."

Harper could see the intense angst on Taralyn's face. He then looked at Kinley, only to see that his head was buried in his cell phone.

"What are you doing?"

Kin looked up from his phone. "I'm checking to see how bad we're screwed," and immediately looked back down at his phone.

"He's looking to see how badly we're screwed," Harper repeated. He looked at Taralyn and explained, "We use this scale. It goes from 'Couldn't possibly ever die ever' to 'No pulse. Crapped your pants. Peed yourself.' And I think that we are somewhere around 'We found out that Ronald Reagan was our surrogate father' at this point."

Taralyn looked at Harper with a totally confused looked.

He squeezed her hand and smiled. "We're going to help you."

Kinley grunted.

Harp looked at him. "How bad is it?"

"We're probably going to need a change of underwear." Kin passed his cell phone over to Harper as he said, "I was sort of hoping that maybe she was exaggerating a little bit, or perhaps had misread the situation somehow. But that does not seem to be the case...at all."

Harper took possession of Kinley's phone and began reading the news story that he had pulled up. The story backed up everything that Taralyn had said. It also instilled in Harper and Kinley a great deal of uneasiness about the entire situation.

"Taralyn, do you mind giving me and my young comrade here a few minutes to discuss a couple of things?" Devereaux asked the woman.

"Yes, of course," she answered. As she stood up from the table, she gave Harper a worried look, but he was quick to return it with a reassuring look of his own.

Devereaux waited until Taralyn was out of earshot before saying to his friend, "When did she contact you about this?"

"Yesterday afternoon," Rowe replied. "When we had gotten back from picking up John Watkins and his crew at the old airport hangar."

"Did she tell you that this is what was going on? That an entire Eastern European city was looking for this woman and her child, and that she needed us to help her get them to some sort of safe haven?"

"No, she did not."

"So, this really is the first time you're hearing about what she wants from us?"

"Yes, I told you it was."

"And you haven't given her any sort of false promises about us definitely helping her with this mess, right?"

"What are you getting at, dude?"

"Well," Kinley said, bobbing his head slightly, "I don't think this is a job for us to be getting into, ya know?"

"Why wouldn't we?"

"It's just too dangerous. It's little side jobs like these that can get us sidetracked from the big picture and end up landing us in some serious – if not perilous – situations."

"And what exactly is the big picture again?"

"What I told you earlier about Kelly Campbell having a seemingly very legitimate way for you and Chase and me to clear our names so that we can finally go home again."

"You said that it was going to be a couple of days before that happened, though," Harper pointed out.

"Well...yeah."

"So, let's kill some time by doing this then."

Harper handed Devereaux's phone back to him.

"I just don't think we should, Harp. I mean, this is some real danger here."

Harper shook his head in disbelief at his buddy's comment.

"Real danger? What would you call what we just walked away from about three hours ago? We just took on about two hundred soldiers of one of the world's biggest bad guys. And you suddenly think that helping a woman and her child flee a city of millions to someplace – anyplace – safer is more dangerous than that?"

"That is a situation that is one hundred and eighty degrees different from this situation. Taking out del Fuento's goons and his compound is something that had been planned out far, far in advance. Not to mention, we had some serious back-up and a lot of weapons to assist us in all of that. That was us doing what we do best: killing bad guys. This is not what we do. We aren't Harriet Tubman and William Still or any of the heroes of the Underground Railroad. We don't just go to people who are looking to escape a bad spot and usher them to safety. It's not like we just show up to a tenuous situation, and everything, magically, turns out okay."

"Well," Harper started to say as his gaze drifted off into deep thought for a moment.

"Well, what?"

"Well...it kinda does."

"What?"

"When we're together, bad situations seem to turn out okay... no matter how screwed up it tends to get, stuff always – and I don't mean to insinuate that we have magical powers – seems to work out okay. Mexico City, that little stunt we pulled in Atlanta a few nights ago, those terrorists at the nightclub, taking out—"

"Harper, I see where you're going with this, but—"

"But nothing, Kinley. You heard what Taralyn said. You read that story on your cell phone. That woman and child, they, lit'rally, have nowhere to go, and if we don't help them their goose is as good as cooked. Yeah, with our help it's going to be difficult, no doubt, but without our help it is just going to be downright impossible for those two to survive this."

Kinley looked at Harper with disgust because he knew he was right.

"Yeah," Devereaux sighed, "I don't suppose there's much of a point in you and me being able to go back home if we have to live with the guilt of those two on our conscience the rest of our lives."

"Not unless we're looking to while away the hours of our remaining days drinking bad memories off of our minds...which I, for one, do not intend to do." Harper drew in a deep breath, looked at his friend, and said excitedly, "C'mon, man. Let's go save some lives and have a good time doing it. What do you say?"

This time Kinley shook his head in disgust at himself for being so easily swayed.

Before he could answer, Harper cut in, "I can tell by that look on your face that you're disappointed in yourself. Don't be. I have come to accept that this is what you and I do now. We help people."

Devereaux reached across the table and grabbed Harper by the wrist. He gave him a hard look and said, "No. This is not who we are, and this is not what we do. I really, really, really need you to wake up from this little fairy tale world that you seem to have embraced, and please join me back here in reality." He let go of Harper's wrist but held his intense look before asking, "Can you do that for me?"

"And you need to stop denying the fact that you and I are natural born heroes. Sometimes people need our specific set of attributes, and we show up and deliver. Just like we did with Chase, just like we've been doing to stay afloat for the last year and a half, either separately or together."

"You know what you have? An apparent attraction to dying young. Let me tell you who wants to die young, Harp. Nobody...ten seconds after they're dead."

Suddenly, the two men heard a throat being cleared next to them.

"Did I come back at a bad time?" Taralyn asked.

Devereaux looked up at her and smiled. "Absolutely not. Harper and I were just discussing how we're going to help you and your mother-daughter friends." He looked at his buddy. "Weren't we, Harper?"

Harper looked up at Kinley, a bit caught off guard by his friend's statement. Then he looked up at the beautiful Taralyn. "If the man says we're working on a plan, then you can bet your sweet cheeks that is exactly what we're doing."

She pulled a chair out, sat down, and smiled as she asked, "So, what are you guys coming up with so far?"

"Gonna need to make a few phone calls," Dev admitted. "How long is the flight to Prague?"

Laurie Chase, Big James, and Diego

Laurie Chase drove her van through the weed-infested, broken pavement surrounding the abandoned warehouse that she had been calling home for the last year and a half. She pulled into the hidden parking area inside the structure, placing her vehicle out of sight from any unwanted observers that might be flying overhead or, for some inexplicable reason, trespassing on her property.

The night could not have gone better. Laurie was all smiles as she entered the warehouse. For the most part it was dark, but she saw lights on in a distant room and saw Diego sitting in one of the chairs, waiting for her return. Making her way back, she said to Diego, "We kicked some ass tonight, didn't we?"

Hearing a voice behind her, she practically jumped out of her skin.

"Got that right, we did." It was Big James.

"Holy—" Laurie spun around to face the big man.

"Ease up there, Hawaiian noises. Don't go bangin' on the bongos like a chimpanzee."

"You scared the crap out of me. Why are you here?"

"Eh, I had to drop off the little man, plus I had to use the facilities. So I just decided to stick around and wait for you. Besides, did you think I was going to let you and Diego have all the fun of putting del Fuento in his grave when he returns home?" Big James smiled.

"Really? You think that I am going to have fun killing another human being? I think you must have me confused with some sort of psychopath from another one of—"

Laurie broke out into uncontrollable laughter.

"Sorry, I tried. Heck to the yeahs I am going to love bringing this piece of butt mud all the way to his knees before I watch him breathe his last breath...and I will be pleased as punch if you can help us out with that."

Big James threw his beefy arms around Laurie and gave her a friendly squeeze. Looking at Diego, he said, "C'mon, li'l man, get on in here and get some of this."

Jeb Crool and the Close Call

3:15 A.M. BRST

United States Special Agent Jeb Crool walked down the Rua Visconde de Pirajá in Ipanema, the main drag that ran through the busiest part of Rio de Janeiro. He was headed toward the Espeto Carioca, a night club that had fallen prey to a probable terrorist just two nights prior.

The attack had been a complete failure. The only lives that had been lost were those of the terrorists themselves, due to a supposedly small group of men and women that had caught on to the strike and headed it off. Lives were saved and some bad people were taken down and out of this world.

Some of the club's patrons had filmed the brief incursion with their cell phones. One of these videos had been posted online, catching the attention of Special Agent David Baldwin, sidekick to Special Agent Jeb Crool. The video clearly showed Harper Rowe as one of the heroes that had thwarted the gunmen. That is what had set in motion the events that had Jeb and his team in Rio at the moment.

Jeb did not have any real directions to the club, but he figured that he would know it when he got there. Until then he was more than content to take in Rio's warm winter air and see what the city's wee morning hours had to offer.

And he was hungry.

Crool told himself that at the first decent-looking open restaurant that he came to, he would get something to tide him over for the next few hours. He hated working on an empty stomach. True to his word, the first place he came to – even though he could not pronounce the name of it – was decent enough and open enough for his liking. Inside he went.

He would never know that, had he only walked another two hundred feet, he would have found a quaint little 24-hour café named Boteco Cabidinho. Inside he would have found a friendly atmosphere, reasonable prices, great food...and Harper Rowe and Kinley Devereaux at the genesis of their next great adventure.

GETTING OUT OF RIO

Kinley stood outside of the café for almost twenty minutes talking on the phone to the pilot that had flown him and Harper into Rio just two days prior.

Kin and the pilot – an Irish chap named Bairre Dolan, who was out of Belfast but called the world his home – had already set a time to fly the two assassins out of Rio and into Caracas, Venezuela. When Devereaux had made the initial travel itinerary for the job in Rio, he had little to no clue how things were going to play out. But he figured if things got too screwy, getting himself, Harper, and, if necessary, Laurie Chase to a country that had no extradition laws was about as safe of a play as he could make at that point.

Now, however, it was a completely different ball game. Kinley had to see what Bairre could do as far as getting him and Harper to Prague.

How much?

How long?

"Aye, *mo chara*, it's your dime, brah. You tell me where ya want to go and I take ya there. I get to do wha' I love, and you get to pay me." Bairre's thick Irish brogue highlighted every word that came through Kinley's phone.

"I don't guess you offer a frequent flyer discount, do ya?"

Laughter on the other end was followed by, "I don't suppose ya pay double time, do ya, brah?"

"So, besides money, what do you need?"

"I've got no issue wif takin' you an' your li'l friend from outside o' Rio all the way into the Czech Republic, lad, but there's just no place in tha' town for me ta land. Ya goin' to 'ave ta fin' a place outside o' Prague for me to land ya."

"Give me some time. Call ya back in ten."

Kinley ended the call, gave a worried look to no one in particular, and returned to the table where Harper and Taralyn were sitting.

"How familiar are you with what's outside of Prague?" Devereaux asked Taralyn.

"Me? Not very. However, I do have a best friend that's lived there for a very long time, and she could probably tell you whatever you needed to know."

"Sooner rather than later I'm probably going to need to talk to her, if that's okay. Did you drive here or take a cab? To this café, I mean?" Dev followed up.

"Since I had no idea of what was going to happen once I left the airport, I thought the smart move would to be renting a car. I figured, at the most, I would only be using it for a day. Plus, I get all kinds of Triple-A discounts wherever I go...that whole stewardess-flight attendant thing. The car's parked right across the street. Why? Do we need to leave?"

"We do. I mean, we can give it a few minutes, but yeah, we have to go," Kinley said. "Thing is, Harper and I can't even remotely think about going to a national airport. The kind of eyes that are looking for us right now in this town? Flying commercial's just not an option."

"Because you're wanted," Tharp stated the obvious.

"Fact of the matter is, Harper and I didn't set out to be criminals. I mean, once upon a time we were considered the good guys. Now, though, you mention our names, and it's a three-ring circus."

"We want to help you," Harper picked up where Kinley left off, "but you've come to ask for the help of wanted men, and when it comes to our situation there are a lot of restrictions. Hoops to jump through. A whole bunch of duck and cover."

Kinley sat back in his chair. "Bad criminals...get killed. Good criminals...get caught. Decent criminals make a point with what they do...and then get caught just to make sure the point isn't missed."

"Still, the really great criminals," Harper came in, "are nothing more than legend and the stuff that ghost stories are made of. Kinley and I intend to stay legendary ghosts long enough to clear our names."

"You are going to help me, aren't you?"

"Wouldn't dream of not helping you," Kinley answered obligingly, "but if it's all the same to you, we are going to need a lift to an airstrip about twenty minutes from here. Easy to get to, and it's gonna make our lives a whole lot simpler. With the kind of heat that we have on us right now, we can't afford to show our faces at a major traveling hub of any sort. After you drop us, you can take your rental car back to the Rio airport here in town, catch a flight to Prague, and Harper and I will meet you there…" and Kinley paused for a moment to do the time zone math, "around ten o'clock tonight, Prague time. Sound good?"

"So?" Tara asked, a bit uncertain.

"So, we should probably go now," Harper was quick to explain.

Taralyn looked around nervously. "Are there people here now that are looking for you?"

"Not so much that you would notice, but soon, yes."

"Sooner than you'd think, actually. Go get your car," Kin said flatly.

The woman stood up from her seat – two parts cautious, two parts knowing who she was dealing with. Without a moment's hesitation, Tara casually walked out of the café.

Kinley looked at Harper and said, "I need you to keep your

mouth shut and listen. Can you do that, bub?"

Harper looked around as if he thought he was on some sort of game show. "Am I missing—"

"I need *you* to keep your mouth shut."

"Seems like you really mean it this time."

"You're her boyfriend."

"Whose?"

Kinley took a second before he responded. "Hers. The woman that just left here. You're her boyfriend."

"No," Harp responded, oblivious to Kinley's point. "I mean, I think she's—"

"You're her boyfriend!" Kinley stated strongly. "If she didn't feel some strong connection toward you, then she would've never come calling on the two of us – more to the point – she would've never come calling on you."

"I mean, I like her and everyth—"

"You're her boyfriend, and we are going to go along with whatever she says, okay?" Kinley made no bones about it. "Ya wanna know why?"

"Umm, because you think she's really hot and you want to bo—"

"Because she trusts you," Devereaux came clean, "and because she's going to get us out of here. We'll help her – if we can – but push is coming to shove, Harp, and we need some help to get where we need to be."

"Which is...where?"

"The heat is coming down, brother, so anywhere but here will do."

"You seem rather intent on that now more than ever. Reasons?"

"Just one: while you were mentally undressing and re-dressing Taralyn in a Raggedy Ann outfit, U.S. agents walked into this restaurant. If they were worth half the salt that you and I are, they would have seen us by now...because I'm definitely eyeing up the sorry lot of them. Since they haven't, I think we should take good advantage of their negligence and get the Ram outta Dodge. Ya feelin' me, Cap'n Kirk?"

Harper nodded in understanding. "Beam me up, Scotsman...and let's meander our way out front. Our chariot awaits by now, I'm sure."

Kinley threw a fifty on the table, and he and Harper got up, straightened their shirt tails, and discreetly made their way out of the café.

"That chariot line...seems I've heard it before."

Harper shook his head innocently. "Not from me. I never use the same line twice."

"Oh, is that right, Mr. 'See ya 'round downtown'?"

"Hey...that's not a line," Harper stated, inhaling deeply the Rio night air. "It's a catch phrase."

CHASE REVEALS HER PLAN

It was late. They should have been sleepy. At least, a bit drowsy.

No. They were wide awake and talkative, and they were talking about Tito del Fuento's return to Rio. Big James Gray was asking the questions, Laurie Chase was answering them, and Diego was sitting by and smiling.

"So, what's our next move? Do we just sit here and wait for him to take off from where he is now before we start to do anything?" Gray asked.

"For now, yes," Chase answered. "Don't you think we've done enough already for one night?"

Big James gave a sheepish look and shrugged his shoulders.

"Oh, no, you don't," Laurie said to him. "Don't you even think for a minute that just because you and Diego got slightly averted from the overall plan that you didn't hold up your end of the deal."

"Kinda feels like that." James looked at Diego who, at this point, had stopped smiling. The little man looked at Laurie and agreed with his large cohort, "Ehh, eet kinda duss a leetle beet."

"Well, stop it, both of you. Do I need to remind you about that piece of the plan that was the most important part of our attack? Remember? The part of the plan that had you guys knocking those P-3s out of the sky so that the rest of us could do our jobs and see the attack through to its entirety?"

"Well," Big James began slowly, "I'm not gonna speak for Diego, but that's only because I don't know the Portuguese word for concussion."

"*Concussão*," Diego informed him quickly.

"Right. That."

"Oh my Lord," a startled Chase put her hand to her mouth. "Do you not remember anything about tonight?"

"I have a vague recollection of knocking those birds out of the sky. I remember loading roughly a million dollars into the back of my van even though I think I could have had more. I know that we are here in your mountain warehouse talking to each other. Everything in between those finer plot points has kind of a Scooby-Doo flashback, funhouse mirror sort of sketchiness to it."

"So, when you say that it kinda feels like you didn't do enough tonight, you don't actually remember what you did or didn't do, do you?" Laurie probed.

"No, I don't suppose I do."

"Here's what you two need to remember – and whatever else comes into your head later on be damned – you two are heroes. If not for what you did tonight, we wouldn't be here."

Big James nodded slowly, still looking somewhat confused. "I guess I can get along with telling that story to my grandkids."

"Okay?" Chase looked to Diego.

"Ehh, you might need to remind me again een the morning, but okay." And the smile returned to the little man's face once again.

"In that case, let's get back to going over what we do next with finishing off Tito," James Gray recapitulated.

"We wait, and we watch. I don't know how long it's going to take for word of what happened tonight to get to Tito in Amsterdam, but when it does, I know that he will be flying back here as soon as he can. Once he logs his flight plan, it will come up on the FAA site which I already have pulled up on that computer over there," she pointed.

"And that's because you guys know his FAA flight ID number, right?"

"Exactly."

"What if he changes it?" Big James wondered. "I mean, at some point he's going to figure out that somebody is messing with him in a very real and dangerous way. What if in his paranoia he swaps out flight ID numbers?"

"Ees too much paperwork for heem. Eet would take heem many weeks to do that."

"Right," agreed Chase. "Plus, with the laundry list of people, cartels, and authority types that he'll be going over and over in his head, I'm pretty sure he's not going to think for a moment that the FAA is the one that's out to get him. Right now he is feeling grief-stricken, angry, and confused. In other words, the man isn't thinking real straight. Once he finds out that his compound has been reduced to rubble and ash, he's going to want to get back here as soon as possible...and we'll be waiting for him when he does."

"I'm sure whoever it is that informs him of his place looking like the *after* picture of the Alamo will probably let him know that he won't be able to land on his own runway. How will we know where he's going to be touching down?"

"His flight plan should give us all the information we'll need about that. It would be great if he landed at Rio International. With all the typically heavy passenger traffic in and around that hub, we'd have easy pickin's as far as being able to grab him and his family. But I'm thinking that he'll probably land at another private airstrip. Regardless of where it may be, we'll have plenty of time to track down his arrival destination, do some quick recon, and construct an effective plan of execution."

"And in the interim?"

"Well, it would definitely seem like you and Diego have some sort of concussion syndrome occurring inside those craniums of yours. And if that's the case, then you most certainly do not want to go to sleep. You may never wake up again."

A smile spread across Big James' red goateed face. "Can I go play in your rec room then?"

"Absolutely," Chase said pleasantly. "Go have a ball, big boy."

"Yes!" The big man clapped his hands together and shot up out of his chair like a jack-in-the-box. "Come on, Diego. Let's go get un-concussed together."

Final Instructions to Tara

Taralyn drove the two assassins, as per Kinley's directions, toward the out-of-the-way airstrip where they would be meeting up with Bairre Dolan.

She had rented a sporty little 2015 Dodge Dart SXT. A blue one.

As the case always seemed to be, Kinley sat up front in the passenger's seat while Harper was stretched out in the back.

"You ever notice that we never drive, Kin?" Harper asked from his backseat position.

"Do you even have a driver's license? I mean, I know you've got about a million and seven fake ones, but do you have a real one? A legitimate one? From anywhere?"

Rowe pondered the query for a moment. "Well, technically," he finally said, "they're all legitimate in the aspect that if I were to get pulled over with any of them, no suspicions would be aroused. However, do I have a current driver's license with my name on it from one specific country or another? No, I do not. Mostly because I don't have a legitimate address in any country or another. What about you?"

"My license from when I lived back in D.C. is still active, but it's not like I could ever use it." He looked at Taralyn. "You have a license, right?"

"Yeah, they don't let you rent a car without it," she reminded him.

"Is it a U.S. issued license?"

"It is."

"So, which state is it from?"

"New Mexico. I have lived there for the last three years."

"Santa Fe area, by any chance?"

"Las Cruces, actually."

"Oh, very nice. I've made a few trips to the area myself. Incredible views of nature with those mountains," Kinley recalled.

"Were you there on a mountain climbing expedition?" Tharp asked.

"Umm, no, I wasn't. I was there to kill someone."

"And there's the buzzkill," Harper smarted off from behind them.

"Which is fine," Dev said, "because we need to get back to the matter at hand. We need you to get on the phone with your friend in Prague," he addressed Tara, "to see if she can find a similar landing spot outside of the city for us to, number one – land on when we fly in – and number two – fly out of once we get the mother and daughter out of harm's way from the city. Without that information, we won't even be able to land in that area, much less get any sort of rescue operation underway."

A worried look came across Taralyn's face. "I don't know if she will be able to find that kind of information. She's just not that kind of person. I think she barely knows where the regular airport in Prague is located, and she only lives about ten minutes away from it."

"Well, somebody is going to have to do something. Because without a private landing area for us to come in on, we may as well not even take off from the one we're getting ready to go to," Harper said.

"We won't be able to take off from the one we're headed to," Kin corrected. "My guy isn't going to go flying blind into the Czech Republic with no concrete destination at which to land. He just won't do it."

"I can call her," Tara sighed, "but I really think that it might be an exercise in futility."

"You know anyone that might have some sort of knowledge of the area, Harper?"

Harper leaned back in his seat, tilted his head back and closed his eyes. "Let me think for a minute." He started to hum abstractly which he was prone to do when he was deep in thought. At first, the humming was not too bad, but after some thirty seconds of it droning on, it had Tara giving Kinley a look of irritation.

"Don't worry. This is his normal, deep-thought spiel."

"Worry isn't exactly what I was going for wi—"

"Yes, I do!" Harper shot forward on the car's backseat. "Kendrick Arthur."

"Kendrick Arthur?" Devereaux repeated. "Who's he?"

"A guy I met about two months ago in Johannesburg. He's a map maker. He travels all over the world, researches places, and gets the area onto an updated map. If anyone would know where there is an outlying airstrip around Prague...I think he could be our guy."

"Yeah, but can you get hold of him at this particular hour of the night is the question."

"Johannesburg is six hours ahead of us here so that should make it just before 11 a.m. there. Yeah, I think we've got a shot." Harper smiled.

"Get on it then."

Harper was already scrolling through the contacts on his phone. For as handy as the contacts he had on his phone were, they also served to be a sad reminder to him of all the people that he had to leave behind due to his recent fugitive lifestyle. "Found 'im!" Harp shouted. "Aaaand"—he hit the green send key on his phone—"calling him now."

Kinley looked over at Tara.

"Is he usually this obnoxious when he hangs out with you?"

"Easily," Tara smiled. "Although I don't think he has ever done any deep thinking when he hangs out with me because that whole humming thing he was doing? Could definitely do without having to hear that again."

"Well, the good news is that Harp does deep thinking about as often as he—"

"Kendrick Arthur, m'man!" Harper said from the backseat of the Dodge Dart. "Harper Rowe here. How ya doin', my friend?"

Arthur laughed. "Ahpuh Rowe, seems ahn eternity, my brutha."

"Well, geez, Kendrick, an eternity seems like a really long time. Has it been that long?"

More laughter. "Ooll right, Ahpuh, maybe not an eternity, but fuh sure a mont' of Sundays."

Harper laughed before admitting, "Yeah, it's been a minute."

"Ah, fret not, my brutha. You are coollin' me now. What can I do fuh you here, in dis, your time of need?"

"I need some information. I need to know what you might be able to tell me about any private airstrips outside of Prague – at least, in that general vicinity."

"Let me hov a few moments to check my coord'nits in dot area, old friend, and see what we're workin' wit. Can ya hang on for a minute, *boet*?"

"For this? Yeah, I can hang on for a minute or two, but don't dally. Pretty sure my international calling plan charges me by the nanosecond." Harper heard Kendrick put the phone down and begin to make all kinds of racket rummaging through cupboards and filing cabinets. He heard the Gauteng native muttering under his breath, "Pardubice, Plzeň, Prague...Aha!"

Kendrick picked the phone back up. "I've found what ya needed, Ahpuh," he smiled as he began to unpack his map of the Prague area. "Let me see if I can find duh onsuh you seek."

Kendrick Arthur set the phone down again and spread the map

out on the table in his office. Placing paperweights on each corner, he ran his index finger across the surface of the geographical chart, scanning for a private airstrip that his friend might be able to utilize.

Harper waited quietly for about thirty seconds before Kendrick Arthur noisily picked up the phone. "Yes, I hov found what you needed, Ahpuh Rowe. I can confirm an airstrip dot will potentially give you what you'll need. It is positioned to duh nort'wist of the city along duh waterway dot is known as duh Elbe River. Ah you familiar with duh Elbe River, Ahpuh?"

"The Elbe River? Yes, absolutely. Which side of the river is the airfield on? Are we going to have to cross over?"

"Oh, nah, nah, nah. Duh airfield is on duh near side of duh river, I assure you. I will text duh coord'nits to your phone. Dot will be duh simplest way to do all of dis."

"Yes, that'll be tops. Text those coordinates to my phone, and I will be indebted to you like Willie Nelson to the IRS, my brother."

"Think nothing of it. Godspeed to you and your friend, Ahpuh. Sending duh coord'nates now. Cool me if you need any other favuhs, my bru."

"Thank you, Kendrick," Harper said appreciatively. "Keep it dark, my crazy chine."

Harp hung up and leaned forward to address Kinley.

"I got what we needed, chief. My guy is sending the coordinates to a landing field just outside Prague. We are golden."

"Like a ticket to Willy Wonka's chocolate factory," Devereaux agreed.

Taralyn caught Harper's glance in the Dart's rearview mirror. She smiled at him, shook her head and said, "It's always just that easy for you, isn't it?"

"Oh, I don't know. Sure, in the middle of the night, I might be able to find a guy that can tell me where I can locate all of the hidden airstrips of the world, but ask me to find a late night Chinese place when you're jonesin' for some shrimp toast at two in the morning after a Saturday night house party, and I'd more than likely come up with a grand total of bupkis."

"Okay, Tara, you're going to come up to a dirt road in about half a mile. It'll be on your right. Turn there," Kinley instructed. "Obviously, it's not well lit and hard to see, so you'll want to start slowing down soon."

Taralyn eased her foot off of the accelerator. "I just wanted to thank you, Mr. Devereaux, for being a part of this – for helping me. In all honesty, I wasn't sure that you would agree to be in on this at all, but I just didn't know where else to turn."

"Yeah, Kin, I must admit that for a second or two back there at the café I was thinking that you weren't really going to be on board with this whole operation. What made you change your mind?"

"Eh, it's like she said, who else was she going to get at this juncture. Besides, it's a little kid and her mom against an entire metropolitan authority. What kind of chance do they have? I just figured with me and you on their side that it kinda evened the odds a little bit."

"Well, whatever your reasons," Tara said, "I love you for it. Both of you. I just...there's no other way to express my appreciation. Knowing what you've just been through, the fact that you would turn right around and do this for me...I just love that you would do this."

"Ya hear that, Kin? She loves us," Harper grinned. "Just for the record, I love ya, too, big guy."

Kin turned in his seat and gave Harper a cold smile. "And just so you know...love...is not nearly a strong enough word to describe how I feel about you right now."

"Yeah. I get that," Harper nodded. "So, now that we've gotten our true feelings out on the table, perhaps we should go over the next few steps in our plan of action."

"Oh shoot!" Taralyn exclaimed suddenly. She slammed on the

brakes and jerked the wheel hard to the right. Granted, the car was not going very fast, but with the suddenness of the braking and the hard turn of the steering, Kinley grabbed onto the dashboard, and Harper wrapped his arms around his head to protect himself as he slid wildly across the back seat.

"Sorry," Tara said, righting the car onto the aforementioned dirt road. "I know you told me that it was coming up, yet somehow it still sneaked up on me. Sorry. You guys okay? This is the right road, right?"

"Yes, this is the right road," Kinley said, releasing his grip on the dashboard. "You'll want to stay on this road for what will seem like forever. It will just be about two miles in reality. You'll hit pavement again at some point. That will be your indicator that you're getting close to where we need to be. Of course, I'll realize that, too..."

"Pretty sure we were getting to the point where you were going to tell the two of us what was getting ready to happen next. You know...the plan."

"Tara, you'll drop us off up here. You'll go to the regular airport, turn in your car, of course, and catch the first flight back to Prague. Will your friend be meeting you when you land? What's her name again?"

"Eliska Lukasik, but she goes by Ellie," Tharp answered. "And, yes, I'll give her a call when I'm getting ready for takeoff."

"When we have the details of where we'll be landing and the time of our arrival, Harper can text you the information...and you can come pick us up?"

"Absolutely."

"It's a long flight. Hopefully, it will be long enough for me and the kid to come up with some sort of plan to get that woman and her daughter out of the city and to some place safe."

The three of them felt the bumpiness of the dirt road give way to pavement. The airfield came into view, and just about the time the trio saw the airplane in the distance, Harper's phone went off indicating that he had received a text message.

"Is that your map guy?"

Harper checked his phone for verification. "Yes, it is. He sent the coordinates for the airfield just outside of Prague."

"Go ahead and forward that to me and Tara. That way she'll have it when she lands, and I can forward it to our pilot so he can start getting things prepared for our takeoff."

While Harper did that, Taralyn pulled the Dodge Dart to a stop some fifty yards shy of the tail of the plane that Kinley and Harper would soon be boarding. "So, I guess this is goodbye for now," she said, looking at the two men gratefully.

"For now. We'll see you, hopefully, later on today...about half a world away," Kinley said as he leaned over and gave Taralyn a quick hug.

"Five time zones and just over 6100 miles," she said as she returned in kind.

Devereaux leaned back after a quick second and looked at her. "Ya don't say."

"When you're a flight attendant for as long as I was, all that stuff just kinda gets imprinted into your brain," she smiled. "I'm a blast at parties."

Dev smiled back. "I'll leave you two to say your see ya laters. I'm gonna go talk to the pilot. See you on board, Harp."

After Kinley made his exit from the vehicle, Harper and Taralyn did the same. Standing next to the rental car, Taralyn looked at Harper and smiled yet again. "It's really good to see you again, Harper. I wish it was under different circumstances."

"Almost everybody that has ever met me the last, well – ever – pretty much starts that sentence the same way. The good news is that, barring any Amelia Earhart shenanigans from our pilot or yours, we should see each other again really soon."

Tara laughed and gave him a tight hug. "Thank you," she said softly.

"Don't thank us yet. We haven't done anything."

Taralyn pulled back from the embrace. "You're showing up, aren't you? And I'm pretty sure that once upon a time you were the one that told me that showing up was one-third of every plan."

"Yes. Yes, it is. Showing up, getting the job done, and not dying: the only three steps that any plan ever needs. I mean, any more than that and things just get confusing and unnecessary."

"Do you guys have any idea about what you're going to do to get Jana and Anezka out of the city?"

"No, not really, but like the man said, it's a pretty long flight."

"And once you show up, get the job done, and don't die, do you have any plans for where you'll go next?"

"Actually," Harper said, rubbing a light sheen of sweat that had formed on the back of his neck, "I think we're headed back the U.S."

"What?" Taralyn said, shaking her head so quickly it sent her long brown locks flying. "Why would you do that?"

"Someone that Kinley and I know told him that she may have found someone that can clear our names in everything that happened with Mexico City and Paul Michaels."

"Do you trust this person?"

"I trust Kin, and he trusts her, so, yeah. Plus, I know enough to know that this may be our only chance to finally set the record straight."

"I worry about you, Harper. You're one of the only good people that I have ever met in this life. What if this is all a trap? If something were to happen to you...I don't know. I mean, can't you just let Kinley go and sort this out?"

Harper smiled. He appreciated the amount of concern that his friend had for him. He appreciated that after everything he had been through over these last many months, there was someone else in the world that cared for his well-being. He looked Tara in the eyes and said, "It's not that I can't, sweetie. It's just that I won't."

Before she could object, Harper said, "But that's later. This is now. You need to scoot so you can get out of here and back to Prague in time to pick us up when we land. We'll take this one step at a time. I don't care about the U.S. and getting redemption for something that wasn't even our call in the first place. This...this...is what we have decided to do, and we are going to do it well."

"I know you will." She grabbed his hand and squeezed it tightly for a moment. "You know, you gave me that stupid phone so long ago. I've looked at it at least a hundred times between then and now, and I always knew you'd be there for me. When this is over, I don't know what I'm gonna do."

"Ah, that's the great thing about burner phones, they just keep making them. There will be a million more after today."

"True, but there's only one you, Harper Rowe." With that, she got into the Dodge, shut the door, gave a quick wave and drove off. He watched until she drove out of sight, then turned and double-timed it toward the plane to meet Kinley.

A new adventure was afoot.

NIGHT CLUB INTERROGATION

While Jeb Crool had decided to walk to Espetto Carioca, Agent David Baldwin and the rest of the team of agents that had made the trip to Rio had taken a more practical means of transportation to the crime scene: two rental cars.

Baldwin was interrogating the owner of the club with the aid of a translator named Milfred Wales. Things were not going well.

"What did he just say?" Baldwin asked the interpreter.

"You want the literal translation or my interpretation of what he just said?" the interpreter asked Baldwin.

"I'm going to do you a favor and tell you to please never ask that question to my boss. He's on his way here, and he's pissed. So, it's okay for you to ask me that because I'm not looking for a reason to kill someone 99.4% of the time, but...he is. So, that being said" — Baldwin pretended to flip through his interrogation notebook — "let's just assume you didn't ask that question. You just give me the literal translation, and I'll do the interpreting on my own."

"You need to stop screwing around and find the real bad guys," the interpreter said brashly and smiled.

"What?"

"Hey," the interpreter put up his hands in protest, "that is the literal translation of what this man just said."

"Really?" Baldwin asked. "Then maybe you can ask him who the real bad guys are."

The interpreter turned to the man, Adalberto Palmeiro, owner of Espetto Carioca. "*Quem o compra muito ruim?*"

"What did you just ask him?" Baldwin was looking over his own shoulder every chance that he could. He was done dealing with this interpreter and wanted Jeb to show up now more than ever.

"What you asked me to ask him. I asked him who the real bad guys were."

"And what did he say?"

"Well, you never gave him a chance to answer, boss," the interpreter smarted off. "Maybe you should just back off and let me do my job, huh?"

Suddenly the front doors to Espetto Carioca slammed open and Jeb Crool walked in. To most that were in the establishment, he looked pissed.

To David Baldwin, Jeb looked surprisingly levelheaded and calm.

"How we doin', Dave? Get anything yet?"

Baldwin turned to the interpreter and said, "One day, when you're still stuck in the mail room and wondering why your life is just a corn nugget on a piece of donkey dung...it will be because of what is getting ready to happen next." Baldwin shook his head sympathetically because he really did know what was getting ready to happen next.

"Why so down, Dave?" Jeb asked, walking towards Baldwin. "Who's gvin' ya lip and not wanting to cooperate, buddy?"

"Well, I hate to be that guy, but..."

"Oh, by all means, Agent Baldwin, please...be that guy. Who is it that is bugging you tonight, my good man? You know I need answers, and I've got no one better than you to sniff out someone that can give them to me." Crool walked right up to Agent Baldwin, and in the softest of voices said, "Point a finger, give me a smile, and walk the rug on up outta here, Agent Baldwin."

Baldwin hated it when Jeb got all theatrical on the job. Nevertheless, he knew that – theatrical or not – Jeb was the best interrogator that he had ever worked with and probably ever would.

He also knew that if Harper Rowe was going to be caught, it had to be real quick and in a hurry.

So Agent David Baldwin pointed at Milfred Wales.

"This one?" Crool double-checked.

Baldwin nodded and walked away. He knew what was getting ready to happen, and he had seen it enough. Leaving the scene for a quick nap while it all took place seemed like an extremely inviting idea. Nevertheless, Dave decided to stick around.

Jeb Crool walked up to his target.

"How's it goin'?"

"Fine," came the flat, unimpressed answer from Wales.

"Good. That's good. I'm afraid I didn't catch your name upon entry. I'm United States Special Agent Jeb Crool," Jeb said as he extended his hand toward the translator.

"Milfred Wales," was the cold response. He did not bother to shake Jeb's hand.

"Alright," Jeb smiled, taking his hand and patting the interpreter on the shoulder. "Here's the deal, Mr. Wales. I don't like to put timeframes on things, but I need to capture a guy that was needing to be captured about 187 seconds before I asked you about said guy. You get the reference, right....Mr. Wales? The 1-8-7 seconds? And what it means?"

The interpreter just laughed quietly and shook his head, "I *really* do not know what it is that makes you Washington types come down here and think that you can just waltz onto a scene and start—"

Jeb grabbed the interpreter by the throat, then kicked him in the groin.

"Really?" Jeb laughed, "Ya don't know?"

The interpreter fell to the ground. Jeb Crool turned to the club owner and put his gun up to the man's forehead. As clearly as he could, he asked, "Where is Harper Rowe?"

The club owner went on in his own language saying all kinds of things that Jeb Crool could not understand. Jeb pulled out a picture of Harper Rowe and showed it to the man.

"Big James...he tell you. Big James...he here earlier too," Palmeiro said nervously.

"And who is this Big James? What is he going to do for me?"

"He know your man," said the frantic owner. "He pay me to lose footage of incident, and he—"

"Where's the footage?" Crool cocked the pistol.

"I don't know," the club owner trembled. "Erased."

"Ya sure?" Crool asked coldly. "Because here's the thing. I'm going to pull this trigger if you don't give me something. I mean, why on God's green earth would I let you live?"

Jeb hesitated for just a moment before he answered his own question, "Oh that's right. I won't let you live. So tell me what I need to know...or else." Then he pointed to the gun he held in his right hand and explained, "Just in case you're unsure as to what 'else' is"—he waved the gun around—"this is else."

The club owner just gave him a scared, confused look. "Erased." Then the man made the sign of the cross, looked upward and began muttering in Portuguese what Jeb could only assume was some sort of prayer for mercy.

"Hey, interpreter guy," Jeb said to the man that was still writhing on the floor in pain from the previous groin shot, "I'm gonna need you to get back up here and tell this guy that his security footage isn't erased. He may think it is, but it's not. I got guys here that can retrieve stuff like that from the bottom of the ocean if need be. So, get up here and find out where his security room is so we can go to work."

"Screw you," the interpreter moaned.

"Hmm, well, that wasn't very kind. Believe me, ya little jerk, getting kicked in the chads is gonna feel like a picnic when put in comparison to my shooting you in the kneecaps. Now suck it up, tell one of these *cholos* to get ya a bag of frozen peas from the kitchen, and get up here and find out where this guy's security room is."

When the interpreter made no attempt to move, Agent Crool moved the gun away from the club owner's face and aimed it at the interpreter's right knee. "You literally have 2.9 seconds until I count to 3, and then I am pulling the trigger."

"Oh, good Lord," the interpreter whined as he rolled around on the floor, "you are the worst person that I've ever met."

"He'll just take that as a compliment," Baldwin said, reaching down to give the interpreter a hand up. "Having worked with Jeb for the last several years, my advice to you at this point would just be to do what the guy asks, and things will go a lot smoother."

The interpreter gave Dave a perturbed look and said, "You couldn't have given me that advice earlier?"

"I could've," the agent shrugged, "but you were being a dick to me, so I decided to hold off on that particular shred of advice for a bit." Baldwin helped the man up from the floor and onto his feet. "But I'm tellin' ya now."

Crool's patience was running short. "Hey, can we step it up a bit, chief? I'd like to try to get out of here before next New Year's Eve gets here."

"Fine, fine. What do you want to know?"

"This guy"—Jeb pointed to the club owner—"security room. Where is it?"

"*Onde é a sala de segurança, seu palhaço?*"asked the troubled and tortured translator.

The club owner gave him a cross look before he answered a bit begrudgingly, "*Pela cozinha e suba as escadas de trás. A porta da esquerda é a sala de segurança.*" Then he spit in the linguist's face.

The move proved to be the breaking point for Milfred Wales. He wiped the saliva from his face, raised his fist, and took a wild swing at the club owner. Agent Baldwin quickly grabbed Wales from behind and secured him in a guarded hold.

Jeb Crool grabbed the club owner by the shirt collar, then drove him some five feet backwards into the nearest wall. Jamming his his left forearm up into the throat of the man, Crool held him tightly against said wall.

"Congratulations, ya dumb jackhole. That's assault," Crool explained. He turned to see that a handful of the local police were already moving in with their weapons drawn and their cuffs ready. Jeb looked at Milfred Wales. "Did he tell you where that security room is?"

"Yeah," Wales said, jerking away from Baldwin's grasp, "He told me."

Jeb removed his forearm from the club owner's throat. "Take this piece of fecal matter out of my sight before I get my own ass locked up." As he walked over to the interpreter, Jeb pulled a hand-kerchief from his pocket and handed it to the guy. "For the life of me I cannot figure out why that guy spit on you and not on me."

Milfred snatched the hankie out of Jeb's hand and wiped his face clean of any residual sputum. "I don't know. Must just not be my day." Wales held the kerchief up to his mouth, discharged a rather large amount of spew into it, and handed it back to Jeb.

"Nah, you keep it," Crool declined. "I'm a bit of a germaphobe."

"I hate to break up this little love fest," Baldwin interjected, "but I think there's a security room that we need to get to."

A Prayer with Wings Attached to It

"So we've no real idea how we're going to get this mother-daughter duo out of Prague, do we?"

"No. Not yet, at least," Kinley Devereaux answered his friend's question. "But it is like I told your girlfriend, Taralyn. It's a long flight. We'll come up with something."

"She's not my girlfriend," Harper corrected, "but I appreciate the assumption."

"Then why are we here? I mean, seriously, if she's not some sort of love interest of yours, then why are you doing this?"

"Oh, dear John, please don't tell me that you're one of those people that think men and women can't be just friends. One of those people that thinks that if a man is doing something for a woman, there has to be some sort of sexual circumstances involved. That's not you, is it?"

"Is that your inference?"

"Is that what you're implying?"

"Depends on what you're insinuating?"

"It just sounds like your presupposition is that I'm something of a male whore doing jobs that are insanely dangerous just because I'm getting a piece of tail."

"Okay," Kinley said, holding up his right hand just inches away from Harper's face. "Number one, that's not even close to what I'm saying. And number two, your use of the term 'male whore' is absurd as the term 'whore' in and of itself refers to the female gender. Feel free to look it up."

"Yeah, I get that. Point taken. I guess you'd classify that under the heading of oxymoron."

"And I'm not making the connotation that you're a gigolo – which would be the male equivalent to a whore – but even you must admit that your proclivity for bandying from one woman to the next is at a level that even Larry King would find somewhat astounding."

"Okay, okay, I see where you would get the notion that I'm bedding down a lot of the opposite sex for personal gain, but I assure you that you are wrong. Have I used a decent amount of women to help keep myself discreetly out of the public eye and hidden from the overall view of the big brother we know as the American government?"

"I'm pretty sure we both know the answer to that particular interrogatory would be a resounding yes."

"Correct, but while we jump to that specific conclusion, I would just like to point out that the term 'used' does not axiomatically mean that I was sexing up said women. In reality," Harper continued, "I was actually procuring their accommodations and favors with acts of kindness and generosity...and listening. Which, as it turns out, most women seemingly appreciate more than a proper rogering."

"Ya think?" Devereaux asked with a furrowed brow.

"Seemingly."

Kinley pursed his lips and stroked his chin, pondering Harper's words.

"I digress, however. Getting back to your original question: Why are we here? Well, I am here because about a year ago Taralyn did me a favor of major proportions that might only be equaled by that of Sydney Carton in Dickens' *A Tale of Two Cities*, with the exception being that Taralyn is still among the living. But I'm sure you get my point."

"I will as soon as I google it," Kinley said.

"I try not to rank my friends or put them in some sort of pecking order. The term 'best friend' makes me shudder just a bit because then I have to wonder if the person that said that has a second-best friend and a third-best friend, and is the whole thing like a car race where their friends are vying for some sort of pole position."

"Your point being?"

"My point being that I don't have a lot of people that I can call a friend. I can, lit'rally, count them on the ten fingers on my two hands. But just because when I rattle off your name when I happen to be pointing at the ring finger on my right hand as opposed to the name I say when I am pointing to the index finger on my left hand... it doesn't mean that you have any lesser or greater importance to me than any other friend I have in my life. Just like I don't have a best finger that I favor over another finger, I don't have best friends because all of my friends – to me – are the best."

"Still not seeing where you're going with this."

"I just don't want you to feel slighted when I say that Taralyn is a friend, and that is why I'm doing this. It's for the same reason that you're here. You can dress up your reasoning all you want, but in the end you're here because I'm your friend, and you know that I can't do this without you."

"I would just like to go on record as saying that I am officially not slighted. Because, say what you will about her being your friend and me being your friend, I'm just grateful that you and I never joined the Mile High Club like you and she did. I don't care how close we get, Harper...we ain't never gett'n' that close. Ya dig?"

"I do dig. I just feel bad that the only part of the relationship that Tara and I have that you know of is that part on the plane ride to Mexico City. Honestly, that's why I went and tracked her down.

To apologize for the '*wham, bam, thank ya, ma'am*' actions I took on the plane. Not gonna lie to ya, Kin, when we were on that plane ride I really had the feeling that we were gonna die."

"I know what you mean. I kinda get that same feeling whenever I spend too much time with you which, oddly enough, is usually about ten seconds after we're together."

"Joke all ya want, but I think what I'm really trying to tell you, my friend, is that while Taralyn is also my friend...that doctor... Mercedes Lara?"

"Merc? Yes."

"I think she might be more than a friend. I think my feelings for her are different."

"Think? Or know?"

"Know."

"And you're basing this on...?"

"What we do, I know we're in the right. What we did with Paul Michaels, I knew we were in the right. So, when you told me that we had a chance to go back to the States and clear our name, the first thought in my head should have been 'Yes, let's do this so I can finally go home again because we aren't the bad guys in all of this.' But instead my first thought was 'Maybe I can see Dr. Lara again sooner rather than later and find out if what happened in Rio can happen in other places, too.' And I did have to ask myself if that was what I was really thinking...and I...I really was."

"Funny how the realization of being human can be so fulfilling and so unsettling all at the same time. I get what you're saying, though, because I had the same thoughts about Laurie once I accepted that she was my one. I suddenly wanted to do whatever it would take to be with her. By the way, just for the record, if I wasn't on this little objective with you, I would be with my most cherished right now."

"Yeah, and speaking of objective, we should probably start engineering a strategy to get Taralyn's two friends out of Prague."

"Right." Kinley agreed. "I think after I google Sydney Carton, I'll also look up 'plans with no earthly chance of working'. Pretty sure if it's not there yet, our plan for getting this mother and daughter out of Czechia will be showing up really soon as a prime example of just that."

KILLING TIME IN A NON-VIOLENT WAY

Big James and Diego walked back into the area of the huge abandoned warehouse where Laurie Chase was typing away on her computer so intently that she failed to see the two men approaching.

She jumped a little when Big James asked, "Whatcha lookin at, Mistress of Distress?"

Laurie spun around in her office chair and gave the two men a good visual inspection. Big James and the much, much smaller Diego were both covered in sweat from head to toe.

"Soooo..." she started suspiciously. "What exactly were you guys playing back there?" She cocked her head to the left while shifting her glance back and forth between the Brothers Grime.

"Whoa, whoa, whoa," Big James protested, "before you go getting your mind covered in wet leaves, let's just get it out of the gutter right now. Number one, there's not a lot of ventilation back in that room – or anywhere in here, really – so you can work up a pretty pristine sheen back there just from sneezing too hard. Number two, we were playing Dance Dance Revolution, and unless you're playing it outside in the snow – which would be weird – if you're not sweating like a porn star on Judgment Day by the time you finish your turn then you're not playing to win. And number three, I'm a large, fat, pasty white guy, and Diego is Hispanic. We sweat a lot. We are people of perspiration. Get over it"—Big James stretched his arms out wide and smiled—"and get over here and give us a big hug."

"Eww, gross," she made a sour face. "I'd rather hug a serial killer with dried blood on his hands than to hug you right now. No offense."

"No offense?" James asked, making a Gloomy Gus face. "How or why would anyone take offense to that statement? That you'd rather hug a serial killer than a big ole lovable arms dealer." Big James hung his head in pseudo shame.

Chase was glad that she knew Big James well enough to know that he was just giving her a hard time. This was clearly evidenced when he suddenly lifted his head and asked, "So what did you say you were working on?"

"Just keeping one eye on Tito and the Amsterdam situation, and the other eye on the FAA page to see when Tito puts up his flight plan to come back to Rio."

"What if he doesn't do that?"

"Do what?"

"What if he doesn't put up a flight plan? Dragon's Men don't always put up a flight plan. Lord knows your boyfriend and Harper Rowe are always flying from here, there, and everywhere. They sure as Hellman's mayonnaise don't put up a flight plan."

"A valid point, to be sure," Laurie leaned back in her chair and looked up at the lovable lout towering over her. "However, they can get away with that because they aren't taking off from or landing at a commercial airport. Not that it makes it any less illegal, mind you, but it does make it a lot easier to get away with. However, such is not the case with Tito and his brood. They will be taking off from the Amsterdam airport. It's not like the authorities there don't know who he is. With all that has taken place in the last several hours, they will be watching his every move."

"With everybody watching his every move, whether it be here or there, isn't that going to make it even tougher for us to make a move on Tito and his family when the time comes?"

Laurie raised her eyebrows in speculation. "Probably," she agreed, "but if it was easy then anyone could do it."

"Meess Laurie?" Diego spoke up. "Eet seems that Tito weell have much to do weeth arranging the transport of all the bodies of all the men that were on the other plane that exploded yesterday, eet could be some time before he comes home. Eet could be days."

"Yeah, I get that, but," Chase held up her hand in slight protest, "I really don't think there's going to be a lot of bodies to actually arrange for transport, though."

"Ya know that's right," Big James acknowledged. "Seriously, though, is it gonna be days? Because if it is, I'm probably going to need to go home and get some sleep. Probably shower. Get something to eat. Check my messages, emails, things like that."

"Can't you check stuff like that on your phone?"

The big man shook his head back and forth like a dog emerging from a swimming pool." Are you serious?"

"Should I not be?" She seemed confused.

"Did you know that there are third-world countries that still eat rice and mud pies as their main meal of the day, and those countries have enough technology to track a cell phone? So imagine what a second-world or first-world country can do to your cell phone. You know why they call them 'smartphones'? It's a ploy, a trick, a slick tactic to make the average human want one. I mean, who wouldn't want a phone that's smart? People want to give off the impression that they are smart, that their spouse is smart, that their kids are smart, that their dogs are smart. What better way to show others how smart your entire household is than to get a smartphone for the whole lot of 'em? When the average human gets a smartphone and realizes all the different things it can do, well, they put every little piece of information about their stupid little lives that they can possibly fit onto their smartphones, and countries whose technology has barely breached that of an abacus and a rotary phone can gain access to whatever it is that they so desire about that average human being.

"Since that really is the way that reality works, a guy like me – a guy that isn't quite average because what he does for a living is not only dangerous but also illegal on all seven continents and most waterways – can't afford to be real pedestrian about where he takes his illegal weapons orders and arranges his meet-ups with other people that are buying arms illegally on the black market.

"Did you know that since the very first smartphone was introduced, arrest rates around the world are up by over thirty percent?" James suddenly got very quiet. He realized that his answer to Laurie's question had become a bit long. He bowed his head and folded his hands across his big belly and said, "So, no, I don't check stuff like that on my phone."

"Okay," Laurie answered, suddenly feeling paranoid about anything and everything she had ever done on her phone. "So, you're gonna go home?"

"For a bit, yeah. Sure, I know that you've got most of the amenities here that I have at my house, but I definitely need a fresh set of duds. I'm relatively confident that you don't have anything my size. Heck, I could probably wear a pair of your jeans for a sock."

"If something happens while you're gone, how do you want me to get in touch with you?"

"I don't care," the big man shrugged. "Text me."

CROOL 24/7

The group at Espetto Carioca followed the instructions of the club owner, heading through the kitchen and up the backstairs to the security room.

Crool was kind enough to let Milfred Wales lead the way. After all, it was Milfred that finally got the club owner to give up where the security room was.

Jeb was about halfway up the stairs when he felt a tug on the cuff of his shirt sleeve. He instinctively pulled his hand away from the annoyance only to look down and see that it was Dave.

"What? What are you doing?" Crool asked in a loud whisper.

"Can we step away for a few?"

"And do what? Search the disco ball for hidden mirrors?"

"If you must know"—Baldwin scowled at Jeb—"I think we need to talk about how we handle any evidence that we may come across in that security room. There are rules."

Without changing his position in the stairwell, Crool retorted, "Do you think Harper Rowe plays by the rules?"

"No, I'm pretty sure he doesn't, but Harper Rowe is not trying to capture and bring Harper Rowe to justice. We are."

Jeb rubbed his forehead as several of his men made their way past him up the stairs to the security room.

"Come on, boss," Agent Baldwin urged, "we haven't spent the last year and a half trying to get this guy just to see it thrown out of court on a technicality. Let's make sure we get this right."

Crool made his way back down the steps toward Baldwin. As he did, he hollered to his men, "Retrieve the video of what happened over the last several hours. Retrieve it. Don't do anything with it 'til Agent Baldwin and I get there. We're dealing with international policies here, people. Whole different ball game from what some of you might be used to."

Crool moved in close enough to Baldwin for only him to hear. "Things of this nature...this is why I brought you on board this team."

"And here I thought all along it was so that we could carpool and play whack the penguin."

"Get upstairs and make sure none of the evidence is tainted."

"Where are you going to go?" Dave asked.

"Gonna go see if they've taken away the club owner yet. If not, I'm gonna take another run at 'im."

"Meaning what?"

"Meaning that if I do get another run at 'im, I don't need you, Mr. Conscience, to be standing there like a little angel on my shoulder telling me that I'm breaking protocol."

"Are you going to break protocol?"

Jeb smiled an eerily calm smile. "Oh, I'm gonna break something all right."

"Can it not be the law?"

"Let me tell ya somethin', Dave"—Jeb put his hand on Baldwin's shoulder—"I didn't come down here to play footsie with these chuckleheads. This is as close as we have been to Harper Rowe – maybe ever – so if I've gotta bend a few rules, skirt a few guidelines, or test the limits of one man's willingness to withhold information, then that's what I'm gonna do."

"Hey, if that's how you wanna play it..."

"That's how I'm gonna play it."

"...then don't get upset when all of this gets thrown out of court—"

"Seriously?" Jeb interrupted Agent Baldwin's tirade. "If you think that Harper Rowe is ever going to see the inside of a courtroom, you're delusional."

"Meaning what?"

"Meaning that there's blood in the water, Dave, and the American people are the sharks. They aren't giving good, level-headed thought to what happened with the Secretary of Defense. They just want justice. And let me tell ya something. Their version of justice and the actual truth? It doesn't have to be the same thing."

"So, what are you saying, Jeb?"

"I'm saying that Harper Rowe probably isn't going to get a fair shake if this all goes to legalese. And, just this one time, in this particular instance, I'd like to know what really happened. And the only chance of that coming to fruition is if we can get to the guy first. I really don't want Harper Rowe to be the next Lee Harvey Oswald – a patsy, a stooge, a fall guy – just to feed the frenzied public's voracious appetite to put a face to the villain. I'm not gonna let that happen on my watch. So, I may not like the results, and I may not like the truth, but the truth is the only thing that's going to let me look myself in the mirror every morning and not wanna puke my breakfast."

Baldwin let out a long sigh. "Well, then I guess I better get upstairs before somebody taints the evidence."

11

PLAN OR SLEEP?

Harper was nodding off. Actually, he had nodded off a few times already only to be awakened by Kinley's loud, abrupt swearing every time he read another news article about the situation in Prague that he and Harper were heading toward.

"Seriously, Harp, we really need to make a plan about how we're gonna get this mom and kid to safe haven. The way things are looking right now...we'll be lucky to get our own selves out of this mess alive."

"Kin, we can try to come up with something that halfway looks like a plan and then go to sleep only to wake up later and realize that our attempt at a plan is complete garbage. Or we can just get some sleep and see what we can do once we wake up"

"You've been over there sawing logs for the last hour and a half. I'd really appreciate your help on this journey that you've invited me on. Give me something. Anything."

Harper sat up in his seat, wiped his eyes, and sniffed his somewhat clogged nose. "Fine," he said, "I'll give you this. If you were me and I were you, you'd tell me what I'm getting ready to say to you now. Go to sleep. It's been – and I'm not sure what time zone we are flying through right now – days since we've gotten any real, quality sleep."

Kinley stared blankly at his friend. "It often amazes me how properly right you can be when you speak utter nonsense."

"If it makes you feel any better, I'm working on a plan on evacuating the mom and daughter, but I do need some sleep to be sure the whole idea actually holds water."

Harper closed his eyes and laid his head back down waiting for Kinley's answer. But he fell asleep before it came.

It would be six hours before he or Devereaux would wake up. Which was good. They both needed some effective dream time.

The Reality of Time And Exhaustion

"Oi," **Bairre Dolan said** loudly. "Ya got about four ayres til we land at the coordinates ya gave to me earlier. I took the liberty o' checkin' the wedder fercast for that area...we got airselves a blizzard that be headin' air way, lads."

Harper opened his sleepy eyes about halfway to see the pilot standing over him and Kinley. "Hey, if you're out here talking to us, who's flying the plane?" Harper asked groggily.

"She's got autopilot, Harper. I just taught I would give meself a bit of a break and come back here to see what ya byes was gettin' tuhgedder as far as a plan to get that young mudder and her li'l gairl out o' Czechia." Dolan's thick brogue made his words very hard to understand, especially for two guys that had just been sound asleep moments earlier.

"I'm figurin' that you're goin' to nayd me to fly ya where you're naydin' to be takin' them, yes?" He stopped talking for a moment as if he were waiting for an answer from either Kinley or Harper, but the two men realized that was not the case at all. Apparently, Bairre had just stopped long enough to catch his breath before he was off and yammering away again. "But, noooo, I come back here to find the two o' ya saw'n' logs lake a couple o' first class lumberjacks. Did ya bodder to come up with ayven a rough draft or an outline of a plan before you daycided to knock off like a couple o' Rip Van Wankers?"

Kinley was awake now. "Did I hear you say that we're just four hours away from landing?"

"Indayd, I did."

"And did you say we were heading into a blizzard?"

"Indayd, we will be."

"Geez, how long did we sleep? It feels like I've only been asleep for about twenty minutes," Harper said trying to rub his eyes into focus.

"We been up in the air fer almost ten ayres, so you tell me." Bairre gave a look to both men that was equal parts disapproval and disappointment. "I'll be up in the cockpit whenever the two o' ya decide that it's tame to get doan to business."

As the tall, lanky Irishman walked back toward the front of the plane, Kin and Harp looked at each other, exchanging tired expressions.

"Did he just scold us?"

"I do believe he did. Sometimes he gets to talking so fast I can't really make out what he's saying, but he definitely was using a scolding tone."

"Eh, we slept longer than I was planning, but it's only because we needed it," Harper admitted. "Now I guess we better start putting some semblance of a plan together."

"Where do we even begin? I'm definitely concerned about flying into a blizzard. First of all, I'm sure that where we're landing isn't going to be any kind of cleared off. So, that's dangerous. Second, I have to wonder what kind of shape the roads are going to be like leading in and out of where we'll be landing. In my experience it's usually a secondary road or worse that service most private airstrips. So, that's dangerous."

"I seem to be picking up on a recurring theme here."

"Any idea how adept your girl Taralyn is at driving in the snow?"

"Can't say that I do. But I do know that she grew up in Colorado, and it snows a decent amount there. So I would say that the odds are in our favor that she has some inkling as to what she's doing."

Kinley stared down at the floor, deep in thought.

Harper figured he would give his friend some time to contemplate things on his own. He stood from his seat, stretched quietly, and began walking toward the plane's bathroom at the back of the craft.

When Kinley finally snapped out of his cogitative state, he looked up to see that he was alone.

"Harp?" Dev looked around. "You didn't grab the last parachute, did ya?"

"I'm in the can," came the muffled response from the back of the plane.

"Time did the man?!" Kinley yelled, not understanding what Harper had said, nor from where he had said it.

A good ten seconds of silence elapsed before Harper emerged and went out of his way to over-enunciate, "I'm...in...the...can."

By now Devereaux had gotten used to letting Harper's irritable remarks wash over him, and this particular time was no different. Unperturbed by Harper's latest barb, he said, "I gotta tell ya, my wanting to do the right thing is starting to be overtaken by my will to survive, and it's really—"

Kinley's cell phone sounded off with the Muzak version of "Twinkle, Twinkle, Little Star." He began patting himself down in an attempt to find the phone and answer it.

"It's by the window," Harper pointed.

Kinley's cell phone was set to get louder the longer it rang.

"What?" Kin asked over the increasing volume of the phone's ringing.

"There"—Harper pointed more fervently—"by the window. It's on your charger."

Finally realizing what his partner was indicating, Kinley frantically answered his phone. "Hello?"

"Hiya, baby. It's Kelly. Got a few minutes to talk?"

A GREAT PHONE CALL AT A BAD TIME

"Kelly," **Devereaux said, trying** to sound excited. As soon as he said her name, he braced himself for Harper to say something smart alecky.

Surprisingly, Harper just returned to his seat and quietly whispered, "Can you put that on speaker?" Devereaux pressed the cell phone's speaker button.

"Yeah," he responded to Kelly Campbell, the former handler of both Kinley and Harper back in their glory days of United States wetwork. "I've got a few minutes. Probably even several minutes. By the way, you're on speaker with me and Harper. Ya good with that?"

"Haarperr!"she said in a voice so shrill that it made Devereaux's cell phone vibrate. "How are you, sweetie?"

"Well, now that you've just removed all the excess wax in my ears...good. Doin' good."

"I'm so glad that you're both on the line because what I have to say absolutely concerns both of you. I've located someone that can verify everything that Paul Michaels was doing and did that got the two of you in the position that you're currently in. I'm meeting with her later today, and I'm going to see for myself just what she has. If it looks like it's enough to take before a Senate hearing committee, then I'm going to have both of you get back here to the States ASAP and get you cleared of any wrongdoing and make you look like the heroes that you are for what you did to that son of a bitch."

Kinley said nothing. He looked over at Harper to see if he had any sort of immediate response which, of course, he did.

"Well, that all sounds like a fantastic trailer to the sequel of a movie that nobody's ever seen before, but, if you don't mind me asking...what are you talking about?"

"Kinnleeyy," she said, sounding like an embarrassed lover, "didn't you tell Harper that you and I talked about this already?"

"I did tell Harper, and, yes, you and I talked briefly about this, but you were as vague to me then as you're being now. You told me that you thought you had tracked down someone that might have evidence that could clear our names. But that was about as specific as you got."

"Where are you two right now?" she asked.

"We're on a plane."

"Headed where?"

"Probably best if you don't know."

"Okay, Mr. Secretive, can you at least tell me how long you're going to be doing whatever it is that I'm best not knowing about?"

"I can't," Kinley sighed, "and it's not because I don't want to. It's because I really just don't know."

"Does your buddy know?" Kelly's attitude was becoming short. The excitement that had filled her timbre just seconds before was now completely gone.

"If he knew, he would have told me. And if he had told me, then I would know. And if I knew, then I would have told you. We really don't know how long we're going to be. And, for that matter, we really don't know where we're going to go once we finish up doing whatever it is that we're getting ready to do."

"So that's us." Harper said. "What about you? Who are you going to meet, and what kind of timeframe are you working with today?"

"Who I'm going to meet is probably best left off the table." Kin and Harp looked at each other, both thinking the same thing: Sure, maybe Kelly was being mum on the whole topic to keep the two of them clean. But both men could not help but feel that part of her charade was just out of sheer spite.

"I'm meeting her in about seven hours. Once I see what I need to see and hear what I need to hear, I might think about calling you two back and letting you know."

"Kelly," Devereaux pleaded, "don't be like that. It's not what any of us need right now."

"Ya know what I need, Kinley?"

"Tell me."

"I need for you and your partner to start showing me a little more appreciation for what I've done and for what I'm getting ready to do," she whined.

"Kells, we do. We definitely do."

"Then why can't you tell me where you are?"

"Kelly," Harper spoke up, "where have you been for the last year and a half?"

She took her time before answering, "I've been hiding...on the run and scared."

"That's right, and you've had to do that because of us – because of knowing things about us that some really evil dirtbags wanted to get out of you. I know that you and I have a long history of despising each other, but, baby, I love you for what you've gone through and for what you're willing to do for us today." Harper winced a little as he said that.

"That being said, Kinley and I have a quick errand to run because there are some people counting on us as much as we're counting on you. Where we're going and what we're getting ready to do is one of those things that you're safer not knowing...just like you think that Kinley and I are safer not knowing who it is that you are going to be rendezvousing with later on today. Still, if you think that you've garnered from your meeting whatever it is that you think it's going to take to clear our names, you let Kinley know, and I promise you that we will be wherever it is that you need us to be faster than lightning blinks."

"Is what he's saying the truth, baby?"

"Yes, Kelly, it's absolutely true. The boy wonder and I are needed, and you have to know that it's of the utmost importance if it's keeping us from heading straight to you now."

"Okay," she said in a voice that was just above a whisper. "I'll wait to hear from you, and we'll go from there. Talk to you soon."

And the call was over.

"She called you baby." Harper laughed.

"You told her you loved her," Devereaux countered.

"Yeah, well...sometimes a good lie beats a bad truth."

BEND, DON'T BREAK

Adalberto Palmiero owned the Espetto Carioca night club. He had been giving a hard time to just about every law enforcement officer that he encountered, dragging his feet at every turn and putting off the inevitable for as long as he could. Palmiero had already called his lawyer, and he was hoping to hold up the works long enough for the aforementioned lawyer to get to the Espetto Carioca before anyone, especially him, was taken off to jail.

He was pleased with what he had been able to accomplish thus far. He would not be for long.

Jeb Crool thumbed through his pocket-sized Portuguese dictionary, trying to put together the phrases he was going to need.

The translator that he had roughed up earlier was upstairs in the security room with the rest of Jeb's boys helping them recover what video footage they could from the terrorist attack the night previous. Even if he had been available, Jeb figured he would not get much help from the guy anyway. Jeb was on his own and left to fend for himself amongst the Rio authorities.

He approached one of the officers and stammered, "Yeah, hi... um...*Quem...está no comando...aqui?*"

The officer turned and pointed to an attractive older woman that was wearing a sleeveless black blouse and tattered black jeans.

"*Ela está no comando*," the officer said. "*Tenente Aline Rapido*."

Jeb nodded in understanding. "Okay, thanks – I mean, uh"—he thumbed through the Portuguese dictionary until he found the word he was looking for—"*Obrigado*." He headed toward the identified woman.

She was conversing with two uniformed officers at the moment, so Jeb stood back and waited for his turn. While he waited, he scanned the crowded crime scene for Adalberto Palmeiro. He was impressed with how many different groups of Rio de Janeiro law enforcement were represented at a crime scene that was well over 24 hours old. It said to him that the Brazilians were taking this just as seriously as he and his team was.

"*Posso te ajudar?*" came a woman's voice from behind him.

Jeb spun around quickly to see that it was Lieutenant Aline Rapido, the agent in charge. While small in stature, she had a presence about her that commanded both respect and attention.

"May I help you?" she repeated, this time in English. "It looked like you wanted to ask me or tell me something just a moment ago."

"I was wanting to inquire about the whereabouts of the club owner. Do you know if he's been taken from the scene yet?"

"May I ask why you're wanting to know?"

"Just had a few more questions that I wanted to ask him about what happened last night...two nights ago, I mean. Sorry. Not used to being up this late in a different time zone trying to stumble my way through a language I don't know. It seems to have knocked me off my game a little."

"If he's not here, he's been taken to the local BLRT building for further questioning."

"BLRT?"

"Yes, the BLRT. It would be our version of the American counterterrorist unit. The Brazilian Legal Regime against Terrorism."

"Ah, yes, right," Jeb nodded. "Well, my questions are going to be more along the lines of what else I might be able to get out of him as far as Harper Rowe is concerned. Not so much about the terrorist attack itself."

"Do you think that we, the Rio authorities, were not planning to get around to that line of questioning?"

"Well, I think you just said it yourself right there: you all will get around to it, I have no doubt, but that might be – what? – a day or two? Maybe longer? I was hoping to ask him a few quick, pertinent questions so that me and my team could be on about our investigation."

"And why did you not ask this club owner these 'quick, pertinent questions' when you had the chance earlier?"

"Oh, you know how it is, Lieutenant…"

"*Tenente.*"

"I'm sorry?" Jeb was uncertain.

"You called me 'Lieutenant' which is the American term for my position, but the Portuguese term is *Tenente*. Feel free to call me *Tenente* Aline Rapido."

"Oh, gosh. Sorry. Like I was saying *Tenente* Rapido, some questions you can ask prior to an arrest, but others have to be held off until a suspect is in custody. You probably don't know this about me, but I'm a stickler for procedure."

Tenente Rapido gave Crool an apprehensive look. "I somehow doubt that. It's been my experience that when officers are sticklers about anything they don't usually go around advertising it. Being a stickler about something usually speaks for itself."

Jeb did not mind that she called his bluff, nor did he mind that she was giving him the ninth degree about why he wanted to further question the club owner. But what was starting to get under his skin was that every line of dialogue that he traded with this spitfire of a lieutenant was another moment that he was not getting any closer to Harper Rowe, and another moment that Harper Rowe was getting further away from him.

"Ma'am," he said politely, "Adalberto Palmeiro? Is he still here?"

"Ernesto!" she yelled, looking around the club for the man she knew to be Ernesto Reis.

"*Tenente?*" came a man's voice from a vague direction.

"*Onde está o Adalberto Palmeiro? Ele está ainda nas instalações?*"

It took a moment before Ernesto responded with, "*Ele está na cozinha a falar com uns caras de combate ao crime.*"

Aline pointed Jeb toward the kitchen. "You'll find him in there talking to a couple of officers. When they are finished, let them know that I said it was good for you to talk to him next." She hesitated before asking, "I'll assume that you are going to want to talk to him alone?"

"I am," Jeb answered slowly.

"Try not to leave any marks."

AWAITED MOVEMENT

Laurie Chase opened her eyes and found herself still sitting in front of her computer, her head buried in her arms. Slowly lifting her head, it became apparent to her that she had been asleep for a while. Her mouth was cottony, her neck was stiff, and her back was achy.

"Diego," she tried to yell, but only a choking cough emerged. After a few seconds of hacking and clearing her throat, she heard Diego del Fuento's voice from behind her.

"You okay, Meess Laurie?" he asked. "Eet sounded like you were choking."

She turned to face him, her eyes watering and her face red. "How long was I sleeping?"

"Oh, eet was a while. Do you want some water, Meess Laurie?"

"Um," she thought for a second, "yes, some water would be great. Thank you."

While Diego retrieved water from the kitchen, Laurie tried to get her thoughts flowing once again. She stood up and stretched, cracking her knuckles. Seeing the sun shining outside, she checked her watch to see how long she really *had* been sleeping. Close to seven hours.

Holy crap, she said to herself, *no wonder I'm so stiff*. She walked around for a few seconds, taking some exaggerated high steps to loosen herself up.

When Diego returned with a cold bottle of water, seeing one del Fuego prompted her to check on the return of the other del Fuego. She headed back to her computer to see if anything might have changed on the FAA website to indicate that Tito would soon be making his return to Rio de Janeiro.

She punched a few keys on the computer keyboard, and there it was...the change that she had been waiting to see for the last several hours. The change that made her say aloud, "Trouble has saddled up its horse." The change that would set in motion the final part to her plan of wrecking the once great and powerful drug kingpin, Tito del Fuento. The change that was, indeed, Tito filing his flight plan to return back home.

Laurie picked up her cell phone and texted the news to Big James.

Turning to Diego, she said, "Won't be long now, my friend. This will all be over, and we can start moving on with our lives."

"*Sim*, Meess Laurie. *Sim*," Diego nodded solemnly, "and eet's been a long time coming." He walked over and gave her a comforting pat on her shoulder. "Ees Mees'er James coming over soon?"

"Yeah, it won't be too long before he gets here."

"And then I guess we weel put together one las' plan, eh, Meess Laurie?"

"Yeah, Diego. One last plan. One last time."

A Plan That Makes All Other
Plans Seem Like Sheer Genius

"Sometimes it seems like we just can't catch a break. Other times it seems like we're living with a horseshoe firmly entrenched in our backsides." Kinley Devereaux said. He and Harper had been discussing the phone call that they had just received from Kelly Campbell.

"Well, I hope they're new and shiny horseshoes, and not all old and rusty. That could lead to a serious infection. Might cause sepsis or some other unwanted side effect."

"I'm just saying that we get a call saying there might be a legitimate shot at the reinstatement of our good names, a real chance that we can go back home to stay, sleep with both eyes shut for a change, ya know, and you'd think that we would be making a beeline right there right now. But we can't even do that. I mean, that seems insane, doesn't it?"

"Well, I do recall just before Kelly called that you were saying something about your desire to do the right thing was being overtaken by your will to survive. What exactly was that about? Is this blizzard giving you cold feet?"

"Believe me, Harp, I had cold feet long before hearing about the blizzard." Kinley shifted in his seat to get more comfortable. "No, the blizzard is just another in a long list of hurdles that we're going to have to get over for this whole extraction to work."

"You have any people in or around the immediate Prague area?"

"I used to have a paper guy, but I haven't been to Prague in so long, I'm not even sure he is still in the area, or if he's even doing business, for that matter. What about you? Any contacts that might be able to lend us a hand on this one?"

"I don't have any business contacts, but I do have a pretty good friend that lives near Prague Square. She runs a modeling agency. It's small but very successful. Still, not sure what kind of help she might be able to offer. Too bad our mom and daughter aren't two 23-year-olds that are six feet tall, curvy, and of ample bosom."

"Wait a second," Devereaux said. He began to shake his index finger at Harper, but he did not say a word. Twelve feet deep in thought, Kinley finally confessed, "I might have something here."

"Oh? Something...as in a plan?"

"Your model friend, how close are you with her?"

"I talk to her a few times a month. She's aware that I am on the run from the U.S. for the time being."

"Do you think she would be willing to help us out with our current dilemma?"

"Maybe. I know she's got a big heart for those less fortunate. She has several charities that she operates for orphaned children. Why are you asking anyway?"

Kinley started messing around with his phone. Pressing buttons. Swiping screens. Searching.

"Got it." A second later he had the phone up to his ear.

"Who you callin'?" Harper asked. But his question was met with Kinley making the international sign for "shut up." So Harper Rowe shut up and waited with great anticipation to see with whom his friend was getting ready to speak.

He waited. And waited. Then, Harper being Harper, he could not hold his patience any longer.

"Who are you...?"

Kin, once again, gave him the "shut up" gesture. To which Harper gave an exasperated sigh.

"Uh, yes, I am trying to reach Karel Josef. Not sure if I have the right number or..."

Kinley went silent, listening to the person on the other end.

A few moments, then, "Yes, my name is Peter Krug." The other person spoke again. Kin's face remained completely stoic, listening.

Harper was intent like an eight-year-old watching cartoons on Saturday morning.

"If he's there then just tell him my name. He'll want to talk to me," Kinley finally said.

Then...more silence.

Harper caught eye contact with Dev. He nodded his head up and down letting Harp know that whatever it was that he was up to was coming to fruition.

A silence that seemed to last just slightly longer than a Michener novel was ultimately ended with Devereaux letting out a long sigh and saying, "Yeah, it's really me, Karel."

Kin listened and smiled as the conversation progressed in this nature:

"Peter Krug, my good friend," Karel Josef's Eastern European accent was barely noticeable at all, "I cannot believe it is you. How long has it been?"

"I wish I could say that it's been a few months, but I'm pretty certain that it's been more like a few years."

"So, I take it that you are not calling me for catching up purposes?"

"Tragically, no," Kinley admitted.

"Is okay, my friend. You have always been a good business associate. You pay good money and keep your mouth shut. Is more than I get from even my family," Karel laughed. "So, what it is I can do for you, Peter Krug?"

"I remember this being a secure line to talk to you on. Is it still?"

"Believe me, Peter, if it were not, we would not be talking even now."

"Good, good," the concerned look that had shrouded Kinley's face dissipated into a good-natured smile. "Then let me get down to it. Are you still in the paper and document business?"

"Ha ha!" Josef laughed. "Does manure draw flies? Does a clown make people uneasy? Yes to all of them. What kind of papers do you need, my buddy?"

"I'm going to need travel visas for a woman and a little girl."

"Oh, no."

"Oh, no? Why 'oh, no'?"

"Please tell me that you do not mean the mother and daughter that all of Prague is searching for."

"Yeah, that's who I'm talking about."

"My friend, Peter, you need to run. Get as far away from situation as possible."

"Why? How bad is this *situation*?"

"Is very bad. If mother and daughter are found...is not good for them or for people that help them."

"And why are they wanted so badly, Karel? Do you know?"

"Czechia media says they are wanted for ties to capital murder." Karel Josef said.

His tone was bleak, his mood somber.

"And what if I told you that was a lie?"

"You know this how?"

"Karel, trust me. I know, and I know what the news is saying. It's saying that they're wanted for connection in a capital offense, but that's just not true."

"And how do you know these things, Peter?"

"I don't think it would be such a hot idea for me to tell you that...for your own safety."

"Peter, you do not call me. I do not hear from you for years, and now you reach out to me for this? It is crazy for me to help you!"

"I have money, Karel. Name your price. I need your help, and I am desperate."

"What do you need, and I will tell you my price."

"I need visas from the U.S., and passports...for that mother and daughter. Is that doable?"

"Peter, this situation with mother and daughter, I need you to understand that—"

"Karel," Kinley said, trying to be patient, "I understand. I just need to hear one of two words from you: *yes* or *no*."

After a brief hesitation, Karel Josef said, "You leave me in no-win situation, my friend. I am afraid that I just—"

"I'll pay you a million dollars – U.S."

Again, another brief hesitation. "Like I was trying to say, I am afraid that I just have no option but to help you."

"That's what I thought," Kinley said, "and I can count on you to expedite this, right?"

"Whenever I have let you down, Peter?" Josef asked.

"Never, but, I assure you, Karel, now is not the time to start."

"Are you in Prague city now?"

"I'm on a plane – a few hours out. Can I reach you at this number when I land?"

"I will be waiting your call, my friend. In meantime, safe journeys to you."

Devereaux disconnected the call and looked over to Harper, who was just staring at him, mouth agape. "What...did you just do?"

"Just trying to lay the groundwork for some semblance of a plan," Kin answered. "That was my papers guy. He can get us all the necessary documentation to take mother and child back to the

States with us when we go."

"Yeah, but you just told him that you would pay him a million bucks. We don't have a million bucks...do we?"

"Not sure if you're forgetting the boat load of money we just came into at del Fuento's place. Even without that, I don't know what you did with your money, but me being 'dead' over the last year and a half, I've got a million-plus in several offshore accounts. With digital banking being what it is these days, I don't need a million dollars to pay the man. I just need a computer."

"Yeah, I guess what they say is true: Dead men tell no tales. And they also don't do a lot of online shopping at Bath & Body Works either."

"Yeah, I really hate that over the last eighteen months I haven't been able to smell like a dandelion in spring that's covered in freshly washed linens."

"You're a real hoot, Woodsy Owl, but seriously," Harper scooted up in his seat and leaned forward for emphasis. "How is having visas and passports for these two going to make it any easier to get them out of Prague and on a plane with us to the United States?"

"Because you are going to talk to your model friend and convince her to help us. I need you to turn on that Harper Rowe charm of yours so that we can get the mother, the kid, and me and you out of Prague and on our way home."

"And just what is your plan? What do you want me to say to her?"

"She runs a modeling agency, right?"

"Pretty sure we covered this before, but, yes."

"Running a modeling agency must involve her bringing women in and out of the country all the time, don't ya think?"

"It would tend to reason, yes."

"When's the last time you spoke to her? Recently?"

"About two – two and a half weeks ago, I guess."

"Think you can give her a call to see if she might be willing to help?"

"Call her and say what?" Harper asked.

"Let's face it, if we try to sneak these two out of Prague, and we get caught, those two are probably dead. You and I will, at the very least, be imprisoned and, if we're lucky, they might turn us over to the U.S. authorities. And I don't have to tell you what's going to happen if that occurs," Kinley stated grimly. "Maybe if your friend... what is her name?"

"Constance Ondracek."

"Right. So instead of trying to sneak them out, you could call Constance to see if she might be able to set up some models for an imaginary photo shoot, and mom and daughter can go along as part of the crew. We'll walk them out right underneath their noses."

"I don't know, Kin. I mean, it certainly sounds good on paper, and you and I can probably pull something like that, but my friend, Constance, she's not like us. I don't know how comfortable I am putting the bullseye on her like that. Her and her models."

"So...you're not even going to try to call her? Just ask?"

"Ugh," Harper groaned, "walk me through what you have in mind. If it seems like something that I can run up her flag pole without her laughing or wanting to annul our friendship, yeah, I'll do it."

"Well, I've got a rough draft of a plan. Between me and you, we can put our heads together, suss it out, slice it up, and make some sort of heads or tails out of this thing, but...it really is going to take your friend's help for us to get ever relatively close to something that might actually work." Kin smiled a wry smile. "Not to put any undue pressure on ya or anything."

"Okay. Fire away."

"Here's my premise. Your friend gets a last-minute call to do a fashion shoot or, whatever, in the States. So she has to pull a few models together to take a trip to America. If she runs a modeling agency like you say she does, then something like this has probably happened before. And she has probably dealt with it a time or two before, as well."

Kinley paused for a moment to get a read on Harper's face as to what he was thinking about the plan thus far. He seemed to still be listening, so Kinley continued.

"My thought is to see if we can't get the mother of our mother/ daughter duo looking good enough to pass her off as one of the models. She can say that with the whole thing being last minute and everything, she was left with no other option than to bring her daughter with her on the trip."

Devereaux went silent again to see if he could read Harper's thoughts on the idea. This time, however, Harper Rowe was not silent.

"So hold up, chief. Do you seriously want me to ask someone that I consider a friend to jeopardize not only her career, but also her very freedom, in order for us to get two people that she has never met in her lifetime"—Rowe shook his head back and forth slowly—"yeah, I'm pretty sure that's not going to happen."

"Which is why I said that I need you to really pour on the ol' Harper Rowe charm," Devereaux smiled. "I've seen you do it before. I know you can do it again. And don't forget, this is your idea – me and you doing this whole operation of getting the mom and daughter out of the Czech Republic. Think you're up to the task?"

"Oh, you mean the task where I throw out all my morals and see if I can get my friend to not only lose her business and her freedom, but very well her life? Is that the task you're referencing?"

"Well...when you put it like that..."

"I'll call her. She's got a heart the size of Texas. If she will help, it will be because she wants to and not because I charmed her into it."

"Can you call her now?" Kin asked. "Because if she isn't going to help us, then we'll need to start coming up with another plan."

Harper pulled out his cell phone, gave it a quick glance, and made a sour face.

"Something wrong?"

"My phone's getting ready to die. It's blinking at me."

"You better get her number off of there if you don't know it," Kinley advised.

"Oh, shoot." Harper's fingers began flying wildly across the face of the phone. "Oh, shoot, shoot, shoot. Come on, already!" He searched frantically for Constance's phone number and finally blurted out "011420289484093." No sooner had he said the last digit when the final chirps of his own cell phone sounded, indicating the last of the battery life. He looked at Kinley. "Did you catch all that?"

"011420289484093," Devereaux rattled off, then smiled an evil smile. "Yeah, I got it."

"Mind if I borrow your phone?"

CROOL'S NEXT MOVE

He had broken him.

Not, literally, mind you. But in the figurative sense of the word, Jeb had gotten the nightclub owner, Adalberto Palmeiro, to finally give him some pertinent information about Harper Rowe and the merry band of men and women that had helped him stuff a sock in the plans that some terrorists had made to cause a scene at the Espetto Carioca.

Yes, Jeb had gotten the man to break, and without even doing any breaking of his own. With the help of the interpreter, Crool had laid out for the man a rather bleak future unless some cooperation was shown. Besides, Jeb told the club owner, with the amount of time that had already passed, Harper and his crew were probably well into the wind by now. The agent commended Adalberto on the fine job he had done to this point of keeping his mouth shut in the face of such mounting pressure. But now the time for playing hero had passed. The time to step up to the plate and be smart had arrived.

Palmeiro had agreed. Within just a few minutes he had agreed to help, and just a few minutes after that he was writing everything down.

Pleased with the information he had received, Jeb headed back toward Baldwin and his men in the video surveillance room. He called ahead.

"Dave, it's Jeb. How are we coming along there on your end?"

"Just about wrapped up. This is some amazing footage to watch – the way these guys took down the terror suspects. Impressive."

"Did you recognize any of the other players with Rowe?"

"I did. Kinley Devereaux cleaned himself, and there's no doubt that he is back in the game. The DEA agent, Laurie Chase, is with them. Four other men and a woman are in the mix, too. I got some clean head shots of them and have already sent those back to D.C. to be run through facial recognition to see if we can get an ID."

"Is one of those four men a rather hefty looking fellow? Big, brawny, massive?"

"Sure is. You know something about him?"

"I got Palmeiro to talk. He said that big fellow came to him and paid him a rather handsome sum for the surveillance footage and asked Palmeiro to keep a lid on the identities of everyone. The big guy's name is James Gray. I've got an address. Figured we could leave our guys here to bag and tag everything while you and I head out to pay Mr. Gray a visit."

"Palmeiro happen to give names for any of the other participants in this little shindig?"

"No. The only person in the crew that he knew was this James Gray fella. All the rest were friends of Gray's." By then Jeb had reached the surveillance room so he hung up his phone and resumed the conversation with Baldwin face-to-face. "I'm hoping we can find this guy at home and try to get the names of everyone else from him personally."

"Well, let's get to it then," Baldwin said. He reached into his jacket pocket and pulled out his keys. "The car's out back."

Crool turned his attention to the rest of his agents in the room. "Okay, boys, Agent Baldwin and I are going to go follow up on a lead. Jamison, you're in charge. Coordinate with whichever investigative agencies are here to make sure we don't step on any toes, but get as much of the hard evidence as you can back to the plane. Whatever you can't take, get pictures. If you haven't heard from us by the time you finish all that up, sit tight and enjoy the air."

Crool and Baldwin headed back down the stairs, through the kitchen, through the dining area, past the bar and out the door.

"So, James Gray? That name doesn't sound like he's a local," Baldwin noted.

"No, it does not. I've got my laptop in the car. I'll see what I can find on him while we head to his place."

"Sounds good."

Jeb's cell phone began to ring. Baldwin recognized the ringtone as "Mother" by Danzig.

"Incredibly Special Agent Jeb Crool," the bald man answered.

"Jeb, it's Susan Lincoln over at Justice. Hey, I know that you and your crew are down there in Rio and probably up to your eyeballs in it, but I just had something come across my desk that I thought might interest you."

"Oh, hey, Susan," Crool said as he waited for David Baldwin to unlock the doors to the beige Chevrolet Malibu rental car. "Whatcha got for me?"

"The name Kelly Campbell mean anything to you?"

"Kelly Campbell. Kelly Campbell," Jeb muttered to himself. He heard the locks on the rental car pop and was just about to get in when the significance of the name registered in his mind. "Oh wait, yeah, Kelly Campbell. Right. She was the handler for Rowe and Devereaux. Her car blew up in her garage and took out the rest of the house with it."

"That's the one," Lincoln acknowledged.

"They never found a body – hers or anyone else's – in all the wreckage. But she hasn't been seen or heard from since, if I'm not mistaken."

"Well, you wouldn't have been mistaken...up until about twenty minutes ago."

"Really," Jeb said. "And what was it that happened twenty minutes ago?"

"We had a confirmed sighting of her at the Minneapolis-St. Paul International Airport. Security cameras there picked her up coming off of an international flight from Brussels. She was flying under the name of Lydia Johnson."

"Did you pick her up?"

"No, not yet. By the time we realized who it was, she had already hit the road. We've got people checking other cameras to see if she left with anyone, or if she rented a car, which direction she went when she left. You know the drill."

"Well, I appreciate the update, Susan. You'll get back to me when you find anything else out, I'm sure."

"Absolutely, Jeb. Talk to you then."

Crool put the phone back in his pocket, got in the car, and buckled up his seat belt for safety.

"Well, well, well," he said. "Kelly Campbell just got flagged by security cameras at the Minneapolis-St. Paul Airport. She was flying in from Brussels under an assumed name."

"Do they have her in custody?"

"No, but they're on it."

"You got that address we're headed to? I need to punch it into the GPS."

"Right. Sorry. I got it." Jeb took the GPS navigator that was sitting on the dashboard and began programming it accordingly.

"So, in the course of just a very few days Kinley Devereaux and Laurie Chase show up. And now here comes Kelly Campbell. Three people of definite interest in the case of Secretary of Defense Paul Michaels, but three people that were all thought to be dead, too." Agent Baldwin paused for a moment and looked at his boss. "What do you make of it all?"

Crool handed the GPS device back to him. "Something," he shrugged imperceptibly. "I don't know just what. But...something."

Constance Ondracek

Constance Ondracek had the perfect looks for an Eastern European model: long, toned legs, long blond hair, and eyes so shockingly blue that they could clean a pool. Besides her attractive features, she had also been blessed with an incredible mind that she used to its fullest extent. She could speak fluently in six different languages. She had started in the modeling business when she was just fifteen years old, and after taking crap for eight years, she started her own modeling agency. After only four years it was now the most lucrative agency of its type in the Czech Republic; for the last two it had ranked in the top ten modeling agencies in all of Eastern Europe.

Not bad for a woman that had never attended high school.

Harper Rowe had been introduced to Constance Ondracek through a mutual friend several years ago. He was fascinated with her, to be sure. Not so much due to her looks or her mental acumen, but much more because of the charity work that she had been doing with children's homes in underdeveloped countries all around the globe. It was because of this philanthropy that Harper Rowe had been introduced to Ms. Ondracek.

Most of Constance's efforts were done in total anonymity. She did not seek praise or humanitarian awards, or anything of the like.

She did it because it was something that needed to be done and, more to the point, done honestly.

Not only were there humanitarian organizations that were defrauding the system when it came to running orphanages and homes abroad, but entire countries, as well, that were cooking the books and stealing funds that were to be spent on less-fortunate children. As it turned out, when more benevolent forces from outside of those countries tried to circumvent the corrupt governments and get the necessary funds to those in need, members of those governments would employ chicanerous and deplorable tactics to make sure that these benevolent associations understood that what they were doing was not appreciated and that further action would – and often did – result in physical violence.

In order to proceed with any sort of meaningful charity work in instances like these, backroom deals had to be made, workers had to be smuggled in and out of the countries, paperwork and monies were covertly dealt with, and protection was given to those who were in danger. It just so happened that at one particular time during one particular instance, Constance Ondracek was the one that needed the protecting. And Harper Rowe was the one that had been given the task of doing the protecting. Which he did...and did well.

All of that was about four years ago, back when Harper and Kinley were at the top of the "most wanted for a wetwork job" list, and not at the top of the "most wanted by every major investigative agency in America" list. Ever since then, Constance and Harper had a great friendship, a wonderful kinship, and a deep respect for what the other was doing for the world. Even though they had only ever met face-to-face three times in their lives, the relationship they shared was stronger than most.

"So, it sounds like she owes ya one. I mean, with you saving her life and everything," Kinley said.

"Yeah, but I didn't save her life so that she would owe me one.

I did it because that was the job I was hired to do."

"Hey, put that on speaker. I want to hear how this goes."

Harp had dialed the number to the main office of Ondracek's company, the Ascending Angels Modelling Agency. It was not until the sixth ring that Constance, herself, answered the phone in her native tongue.

"*Dobrý den. Děkujeme vám za volání modelování agentura Angels vzestupně. Jmenuji se Constance Ondracek. Jak vám mohu pomoci?*"

"*Dobrý den, Constance,*" Harper smiled. "*Je to Harper Rowe. Jak se máš?*"

Ondracek's voice took on a tone of excitement as she seamlessly shifted from her native Czech into English, one of the six languages that she spoke comfortably, even if a bit broken at times. "Harper, am glad to hear from you."

"Well, let's hope that you still feel the same way by the time we finish this conversation."

"Oh? Do you have troubles? Where are you?"

"I'm winging my way to Prague as we speak. I should be there in just a few short hours."

"Be very careful, friend. Snowstorm is coming this way."

"I'll be as careful as a guy can be that's riding in a ten-ton jet that's flying through the air at 700 miles an hour into a snowstorm," Harper laughed.

"You make joke but is very serious, Harper. I will pray for you."

One thing that Rowe had learned – and had momentarily forgotten – during his time with Constance was that Eastern Europeans take things very literally and have a totally different sense of humor than most people in the western world are used to. Although he did find it pleasantly surprising that Constance laughed hysterically at *The Three Stooges* episodes that he had shown her – Larry, Moe, and Curly: were there any worlds they could not conquer?

"Thank you, Constance. I appreciate your prayers. Lord knows we're going to need them."

"So, you come to Prague? We can meet together?"

"Yes," Harper answered a bit uneasily. "Yes, we will, and, as a matter of fact, that's why I'm calling you."

"Oh? So you are in trouble?"

"There is trouble, but I'm not the one who's in it...this time."

"Then who?"

"I'm sure you've seen the news about the mother and daughter that are wanted for questioning in a capital murder case there in your city."

"Yes, have seen this."

"Well"—Harper took a deep breath—"I'm with a friend of mine, and we are flying to Prague to get that mother and daughter out of the country and to someplace safe. Constance, those two aren't wanted for questioning about a capital murder case or drug trafficking or even parking tickets. They're wanted because they saw something that they shouldn't have. Something that, apparently, links back to some pretty high-ranking officials in your city."

"Do you know what is they saw?"

"Yes."

"How is it you know of this?"

"I just do. The people that tracked me and my partner down to do this job had to go through a great deal to find us and convince us that these two – the mother and daughter – Anezka and Jana Bucek, were innocent and caught in the most perilous of situations. Plus, I think you know me well enough to understand that if I'm doing this, it's for real, and not some wild goose chase."

"I have lived here very long time. I never hear of such things in Prague."

"Well, that's because there's a real good chance that nothing like this has ever happened in Prague before. But you know better than anyone that corruption can find its way through just the slightest of cracks. You've seen it all over the world. You must know that there's a chance that it could happen in your city. Right?"

Silence filled the line for a good ten-count before Ondracek finally asked, "What is it that you would like for me to do?"

"Okay, here's our plan, or at least a rough draft of it. My partner, Kinley Devereaux, and I were wondering what it would take for you to round up a few of your girls and put together travel plans for a photoshoot. We were thinking that we could get the necessary work visas for the mother and daughter, get them together with your crew, pass them right through security, get on a plane and fly them away to safety."

Harper went silent and waited to hear what Constance would say to this idea, if she even said anything at all. Part of him expected to hear the phone disconnect. Another part of him thought she might laugh out loud at the ludicrous plan. He looked at Kin, who was doing his own fair share of hand wringing as he waited for what would happen next.

"Do you know what you ask of me to do is very dangerous? Could lose modeling agency. Could be arrested. Is very risky what you ask."

Again, the line went silent. Kinley looked at Harper and mouthed, "Is she still there?" But before Rowe could respond, Constance began again.

"But I know what you say is truth. Corruption can get to anyone. No country, no city, no person is immune. Just like nobody's immune to being victim of corruption. I have seen this."

Harper looked at Kinley, smiled, and gave a thumbs up. Kin put his hands out to make the "pumping the brakes" gesture to let Harp know not to get too confident too fast.

"The Lord above, He looks out for this mother and daughter. He has sent you and your friend at right time. I have photo shoot set up in two days in St. Thomas. You know Virgin Islands?"

"I think I read about them in a timeshare brochure once."

As most people were apt to do, Constance dismissed Harper's silly remark. "With snowstorm moving in, I can make reason for us leaving tonight is to fly out before weather is not good."

"When is that snowstorm supposed to start? Is it snowing there already?"

"Storm to come in late this afternoon so will work with little time to do this."

Harper gave Kinley a confused look. "Hang on a second, Constance. I'll be right with you." Harper hit the mute button on Kinley's cell phone and asked his friend, "Didn't Connor McGregor up there just tell us that we were flying into a blizzard?"

"Yeah," Kin nodded, "I think so, but it's like I said: sometimes I fail to properly navigate through his linguistic nuances."

"Okay," Harper shrugged. His demeanor brightened. "Hey, things are turning in our favor already."

He unmuted the phone and informed Constance that he was back.

"How long till plane arrives?"

"Should be there before sunup. We're landing on a private runway to the northeast of the city. We've got someone meeting us there. We'll take care of getting the necessary paperwork for the mother and daughter."

"Have question, Harper. Are mother and little girl pretty like model?"

"Constance, they're Czech. Aren't all Czech women beautiful?"

"If all Czech women beautiful there would be no beautiful Czech women."

Harper squinted his eyes as he pondered what his friend had just told him before finally saying, "Yeah, I get that. Seriously, though, that most recent picture of the two of them that they are brandishing all over the news outlets – well, it is my understanding that as of a few hours ago, Jana and Anezka Bucek no longer look like that."

"Will you bring them here to agency?"

"As of right now they are in a safe place. I'd just as soon keep them there until we absolutely have to move them. When and where that will be?" Rowe paused and furrowed his brow. "I'll let you know when I know."

"I will get everything together here."

"Constance, thank you. I can't begin to tell you how very grateful for—"

"Do not need to thank me. Do nct need to be thanked for doing right thing."

"In that case, my friend, I will see ya 'round downtown...and very soon." Harper hit the end button on the cell phone, handed it back to Kinley.

"You might want to go check on Captain Weather Channel up there and make sure he's even flying us toward the right continent."

"Yeah," Devereaux agreed, "I should probably go do that."

A Meeting with the Senator

Kelly had taken a cab.

She walked out of the Minneapolis-St. Paul International Airport, flagged down one of the many taxi cabs lined up at the curb, and told the driver to take her to 801 Hennepin Avenue, LaSalle Plaza – the Capital Grille. It was the place she had been instructed to go for her meeting with Senator Brenda Cobb-Schmidt.

The cabbie pulled right up to the front door of the Capital Grille and let her out. She tipped him nicely, made it safely across the sidewalk, took a deep breath, and walked into the restaurant.

Kelly was surprised with the way the place looked. She had expected it to resemble most places with the word "grille" in their title: a parking lot full of motorcycles and beat-up pickup trucks, air that reeked of cigarette butts, stale beer, and body odor, and over-tattooed fifty-something waitresses showing way more cleavage than should be allowed by law.

That is what she expected, but one step inside the door of Capital Grille, and she realized that she could not have been more wrong.

Kelly's first thought upon entering the Capital Grille was that perhaps she had not made it safely across the sidewalk after all, because the entire place had a heavenly glow to it. Overhead lighting lent a golden hue to spotless tile floors, a sleek onyx bar, and polished leather booths with perfectly-tucked white tablecloths. Each table was adorned with place settings straight from a Judith Martin how-to manual.

Kelly's initial impression fell away the minute she spotted the person that she was here to meet: Brenda Cobb-Schmidt, Senator of Minnesota. The Senator was sitting in the last booth, all the way in the back of the restaurant.

Upon meeting eyes with Campbell, the politician stood up and waited politely as Kelly approached. At the appropriate time she took a few steps forward and extended her hand.

"Ms. Campbell, it's a pleasure."

"Likewise, Senator. I really appreciate your meeting with me."

"Of course. Please, sit down."

The two ladies seated themselves in the booth, facing each other.

Senator Cobb-Schmidt let out a long breath and said, "Well... it's been an interesting couple of days, wouldn't you say?"

Kelly was not sure how to respond to that statement. So she just countered with, "How so?"

"Well, it was no secret that Harper Rowe was out there running amuck, but now to find out that Kinley Devereaux and Laurie Chase have also been alive this whole time? And then there's you. I know that I, for one, thought you were dead and gone quite some time ago. And yet...here you are."

"Who was it that said, 'The rumors of my death have been greatly exaggerated'?"

"I believe that was Mark Twain," the Senator smiled.

"It's a rare day that an independent black woman such as myself associates with a bigoted, racist, southern writer like Mark Twain, wouldn't you say?"

"What I would say is that these are rare days that we are living in, Ms. Campbell. Still, don't get me wrong. I cannot imagine the kind of hell that you must've been going through. Two of your men out there – one believed to be dead, one responsible for the biggest assassination in U.S. history since Kennedy. I guess if I were you, I would've stayed hidden, too."

"I'm sorry, Senator. Had I known that this meeting was nothing more than an assassination of my character, I would've been more than happy to tell you to go screw yourself," Kelly said. "However, I do believe that it was you that asked for this meeting. So, do we have something to talk about, or are you just wasting my time?"

"We have something to talk about," Cobb-Schmidt acknowledged. "You want to bring your boys home, and I want to help you do it."

"And you mind tellin' me why you wanna help me, or, for that matter, why you wanna help Kinley Devereaux and Harper Rowe?"

"Because I, much like you, know that they are American heroes. I want to bring them home. I want the American people to know their story. And I think that with the information that I have, we can do that. You and I can do that. It's time to set the record straight, Ms. Campbell."

"Then I guess it's time to put our cards on the table. You tell me what it is that you can bring to the party that will make me want to bring Kinley and Harper along for the ride, as well."

"I was part of a Senate inquiry committee that looked into the Paul Michaels assassination. We found out a lot things. We just never were able to piece together exactly what happened on that day. There were five dead snipers found around the area, but none of them had fired their weapon."

"So there was a sixth shooter then."

"Yeah, and whoever he or she was took out Secretary Michaels as well as the other five snipers. The bullets all came from the same gun. Forensics also proved that because of the trajectory and point of impact of the bullets that they were all fired from the same point of origin. Here's the real pip: besides digging a sniper's bullet out of Michaels, they also found fragments of a thumb drive embedded in his body."

"A thumb drive?" Campbell asked as she squinted her eyes. "Wait. Was it the thumb drive that had been stolen from the Hopkins' house? The one that Kinley Devereaux and Harper Rowe were sent to retrieve from Mexico City? The same thumb drive that got my boss - and almost me - killed?"

"Unfortunately, there just wasn't enough left of the drive to piece it back together in any way, shape, or form. But, yes, that was what we surmised. We wanted to look at Secretary Michael's computer to see what we could find on it, but by the time we got to that point, his computer was gone."

"Gone?"

"Without a trace." Senator Cobb-Schmidt nodded. "And we questioned his entire staff, family members, anyone and everyone that had access to his office and files. We not only questioned them, but we gave each of them polygraph tests. Most of them passed without a glitch. But a couple of them – whether it was nerves or whatever – two or three of them had some inconsistent results. They didn't actually fail the test, but they made the needle jump a little more than it should.

Still, the end result was that none of them admitted to taking or even knowing where Paul Michaels' computer was. It wasn't too long afterward that the inquiry ended, and we decided that there were just too many questions that we couldn't get the answers to."

"Not sure if you remember my question or not, Senator, but I was wondering what you had that could clear the names of Kinley Devereaux and Harper Rowe? You told me over the phone that you had something, but so far you haven't told me anything that sounds even remotely like new evidence that could help their cause."

"Well, I'm not *quite* finished yet," the Senator smiled.

Kelly gave the Senator a skeptical look. "I'm still listening, but I hope that you aren't leading me down some rabbit hole."

A waitress showed up to their booth. "Good evening, Senator. Ma'am. Can I start you off with something to drink tonight? Maybe an appetizer?"

The Senator motioned to Kelly Campbell to answer first.

"I haven't really had a chance to look at the menu, but could I get a diet cranberry ginger ale and seltzer, please?" Kelly asked.

"Absolutely, ma'am," the waitress smiled, jotted down the order and then went to Brenda Cobb-Schmidt. "And for you, Senator?"

"Coffee, black. Decaf, please." She looked at Campbell and confessed, "Anymore if I have caffeine at this late hour, I won't sleep a wink." She then looked back to the waitress and continued her order, "Also, we will take the prosciutto wrapped mozzarella to start, but give us a few minutes before coming back. My friend and I have some things to discuss, and it is of a sensitive nature. Give us ten minutes?"

"Absolutely, Senator. Take your time."

The waitress walked away and left the two women to finish their conversation. Cobb-Schmidt spoke first, "I assure you that I am not wasting your time because here's what happened next: After the senate inquiry committee published what we had found...and hadn't found...I hired three private investigators to go to work for me."

"Doing what?"

"Surveillance. I had them watching the three people that had the skewed results on the polygraph. I just had a feeling that one of them – maybe all of them – knew something. Somebody had to know something, and I needed to know who and what it was."

"And...?"

"And I was right," Brenda smiled smugly.

"Okay. So, who was it, and what did they know?"

"Paul Michaels' wife...and his secretary. His secretary took the computer immediately upon hearing of Paul's death. When the wife came looking for it and it was nowhere to be found, she knew that the secretary had to have it. She's the only one that could've possibly gotten it out of his office that fast.

So Michaels' wife goes to the secretary, and the two of them go into cahoots together to keep the computer hidden away. Thing is, the secretary didn't really know what was on there, but the wife did. She made backup copies of the files and then had the computer bleached clean."

"Bleached clean?" Kelly asked. Of course, Kelly Campbell knew what "bleached clean" meant, but she needed to make sure that her definition was the same as the Senator's definition.

"You know how you delete files from your computer, and they appear to be gone, but there are certain types of computer people that can still find them because they will be quick to tell you that nothing is ever truly deleted from a computer?"

"Okay."

"When you *bleach* a computer...everything really is gone. There's no way to trace it or find a ghost file of it somewhere in the deep, dark, nether regions of the computer. Everything, everything... is gone."

"Okay," Campbell responded. The Senator's definition of the term was, indeed, the same as her definition. "So, if she wiped the files from Secretary Michaels' computer, then why not just conveniently leave it somewhere that it would be found? Be done with it."

"Paranoia. Fear. Maybe she thought she was being watched."

"So you figured out who had the computer. What is it that you got from all of it that's going to help my boys?"

"I found out what was on the thumb drive, is what I got. I found out what was on it, and Michaels' wife told me what he was planning on doing with it."

"What was on the drive?"

"You don't know?" Brenda seemed surprised.

"Not even a little."

"Can I ask you something real quick, Ms. Campbell?"

"If you don't like my answer are you going to hook me up to a lie detector?" she laughed.

"Be completely honest...how long have you known that Kinley Devereaux was alive?"

"Honestly, I found out a few days ago when the team of investigators that have been tracking Harper Rowe happened to see Kinley in the video footage of a police precinct bombing in Atlanta, Georgia. A member of the investigative team, who shall remain nameless, notified me upon discovery."

"I'm guessing that it's the same member that just a couple of weeks ago notified me that you were still alive."

"So, what was on the thumb drive, Madame Senator?"

"Blueprints."

"For what?"

"Blueprints for a state-of-the-art space shuttle that would have been unlike anything anyone has ever seen before. It would have revolutionized space travel by leaps and bounds past anything we've ever known."

"And what was Michaels planning on doing with these blueprints? I certainly hope not sell them to the highest bidder."

"He was going to have one made and then unveil it at his press conference where he announced that he would be running for President of the United States. You see, as Secretary of Defense he was one of the most powerful men in the world. As president of the country, he would have been the most powerful man in the world."

"But I don't understand. How did the thumb drive end up in the safe of Undersecretary Hopkins' house where the thief, Black Ice, could get her hands on it?"

"According to Michaels' wife, the Secretary of Defense was

trying to lure Black Ice out into the open so he could capture her and, in return for her freedom, he was going to put her to work for him."

"What? That's crazy."

"The man had a devious plan to do some bad things. The only thing that kept him from doing it was Kinley Devereaux and Harper Rowe. It's like I said before, your boys are heroes, and they probably don't even know it."

"What's Michaels' wife's name?"

"Lisa."

"And she told you all of this? About the spaceship blueprints, and the Secretary's possible run for president, and his plot to get the thief, Black Ice, to work for him?"

"She did."

Kelly was stunned. She shook her head in absolute disbelief. "I guess my next question is, do you have any proof of what she told you is true?"

"Not really, and it wouldn't matter if I did."

"Wait. What?"

"I hope you don't think that she told me what she did because of a guilty conscience or out of the kindness of her heart. I had to make a deal with her, of course. I told her that for full disclosure I would guarantee that her name would stay out of everything, and that she would never have to worry about being connected in any sort of way should her husband's good name get besmirched if any of this ever came to light."

"Can you make that kind of deal? As a senator?"

"I don't know if you're aware of this or not, Ms. Campbell, but I don't plan on being a U.S. senator for long. I'm running for president, and I don't mind saying...I like my chances."

"Oh, goodness, I'm sorry. I was not aware of your candidacy. But even if you were elected president, could you make a guarantee like that?"

"Without any real proof to back up what she told me, it's not really that much of a guarantee. It's not like I can call a presser and reveal all of this based solely on the word of one woman. I don't care if she's Paul Michaels' wife or the Queen of Sheba, it's all accusations based on the unprovable testimony of one person."

"Well, didn't you get the files that she copied?" Kelly asked. "Or for that matter, did you get the blueprints for that space shuttle? Because I'm thinking that would be a pretty important thing to have."

"Yes, I did get the files that she copied off of his computer, but there were no blueprints of any kind in them. Michaels' wife even told me that she looked for them, specifically, on the computer, in his files, around the house, everywhere. It would seem the only copy of those blueprints was on the thumb drive that I am now very convinced was destroyed when Kinley Devereaux shot the Secretary of Defense dead two summers ago in Washington, D.C.," the senator answered.

"If you have proof of Kinley Devereaux shooting the SOD, then you should show me. I mean, maybe. Maybe he did, but it's like you were saying earlier, if he did, he may have done this country a greater service than we could ever imagine."

"All right then, let's get down to why we're here."

"We probably should," Kelley agreed. "I'm sure that waitress will be back pretty soon."

"So, now that you know Kinley Devereaux is alive, have you contacted him?"

"I have, yes."

"So, you know where he is?"

"Actually, as of right now? No, I don't. I do know that he will be in contact with me soon. He is helping someone that needs him."

"He and Harper Rowe?"

"Yes."

"So, let me see if I got this right," the senator said. "I am going to go ahead and figure that you told the two of them that you were going to talk to me about trying to clear their names, but instead of them coming right here, they're helping someone else first?"

"Pretty much. Although, I did not tell them that it was you, specifically, that I was going to be meeting with. But I did tell them what I was hoping to accomplish at this meeting."

"And they were, like, oh, thank you very much, but we have a previous engagement to save somebody else before we can deal with your thing?"

"Yes."

"Lord, I don't know if that's valor or stupidity." Now it was Senator Cobb-Schmidt that was shaking her head in disbelief. "I guess that will be one of many questions that I will ask them when we meet. I am also extremely curious to know whether or not they made a copy of that thumb drive before the meeting with Michaels. Plus, I'd love to know what they have been doing since the Secretary's assassination. Any clue, Miss Campbell?"

"I don't really know. I would imagine that they were doing the same thing I was doing: surviving."

"God, I can't imagine having to do that...everything you must've gone through...being away from everything you knew."

"Eh, the first two months were hard. I didn't know what was going on. I didn't know if everything that had happened ended when the Secretary was killed. I was constantly in fear and looking over my shoulder. I thought Kinley was dead. It was hard, but then I kinda developed a rhythm, a routine, I made new friends, and I found that, over time, I was thinking less about where I had been and started focusing more on where I was going. I guess it was either adapt to a new life or die hanging onto the old one."

"And now...here you are. A walking, talking testimonial to the triumph of the human spirit. You know, Ms. Campbell, I could definitely use someone like you on my campaign team."

"Senator, one last time, what is it – specifically – that you have to offer up as proof for Kinley Devereaux and Harper Rowe's redemption in the assassination of Paul Michaels. Especially if his wife isn't going to be involved. Will you have enough with the files that you were able to retrieve off of his computer?"

"Absolutely."

"Well"—Kelly looked dissatisfied— "I'm going to need specifics. What is it exactly that you can get from those files that will make Paul Michaels out to be the bad guy, and my two guys out to be the heroes that they are? I believe that is what you called them earlier, yes?"

"There are emails and recordings that are contained in the files that I have. Things that will bring to light just what was going on with the Secretary and his plans toward the end of his days. I assure you, Ms. Campbell, we have plenty enough to bury him and get your guys back in good standing as far as this country is concerned."

Campbell looked at Cobb-Schmidt resolutely. "Thank you, Senator. I appreciate that. I will consider your offer, but right now, my main goal is to see if we can't get Kinley and Harper back home as soon as possible. I'm just glad that somebody is willing to do the right thing and tell the truth about what really happened a year and a half ago. It's been too long coming."

"You should sleep well tonight in knowing that it won't be long now, and Devereaux and Rowe will be right where they need to be."

The waitress returned to the table. "Is everyone ready?"

A Late-Night Caller

It was just past 1:00 a.m. local time, and Big James Gray was fast asleep on his living room couch. It was pitch black outside, and the only light inside the house was coming from the television set that James had been watching just before he finally succumbed to a much-needed slumber.

The remote to the television and Gray's cell phone had both slipped to the floor in front of the sofa. So when Laurie Chase's call set off her personalized ringtone on Gray's cellular device in the wee morning hours of January 6, it caused Gray to suffer such confusion and disorientation that he ended up off the couch and on the floor scrambling awkwardly to find the right mechanism. By the time he managed to answer the phone, the call had gone to voicemail.

"Snapdragons," he muttered. Rolling onto his back, he let his body sprawl across the floor and called Laurie back.

"I'm guessing you were sleeping?" Laurie Chase answered.

"I'd hit you with some sort of smart alec answer, but I know if you're calling at this time of night that things probably are not of a smart alecky nature."

"How soon can you get yourself together and get over here? Tito is on his way back. It's a bit of a flight so we aren't in a time crunch. Still, the sooner you can get over here, the sooner we can start putting our final plan together. It's time to start writing the final chapter on the demise of Tito del Fuento."

Big James let out a long sigh. "Let me shake the sand out of my eyes, and I—"

Gray's sentence was interrupted by a loud knocking at his back door.

"What the—" Big Time flopped over onto his stomach, floundered onto all fours, then perched precariously on the edge of his couch.

"Hello?" asked a confused Laurie Chase. "You still there, James?"

"Yeah," Gray answered, once again out of breath.

"Dude," Laurie said, "you really need to start doing Pilates or something."

"Somebody's at my door," James answered, seemingly unphased by Laurie's dig.

"Late night business meeting?"

"Not that I know of," Gray answered quietly as he stood to his feet and warily began making his way through his kitchen and toward the back door. "No, this is an unplanned knock, whoever it is."

Before he could get to the door, another loud knock came, this time followed with the stern words, "James Gray! I am United States NSA Special Agent Jebediah Crool. I'm here with Special Agent David Baldwin. We would like to speak with you, sir!"

"Laurie," he said quietly, "did you hear that?"

"I heard something," Chase heard herself inexplicably whisper, "but I couldn't make out voices or dialogue. Who is it? What's going on?"

"Who it is, and what's going on is...I think the guys that are after Harper are here at my house."

CLOSING IN ON PRAGUE

He did not realize that Harper was on the phone. So when Kinley returned from the plane's cockpit and said, "Bairre's straight on everything. He said that we misunderstood him about the timing of the storm," his words fell on already-occupied ears.

Harper turned and looked at his friend. Pointing to the phone he had up to his left ear, he lipped the word "Taralyn."

Kinley plopped back down in his seat. "Has she landed yet?"

Harper nodded in the affirmative as he continued listening to Taralyn. Then he whispered, "She said it's not snowing."

"Put her on speaker."

"Ta...Tara," Harper tried to interrupt her. "Tara, sweetie." She kept talking. "Tara, hey, I'm..." She kept talking. Harper finally shrugged and hit the speaker button, catching Taralyn in mid-sentence.

"...so I'm thinking whatever we're going to do, we need to do it fast because the forces of nature seem to be using us as a battering ram."

Kinley gave Harper a quizzical look.

"Taralyn, Kinley is here with us now. I have all three of us on speakerphone."

"Oh. Hey, Kinley!" she said.

"Taralyn," Devereaux replied in a stoic tone, "D'you have a good flight back?"

"I did. It gave me a lot of time to get my thoughts together. Get really focused on what we're about to do here."

"Oh, yeah? So, do you still want to do this?"

"Absolutely."

"Well, then," Dev winced, "you should probably get back on that plane and do some more focusing. Because apparently it didn't work the first time."

Tara laughed. "Believe me, Mr. Devereaux, there were more than a few times during my flight that I had to convince myself that this might work."

"Do you know where we'll be landing?"

"Harper gave me the coordinates, and I'm heading there now."

"What are you driving?"

"A six-passenger all-wheel-drive SUV."

"That works." Kinley looked at Harp and asked, "How much of the plan did you cover with her?"

"Just about none of it," was Rowe's response.

"Then there's no time like the present."

"Agreed."

"Ya ready for this?"

"Let's hear what we're workin' with," Taralyn said.

"Okay. So you pick up me and the kid from the airstrip. From there the three of us are going to pick up an associate of mine. He deals in falsified papers. New IDs, new passports, work visas, the whole nine. And from there the four of us head to wherever your friend has the mother and daughter stashed. With me so far?" Devereaux asked.

"Absolutely," came Tara's response.

Kin leaned toward Harper and quietly said, "I was actually asking you that question."

Harp smiled, then picked up where his friend left off.

"While Kinley and his guy are getting the mom and daughter taken care of, paper-wise, you and I are going to go meet up with a friend of mine. She runs a modeling agency, and she is putting together a modeling crew that will be flying out on an assignment later on today. We need to get them and the mother and daughter together at the airport. We'll get them there, and Kinley will get Anezka and Jana there. We get them coupled up, and your fugitive mother and daughter fly out to a brand new life in a brand new world."

"Wait. What?" asked Tharp. "A modeling crew? That's your endgame? To pass them off as models?"

"Yes. Models. Endgame. Mother and daughter."

"And then what?" she asked. "What about you and Kinley?"

"Our plan is to fly back out on the bird we flew in on. We'll be winging our way to the States," Harper answered. "What about you? Will you be needing a ride home?"

Taralyn laughed. "Gosh, Harper, you act like it's just another day at the office for you."

"I assure you," Kinley cut in, "if he thought it was anything else, I'd be worried like a candidate on election night, but he's not worried. Neither am I. We have a plan, and we're sticking to it."

"Your plan sounds insanely difficult and somewhat preposterous. Nevertheless, it's better than anything that I could ever come up with so...count me in. I'll see the two of you shortly." And without waiting for so much as a goodbye or a see ya later, Taralyn ended the call.

"She's a champ, ain't she?" Harper smiled.

"Well, she seems to have faith in our ineptitude so...I like 'er," Kinley nodded with a small smirk. "Let's go get this thing done and head for home."

"Kinley, my good man, our plan may have a few holes in it, but I don't think that anybody else could have come up with something this good in this situation."

"That's because nobody else would've ever put themselves in this situation."

"Hmm, true," Rowe shrugged. "Point made and taken."

Trying to Break Big James

With the phone still to his ear, Big James opened his back door to find NSA Special Agents Jeb Crool and David Baldwin standing there with their credentials held out to prove that they were who they said they were.

Big James feigned some passing interest in their credentials before saying, "Hey, come on in, guys. Ya kinda caught me at an embarrassing time. I'm on the phone with the local escort service ordering up tonight's entertainment. Can I get you fellas something?"

Jeb Crool, always business efficient, accepted the man's invitation to "come on in," and burst past James Gray into his home.

"Where's Harper Rowe?" Jeb demanded. Like a raging lion, he stomped through Gray's home, kicked around a few loose chairs, and flipped an antique table over.

"Where's Harper Rowe?" he shouted again.

Big James turned back to Agent Baldwin. "Well, he obviously is good to go. May I interest you in a tasty tart – what was it? – Agent Balfour?"

"It's Baldwin, actually, not that you care," David said, leisurely entering James Gray's home. "I will say this: whoever it is that you're talking to on the phone, you should probably hang up because, just in case you didn't pick up on his hints, my boss aims to find out from you where Harper Rowe is."

Laurie Chase, having heard this, said frantically, "What do you need me to do? Should I come over? Even if it's just for the sake of them not beating you to death?"

"Why, thank you, Trixie, but, no, I won't be needing that third order. I'm sure I can handle two just peachy on my own."

"Fine. Then call me back...if you can," replied a nervous Chase.

Gray hung up the phone. "Okay, let's all take a breath here and use that time to get reacquainted. I apologize for rudely being on the phone when you two came barging in. I gladly admit the *mea culpa* there. Now, why don't we just start this interrogation over again. I mean, that is what this is, right? An interrogation? Where you try to get out of me where Harper Rowe is?"

"That's right, Mr. Gray. It can be a simple interrogation, or it can be something like they run in the Middle East when they're looking for something useful," said a finally calmed down Jeb Crool.

Big James was thinking a few things. First of all, he did not just want to give up key information on Harper Rowe, one of his better friends, by telling these two suits what they wanted to know.

Next, he was thinking that helping Laurie Chase finish off her revenge against Tito del Fuento was fast approaching, and that getting into a long, drawn-out, back and forth with his new houseguests was only going to delay his arrival on that particular scene.

Lastly, entrepreneur that he was, James Gray was wondering how much he could bilk these two for, and if it was worth his time to even try.

No time like the present to find out.

"I'm one of those people that thinks that positive reinforcement gets a lot better results than negative reinforcement does. So, that being said, it sounds like the two of you are wanting to know where Harper Rowe is right about now. I can give you a lot more than that. Question is: what can you boys give me?"

"Oh, considering where we are, and how long it might take someone to find you...we can give you one phenomenal beat down," Crool was quick to reply.

"Probably not, Jeb," Dave said. "He's got company heading this way."

"How did you not know that, Jebediah?" asked a bewildered James Gray. "Oh wait. I forgot that when I asked you earlier if you would be interested in one the finer Rio escorts that I know, you were busy taking out some pent-up frustration on some of my nicer furniture."

"Well, when they get here, they're going to find a beaten mass of a man unless you start talking, jackhole!" Jeb threatened, taking a step toward Big James. But when he realized just how big Big James really was, he stepped back and gave the big man the most intimidating look he could muster.

"Ya know, hoss, I'm not sure if you've ever heard the ancient Chinese secret of being able to catch more flies with honey than a flyswatter and burn more bridges with gasoline than sugar, but if you haven't, you should look it up. You may very well need anger management classes."

"Fine. Look, Mr. Gray, I think we both know that I can cause you a lot of problems with...whatever it is you do around here. The NSA is a lousy group of jokers to have on your bad side, so just let me ask you one question, okay? You give me a straight answer, and we'll be on our way. You can spend the rest of your life waking up everyday without fear of ever hearing anything from the NSA again – and if I can have anything to do with it – any other United States agency, for that matter."

"Can I get that in writing?" Gray asked.

"My word is my writing, and you answering my question, looking me eye to eye, will get you my bond. Deal?"

"Well...it's not great, but...okay. Ask your question, Agent Crool."

"Where's Harper Rowe?"

Big James locked eyes with Jeb Crool and looked deeply into them. Then he nodded. "I know where he is, but let me do you a favor," He looked from Crool to Baldwin. "Both of you."

"Oh, and what kind of favor might that be?"

"I'm going to save you a lot of time, effort, and jet lag. Harper Rowe is somewhere far away. I don't know where exactly – Beijing, Prague, Moscow – but wherever it is, he is doing some good. Oh, and I'm pretty sure that you figured out by now that his sidekick, Kinley Devereaux, is with him. Still, that doesn't matter to you, and I will tell you why."

"I am all ears, big boy."

"He and Devereaux are off on a humanitarian mission some-where, and while I really could tell you where they're doing said act of kindness, I would actually be doing you more harm than good."

"And how is that exactly?" Baldwin asked.

"Because you're closer to catching him than you have been in a long time – maybe ever – but the thing is that even if you left here right now and flew to where he and Devereaux are, they'd be gone way before you got there."

Big James stopped to ponder his decision one more time before he said it out loud. "Fact of the matter is, you should go home. The two of them will be coming to you very soon."

Baldwin and Crool both squinted their eyes and shook their heads back and forth. Simultaneously, they asked, "What?"

"I give you full disclosure...then I don't see any Statey's in my rearview? Ever? No lookin' over my shoulder for the likes of you in the near and distant future?"

"I find it hard to believe that you're just going to give up your friend like this, so we'll see how accurate your info is. Its effective-ness will dictate what you see in your rearview," Crool informed the big man.

"Well, fellas, you've hit the jackpot tonight. And, apparently, so have I. I'm not giving up my friend. I'm just telling you what he's going to do, and it don't really matter if I tell you or not, he's still going to do the same thing. But I appreciate you giving me the concessions that y'all have. He and Devereaux are headed back to the States and soon."

"And why would they do that?" asked Crool.

"Now, don't quote me on this, but I do believe the two of them will be going home because they have been informed that there is someone that can clear their names on the whole Paul Michaels shooting situation."

"So, you seriously expect us to believe that Harper Rowe and Kinley Devereaux have been given a chance to clear their names, but instead of heading straight to that chance, they have strayed off onto some sort of humanitarian mission instead?"

"I know, right?" Big James smiled knowingly. "Not the typical actions of anarchistic assassins on the run, is it?"

All three men were silent for several seconds before Jeb Crool said, "I believe him, Dave. Let's go gather the troops and head for home."

Oh...This Should Go Well

"Are you sure that Captain Lucky Charms up there has the coordinates as to where we're supposed to land?"

"Harp," Kinley said, "when have I ever hired the wrong person for a job?"

"I can recall that one time in Guadalajar—"

"It was a rhetorical question," Kinley was quick to point out. "And I already told you that Bairre is solid. He knows right where we're supposed to land, and once we do, he's going to wait for us as long as it takes."

"That all sounds well and good, but if I'm a pilot flying a plane with an unregistered flight plan into a private landing zone into a country that's not too far removed from communism, *and* there's a capital search going on for some felonious types, I might start to feel like the longer I'm immobile in one spot, the more I feel like a sitting duck."

"So? What? Are you afraid that we're going to rendezvous back at the landing site only to find that our ride home is gone?"

"Hmm, well, now that you mention it, yes," Harper nodded like a bobblehead. "That thought is currently crossing my mind as we talk."

"I assure you, for as much as we're paying this guy, he won't be going anywhere without us."

"Question. When you say we, you actually mean me, don't you?"

"Yeah, I do," Kinley affirmed, "but don't worry. We'll be landing soon and jumping out of the frying pan and into the fire. I'm sure once we do that, you'll forget all about how much this random act of kindness is going to cost you."

"Well, it's like the saying goes, 'You can't put a price tag on a human life', although, I've read articles where they have, and, as it turns out, we're not worth nearly as much as we think we are."

"Oh? Pray tell, how much is a human life worth, if you don't mind my inquiring mind wanting to know?"

"About 600 large...according to our U.S. government."

"Based on what?

"Based on what they pay a soldier's family when he or she is killed in battle."

"What about people that aren't American soldiers?"

"A regular citizen in most countries – based on the average life insurance policy that is written on the average person that lives an average lifetime," Harper paused, rolled his eyes up and to the left, thought about it for about ten seconds before answering, "roughly $149,000."

"Oh my. Then you are going to be completely disappointed when you hear how much it's going to cost you to rescue—"

"I'll only be disappointed if we fail," Harper interrupted.

"Well," Kinley smirked, "if we fail that means we probably get killed, too, so I think you're in good shape here, kid."

"Think we should go over the plan again? You know, just to be sure that you and I are on the same page? So as to not killed."

"I most certainly do *not* think we should go back over the plan because, if we do, I'm pretty convinced that one of us will realize what a ruse this whole idea is, and then we'll want to start adding pieces and moving parts which will, eventually, lead to us calling everyone that we have already talked to and telling them about all the changes we've made, and why, and that will lead to them saying, 'Oh...this should go well.' and completely lose all faith in us. We're going to stick with our initial concept. I don't know the rhyming nor the reasoning, but we have a rather strong track record sticking with Plan A. So that's what we're going to do."

Harper sighed, "Okay."

"Besides, I don't think we're going to have enough time to come up with alternate addendums and secondary substitutions. We're getting ready to land. Like I said: It's time to say, 'goodbye, frying pan...hello, fire.'"

"Yeah, I get that. I just hope the burner's on low."

Playing A Hunch

Agent Baldwin had driven about half a mile from Big James' place when Jeb Crool abruptly said, "Pull over here, Dave."

"What?"

"Pull over. I'm giving you a direct order. Pull over. Here. Pull over."

Baldwin knew that when he was given a direct order from his superior, questioning it would get him into a whole lot more trouble than blindly obeying.

Seeing a small interstice off to his right, he braked hard, jerked the wheel to the right, and rigidly skidded to a stop.

"I did what you ordered," he looked at Jeb with bewilderment on his face. "Why are we here? I thought we were going to pick up the rest of the team and head back home to wait for Harper Rowe and Kinley Devereaux."

"Good Lord, Dave," Jeb shook his head. "Did you really buy into all the nonsense that fat man was spouting back there? Because if you did, I've got a Kardashian with a Ph.D. I'd like to sell ya."

"Well, I kinda thought that we left outta there a little—"

"Don't think, Dave," Jeb broke in. "We left because we wanted him to think that we left. I mean, were you really buying that he was on the phone with an escort service? Did you really think he was going to bring in some hookers to bribe a couple NSA agents?"

"He seemed convincing at the time, boss. I mean, c'mon, a guy that fat has got to be paying for it, ya know?"

Jeb took his time before responding.

"Ya see, Agent Baldwin, you look at a guy like James Gray, and you see a red-headed fatso that couldn't possibly score with the ladies on his best day. I look at James Gray, and I see a big, fluffy, teddy bear that knows not only how to work the ladies – but how to work the entire crowd. He's charming, he's smart, he's charismatic, and he's loaded. No, he wasn't on the phone with any escort service. He was on the phone with someone he did not want you and me knowing he was talking to. The whole thing about getting us some poon? Distraction.

"The whole thing about keeping his calm? Distraction.

"Him giving us some info about Harper Rowe and his buddy heading back to the States? *If* it is true, he gave it up way too easily. Which means he just wanted us out of there as quickly as possible."

"Okay, okay," Dave laughed, "but why are we pulling off the road here?"

"I gotta hunch that our big-bellied friend will be making his way toward somewhere and soon. I don't know exactly what we will find at the end of this rainbow, but my gut tells me that it will be worth it to stick around for just a couple more hours. Hey, maybe I'm wrong."

Crool knew that in situations like this he was rarely, if ever, wrong.

Baldwin knew it, too. So he straightened the car and backed it further off the road so that when James Gray came driving by on his way to wherever, the two NSA agents would be virtually impossible to spot.

Look Both Ways and Check

Your Rearview Mirror

Jeb Crool was right.

He and Agent David Baldwin had not been tucked away in their hiding spot more than five minutes before Big James blew past them in a teal minivan at an insane rate of speed.

"Holy crap!" both men howled.

"Hit it, Floyd!" yelled Crool as Dave punched the gas pedal of the Chevy Malibu. "I don't know where he's going, but he's sure in a blaze of blue to get there!"

And just like that, the duo was in hot pursuit.

The road was not paved, nor was it anywhere close to a regulation-sized two-lane thoroughfare, but Baldwin had grown up in the hills of West Virginia where go-karts and four-wheelers were the rule of the day and usually made their own paths through dense woods and thicket. So he was able to hold his own keeping up with Gray.

"You're doin' good, Dave. You're doing real good," Crool encouraged. "This guy's got home field advantage, but you're hanging right with him. Just don't get too close and give away our position."

"Jeb, I'm' doing about 70 mph and barely keeping him in sight.

I don't think my getting too close is going to be an issue."

Even though Big James had a nice lead, Baldwin had to contend with driving through the dust and debris that Gray's minivan was leaving in its wake. Dave had the Malibu hugging the turns, skirting the shoulders – such as they were – and using every ounce of tread and rubber that the vehicle's tires had to give.

Both Dave and Jeb were white-knuckling it through every turn and straightaway of pursuit: Dave on the wheel; Jeb on the dashboard. Both men's focus was fierce. Their adrenaline was high. It was moments like this that made all the boring stakeouts, endless paperwork, and indescribable red tape worth it all. Baldwin hit a straightaway which gave him a chance to look down at the speedometer.

"Sweet baby new year! I'm clockin' 80!"

"Dave, you keep your eyes on the road. I'll keep my eyes on the speedometer!"

The adrenalin.

The situation.

The nerves of steel.

Dave focused on the road. Jeb focused on the speedometer and the road.

Which explained why neither man saw a third car come onto the road behind them when they hit the straightaway. It also explained how the car was able to rocket up behind them, tap their bumper, and send them spinning wildly out of control. The Chevy Malibu spun around several times before leaving what there was of the road to bounce around in the trees like a pinball before coming to rest some 150 feet later. Fortunately, due to all the recent safety measures that had been added to the new model of Malibu, the two men were okay.

Jeb Crool and David Baldwin...like a rock.

"Holy Moses!" Big James yelled. "You made that car spin around more times than a disco ball."

"I know," Laurie Chase replied, "and I barely tapped it!"

Big James had his com in his right ear; Chase had hers in her left.

"Think they're okay?"

"They're probably going to need a shipload of Ben Gay and Ace bandages, maybe some massage therapy. I think once it's all said and done, though, the biggest hurt will be to their egos."

"Well, because I'm not a total cick, I'm gonna go ahead and call it in. Even if they are okay, I don't think they'll be able to find their way back to anything useful for a long, long time if left to their own devices."

"Do it," Chase agreed. "Our job here is done. We're keeping them from catching up with Kinley and Harper, and we're making sure they don't interfere with our final plans for Tito del Fuento. Let's call this one done and done."

WELCOME TO PRAGUE

The sun came up in Prague, but no one was going to notice it. Not today.

It was getting ready to snow, and the sky was changing from black to dark gray to pale gray. Any hope of the sun's rays coming through the clouds would have to wait for another day.

Still, just as the sun tried to make an appearance, Bairre Dolan was landing the plane that Kinley Devereaux and Harper Rowe were in.

Bairre came over the plane's sound system, "All rate, byes. It is time ta get off dis scrap heap an' take care of your bezness."

Kin turned to his buddy and said, "I think this is our stop."

Harper looked out of the nearest window to see what was waiting for them. "Looks kinda peaceful out there...if you like leafless trees, dead grass, and barren skies."

"Is Laurie out there in a white cargo van with a bunch of Mexican cartel guys following her closely and looking to shoot anything that isn't them?"

"I can tell you this," Harper laughed, "Taralyn's out there. Looks like she's by herself. Looks like we're good to get the heck off this bird."

"I miss her," Kinley pined.

"Taralyn?"

"No, ya big dope. Laurs."

Harper stood up from his seat and headed toward the exit door of the plane. "It's nice that you miss Laurie. And by all means, at some point we'll get back to that. But the time has come for you to focus. Like you said: frying pan"—Harp pointed to the floor of the plane, then out the window—"fire."

"Right. Except that given the current weather conditions, it's more like: ice cube tray, freezer." Devereaux stood up. "Let's go rescue that mom and daughter."

Not having on-board luggage, the deplaning process was about as easy as it could get.

"I love traveling light," Kinley said as he and Harper descended the plane steps.

"I know. We save a ton on baggage fees. People would kill to travel like we do. Just kill, I tell ya."

The duo hit the ground and headed toward Taralyn and a new Mazda CX-5. As they neared the SUV, Kinley hollered to Harper, "Take shotgun. I'll take the back seat."

"Cool," Harp yelled back. As he got closer to the vehicle, he signaled for Tara to get into the Mazda, get it started and ready to go. A few seconds later, Harper clambered into the passenger's seat. Devereaux hopped into the back seat behind Harp where he found that, much to his surprise, he was not alone. "Oh, hello," he said slowly.

"Kinley Devereaux, Harper Rowe," Tara addressed them, "meet my oldest and dearest friend, Eliska Lukasik."

"Does she speak English?" Dev asked from the back seat. Then, remembering his manners, he turned to Eliska and asked, "Do you speak English?"

"Is not great," she smiled bashfully.

"She speaks just fine," Tara interjected. "She got me out here to you guys which I definitely couldn't've done if it was just me and Czech TomTom."

"That's good enough for me," Kinley reached out and shook her hand. "It's a pleasure."

Harper turned to Eliska, smiled reassuringly, and said, "Kinley's a fine travel companion. He can play the license plate game better than anyone I know. You're in good hands back there."

After receiving a very confused look from Eliska Lukasik, Rowe turned to Taralyn. "I'm no meteorologist, but I'm pretty sure that this impending snowstorm that's headed our way isn't thinking about slowing down just because the lot of us are on a humanitarian mission."

"Meaning?"

"Drive."

And off they went as the conversation continued.

"Where are we headed?" Tara asked. "Do we know?"

"Where are we right now?"

"About twenty minutes northwest of Florenc, Prague."

"Head toward Prague 6," Kinley said. "Our best laid plan begins there. A man named Karel Josef. He's a paper guy, and he's going to get Anezka and Jana properly documented so that they can fly out of the country this evening with Harp's model friends."

"You can get Anezka and Jana out of country tonight?" Ellie asked excitedly.

"In theory," Harper began tentatively, "we have devised some semblance of a—"

"Yes," Kinley said confidently, shooting an evil glare towards Harper. Then he turned a kind gaze to Ellie and smiled. "Yes, we're going to get them out and get them someplace safe and nice where they can have a fresh start and not have to worry about looking over their shoulders for the rest of their lives."

Eliska grabbed Kinley's hand and said, "Thank you." She then leaned very close to Devereaux, so much so that it made him feel a bit uncomfortable for a moment. But all the uneasiness was quickly alleviated when he heard her whisper in his ear, "Your friend is very much confusing."

Kin whispered back, "Thank you. I can't tell you how nice it is to hear that coming from someone else's mouth for a change."

"You just did," she acknowledged.

"Ellie," Taralyn said, making eye contact with her friend in the rearview mirror, "do you know the way to Prague 6 from here?"

"Yes. You are in right direction. Keep straight for another 8 or 9 kilometers, and you will return into town. I will guide you."

"Were you able to get any sleep on the flight here?" Tara asked Kin and Harp.

"We got some sleep. We came up with a plan. We made a few phone calls. It was a productive flight."

"Ya know what we didn't do?" Harper asked and before anyone could respond, he answered, "We didn't eat anything. Nothing."

"So, you two haven't eaten since I saw you in Rio?"

"That is correct, ma'am. It has been some time, to be sure."

"Yeah," Kinley agreed, "I could definitely go for something." He looked at Eliska. "Any fast food joints on our way to Prague 6?"

"Many places to eat in town. Will find something," she beamed.

Kinley looked at Eliska and tried unsuccessfully not to smile. She had such a joy about her. Her own smile expressed sheer gratitude for was going on at the moment – that he and Harper and Taralyn were here to get her friends out of harm's way to someplace safe, and that she was able to be a part of it all.

"What do we know about the storm that's moving in?" Harper asked. "Also, has your friend been in the back seat the whole time, or did she move back there when you picked us up?"

Taralyn gave Harp an odd look, so he quickly followed up his bizarre question with even more bizarre reasoning. "Hey, I know that you're thinking that's an odd question, but it would be an even weirder thing if you'd had her riding in the back seat the whole time.

You get that...right?"

Taralyn reached over to turn the car radio up so they could all hear it. "You know the language better than I do. You and Ellie let me and Kinley know when you hear something that sounds like weather."

For several minutes, everyone sat silently listening to the radio.

Kin and Tara recognized a few Czech words, but the rest of it may as well have been a fat kid running his index finger up and down on his lips making the "*ubba bubba bubba bubba*" noise.

"Crap, that's not good," Harper said seriously.

"What?" Kinley and Taralyn asked at the same time.

"Storm is only three to four hours away from Prague. Will be bad," Ellie shook her head.

As if they did not believe anything Ellie had said, Kin and Tara looked to Harper.

"Maybe you need me to translate what she just said," Harper smirked. "Ya need to step on it. We've got, at best, four hours to get this done. After that, the city will shut everything down because of snow, and no one will be able to leave. And we don't want that. Worst case scenario would be us getting the mother and daughter into the airport, past security, and then...oops...the airport gets shut down. And the two most-wanted people in all of Prague are trapped in a very secluded spot that the police and security are trolling past every two minutes."

"Well, if we're passing around bad news like it's hot dogs at a baseball game, then I have some not so great news myself," Tara jumped in.

"How not so great?"

"We can take a direct route to where we need to be, but there will be checkpoints that we will have to go through. Or we can go on a roundabout route that will add some twenty to thirty minutes to our trip."

Harper quickly looked at Kinley. "I'd rather go the scenic route.

Better safe than sorry. What do you think, Kin?"

"Here's what I think"—Devereaux let out a long sigh—"At any other time, under any other circumstance, I'd say let's play it safe and go the roundabout route. But on this particular turn, I'm willing to roll the dice that the law in this town has a one-track mind for the mother and daughter. I'd almost be willing to bet that today, and today alone, Harper and I could walk up to the police in this city and try to turn ourselves in, and they would tell us to take a number. I say"—he paused for just a second—"I say we take the direct route and save some time."

Taralyn caught her best friend's eye in the rearview mirror. "This is your town, love. Do you think Kinley is right?"

"Storm is coming, yes. Must need to hurry if all of you make it out of Prague before storm."

"Sounds like we have our plan then," Harper announced.

"No."

All heads turned to look at Kinley – even the driver.

"No," Kin said again. "I'm changing my vote."

"Ohh, don't tell me you're voting for Gore," Harper could not resist.

"No. What?"

"Pay no attention to me nor the man behind the curtain," Harper said. "Why are you changing your vote?"

"Logic."

"Well, thank you for that amazing answer.".

"Pay attention," Kinley said in complete seriousness. "We can go the main roads which are obviously the quicker way, but if they're stopping traffic to check every car that passes by, that, in and of itself, will slow us down to the point of inertia. So I don't see us making up much time going that route. Do you?"

"Well, when you put it in such rational terms like that...no, I don't suppose I do."

"Oh, my sweet luck! Will you two please make up your minds? Where am I going?" asked a frustrated Taralyn.

"We're going to see my friend, Karel Josef."

"Right. I got that part, but where does he live?"

"Well," Kin hesitated, "I'm not sure where he lives, specifically. In Prague 6 somewhere. I just need to make a call or two, and we'll be fine."

Taralyn jerked the car onto the shoulder of the road and shut the engine off. She spun around in the driver's seat like she was the stunt double in The Exorcist. "You just got off a flight that was – like – a gazillion hours long," she said curtly. "You couldn't have made these calls then?"

"I'm going to make a call now," Kin flashed an ersatz smile. He looked at Ellie and asked, "You can get her to Prague 6, right?"

"Yes," Lukasik nodded her blond head.

"She'll get you to Prague 6," Kinley affirmed, "and by the time you get there, I'll have the specific address where you can go." Devereaux sat back in his seat and commenced making a call to Karel Josef.

Ellie scooted forward to lean in between the front bucket seats. Pointing straight ahead, she said, "Go to city on this road. Is fifteen minutes. I will tell you next directions then."

"Do you know this road?" Harper asked Ellie.

"I do not travel this road often. Why do you ask me?"

"Police. We need to go fast, so I was just wondering if you knew whether or not this road is highly policed."

"Do not know," Ellie admitted. "Still, police are busy looking for Anezka and Jana. Search will be in city, not out here on rural road."

Harper turned to Tara. "She makes a good point. Punch it!"

Taralyn pressed the accelerator all the way to the floor. The car zoomed down the road through the biting, morning air.

"Good?" Tharp asked as she smiled at Harper.

"Golden," Harper smiled back.

"Like silence!" Kinley yelled from the back seat.

The radio station started playing Czech music. No one was a fan, so Harp reached down and started to fidget with the radio. "Any idea what station will have the most updated weather?"

"Your grasp of the Czech language is much better than mine," Tara shrugged.

"Ellie!" he turned to his left.

"Yes?"

"Umm...*jaká radiostanice hraje počasí?*"

"Oh!" Ellie smiled. "*rozhlasová stanice 101,1 FM.*"

"Ask and ye shall receive, Taralyn," Harper beamed as he tuned the car's radio to station 101.1 FM. He listened intently to the Prague news station. The story about Anezka and Jana Bucek was the lead story. And the second story. Then there were some commercials.

Then the Buceks made the lead-in out of the commercial break and into the weather.

Ellie smacked Harper. "Here is weather."

Harper smacked her back. "*Ano, jsem si toho vědom.*"

"Fine," she said indignantly.

The two of them listened closely as the station played the information they wanted to hear. They both shook their heads in worry.

"*Pitomče!*" Ellie muttered angrily.

"Judas Priest," Rowe grumbled.

"What?" Taralyn asked.

"It would seem that the weather forecast has changed."

"Already? How?"

"Not for good," Ellie said.

"Kin," Harper was serious. "It looks like our time frame may have just been cut in half."

"What do you mean?"

"Yeah," Taralyn said, "what do you mean?"

Harper looked to Ellie. "*Jak přesný je tento zdroj zpráv?*" he asked looking to validate the news source.

"*Velmi,*" she confirmed.

"A little bit ago we were looking at three to four hours until the snowstorm moved in. But now," Harper grimaced, "we're looking at 90 minutes. Two hours being the best-case scenario."

"Hold on, Karel," Devereaux said. He hit the mute button on his cell phone before starting in on Harper. "What do you want me to do, Harper? We're already moving on my end of this deal. I'm going as fast as I can."

"Right," Harper nodded, and he watched Kinley unmute his phone and return to his call with Karel Josef. Harp turned forward, tapped on the dashboard for a few seconds, and finally said to Taralyn, "When you get into town – into Prague – I am going to need you to let me out."

"Let you out?" Taralyn asked. "No. No. Not even."

"Oddly enough...yes."

"Why? What are you going to do?"

"There are more than just a couple of steps to our plan. And when we thought we had a few hours to work with, taking them one step at a time and being thorough was the prudent way to go. Now, we may not even have half the time that we thought we were working with. Now it's time to take things two steps at a time. I need you to drop me off in the city. I will get a taxi and head over to the modeling agency to see my friend, Constance Ondracek. I'll get her and her people to the airport, and the three of you will take care of the mother and daughter and getting them the paperwork that they need and getting them to the airport. We'll all meet up together in or around the airport and get this thing done. You'll be fine. You'll be with your friend here and with Kinley. You'll be fine."

Ellie leaned forward from the back seat. "No. You should not take Prague taxi. Is very bad and very dangerous."

"Aww, aren't you kind for saying that," Harper looked at her and smiled, "but I assure you that this is not my first rodeo in Prague. I know what the crooked cabbies do here. I know that they have a device that can make make the mileage meter move four times faster than it should."

"Yes, is true," Ellie agreed, "but some cabbies – if you not pay – they have guns. Make you pay."

Harper's eyes widened excitedly. "For real? Some of the cabbies here have guns?"

"Yes," Eliska furrowed her brow. "Is not good. Is bad."

"It will be okay," Harper assured her. "For one, the cabbies only do that accelerated mileage meter thing with tourists. I speak Czech fluently. The cab driver will never have a clue that I am not from around here. For two, if he does have a gun, I'm pretty sure that I won't have a problem relieving him of that burden."

"I don't like this," Taralyn said.

"It's not my favorite thing to do either," Harp admitted, "but desperate times being what they are..." and he just shrugged his shoulders.

Ellie, Taralyn, and Harper fell silent while Kinley continued talking on his cellphone in the backseat. Some thirteen minutes later Kinley finally got off of his call with Karel Josef.

"We're good to go with my guy. He's got his gear ready to go, and he's ready to be picked up."

"Things are working out already," Harper smiled, "and we've only been on the ground for 32 minutes."

"Have you checked in with Constance yet?" Kin asked.

"No, not yet."

Harper pulled out his wallet and removed a few bills from it. Turning to Ellie, he asked, "Do you have any korunas? I can talk like a local till I'm blue in the face, but if I don't have the local currency to back me up, I may as well be talking in rhyming Pig Latin."

Eliska gave a confused expression. "Pig...Latin?"

Harp extended three $20 bills toward her.

She hesitantly took the cash from Rowe, opened up her pocketbook and slid the money into it. She pulled out what korunas she had and counted them. "Only have CZK 37," she said apologetically, timidly handing the bills to Harper.

"Keep the change," the assassin smiled as he accepted the currency and gave Eliska a reassuring wink. "This should be absolutely fine."

"Here, I have a few, too," Taralyn said, fishing a few bills out of the front pocket of her pants.

They had arrived in the city. Harper instructed Taralyn to pull over and let him out.

"Harper, what are you doing?" Kinley asked, unaware of Harper's plan.

"I'm going to take care of my end of the deal – Constance and her crew," Rowe answered as Tara pulled the car over to the side of the road. Harper got out of the car, then stuck his head back inside.

"Kin, I'm leaving you with the smarter and better-looking part of the pack. I'm going to go take care of my people, and we will see you at the airport in about an hour or so. Probably a good idea to put your com in."

"Yeah, I'll put it in now."

"Then I will talk to you soon." With that, Harper shut the door of the Mazda CX-5 and was off into the cold morning air.

Taralyn turned around in the driver's seat to look at Kinley. "So...do we have that address in Prague 6 yet?"

Once Upon A Time There Was This Cabbie In Prague...

Harper waved good-bye as his friends drove away. Then he quickly went about his business.

The first thing he did was to pull out all of the korunas from his billfold and crumple them up inside his fist.

"Alright. Here we go," he said to himself. "Yo, *kabina!*" He waved his arms as he stepped off the sidewalk and into the street. "Taxi!"

A cab pulled over in no time. "*Ahoj,*" he greeted the driver. Climbing in, he gave the cabbie the address of the Ascending Angels Modeling Agency. "*Vzestupné Modelingová agentura Angels, 123 Uhelný trh...Prosím.*"

Harper watched the driver closely as he pulled out into traffic, to see if he did anything to his fare meter.

Nothing.

The cab driver caught Harper's eye in the rearview mirror and smiled a knowing grin. "*Modelingová agentura. Přátel?*" He was fishing to find out if the modeling agency visit was a friendly one or not.

Harper did not want to bring any unwanted business to Constance's modeling agency, but the fact that the cabbie inquired about it meant he had accepted Harper as a local.

"*Ano, nejlepší přítel,*" Rowe answered, making sure the driver knew that this was not some sort of sexual visit. When he saw the dour look on the cabbie's face, Harper knew that this guy was definitely in the market for something. So he took a chance.

"*Mohu vám položit otázku, řidič?*" he asked the cabbie.

"*Ano,*" the driver answered in the affirmative.

"*Opravdu?*" Harper double checked, "*To je nezákonné.*"

This got the driver's attention. The magic words: *To je nezákonné...*It is illegal.

"*Jak nelegální?* "the cab driver asked, trying to gauge just how illegal Harper was talking.

Harper knew the magic words to any crooked cab driver in any country. Money. And a lot of it.

"*Peníze. Spoustu peněz.*"

The cabbie tried to play it cool like he had been here before, but Harper could tell that he had a fish on the line. Now it was just a matter of whether or not the fish had what Harp wanted: a gun.

"*Potřebuji zbraň.*"

"*Zbraň?*" The cab driver looked at Harper in the rearview mirror to confirm.

"*Ano, zbraň,*" Harp acknowledged that he was, indeed, looking for a gun.

"*Mám zbraň.*"

Yeah. Harper had his fish. Now it was just a matter of reeling him in.

Rowe knew how much he was willing to pay for this guy's gun, so the obvious move was to lowball him and see if he could get a deal.

"*Budu vám platit pět set amerických za zbraň,*" Harper Rowe offered $500.

The driver laughed out loud, and without a second thought, he reached underneath his seat and pulled out a Kimber 1911 Stainless 9mm handgun.

The Kimber 1911 Stainless. Wholesale, around 7 bills. Retail, in the neighborhood of 9 C-notes, maybe a grand.

Seeing the product, Harper felt good about his offer of $500 USD.

"*Jak se jmenujete, řidič?*" Harper asked the cabbie for his name.

"*Mé jméno je Dragoslav,*" he answered.

"*Dragoslav, můj příteli, zastavit vozidlo,*" he instructed the cab driver to pull over. Harper had an offer he knew Dragoslav would not turn down: double the retail price of the gun – in American money. Turning around, Harp used his body to keep the cabbie from seeing him pull $2,000 out of his wallet. In an adept sleight-of-hand move, the assassin kept the wallet out of sight while extending to Dragoslav two grand with his left hand and an open palm with his right. Rowe said nothing, not wanting words to cheapen this most magnificent deal.

If the eyes are, indeed, the windows to a man's soul, the look Harper gave Dragoslav was Judgment Day. The Czechian was stoic for a moment, but then a slight grin crept across his lips. Then that slight grin turned into a big smile, and then the big smile became riotous laughter. The cabbie took the cash from Harper's left hand and slapped the Kimber 1911 into his open right palm.

"*Vy, příteli, jsou velmi dobrý vyjednavač!*" Dragoslav commended Harper on his artful negotiating skills.

"*Ještě jedna věc...*"

Harper did need one more thing to go along with the gun: bullets. He was quick to ask for them to be included in the deal. "Kulky?"

Dragoslav opened the taxi's glove box and pulled out three loaded clips for the Kimber 1911. He tossed them to Harper.

"*Kulky, můj bratr.*" The two men exchanged a hearty handshake, then the cabbie turned back in his seat to face forward. As he pulled back onto the road, he looked at Harper in the rearview mirror. "*Pro výrobu této tak dobré ráno, tak vás budu vozit zbytek cesty pro zdarma.*" The driver told Harper that the ride was on the house.

Harper patted Dragoslav on the shoulder and thanked him for picking up the fare. Both men were smiling. Both men were happy.

Dragoslav took his two grand and tucked it into his shirt pocket.

Harper took his newly purchased handgun and tucked it into the back waistband of his pants.

OCTOPUS FOR BREAKFAST

"**Take left here to** go C6," Eliska instructed Taralyn. "Is just few blocks from here."

"Do you have that address, Kinley?" Tharp asked him.

"I do except that it's not an actual physical street address. My guy is very secretive, and being in a business like his, who can blame him?"

"I don't care if we're meeting him at Six Flags under Atlantis, just tell Ellie where we're going so she can tell me how to get there."

"You know where the Hergetova Cihelna restaurant is, Ellie?"

"Oh, yes." Eliska said. "Is favorite restaurant. Is on embankment of Vltava River near Charles Bridge in Mala Strana." She pointed to a road sign. "See? Mala Strana on road sign? We are only a few kilometers away. Can be there just ten minutes."

"Hey," Kin snapped his fingers. "Idea." He pulled his phone out and dialed Karel Josef again.

"Karel, hey it's Peter. Are you at that restaurant already? You are. Great. Hey, can you do a brother a favor? I am starved, but we are short on time. Can you order me something to go there? Excellent. Thank you."

He looked at Eliska and asked her, "What do you recommend?"

She smiled bashfully. "Um, I like...I very much like... the octopus."

"The octopus?" Devereaux and Taralyn asked together.

"Oh, yes, Peter," Karel Josef said through the phone. "The octopus here is the best in the world. I will order it for you now. How long until you arrive?"

"Ten minutes or so. Are they even making octopus at this time of the morning? That does not sound like a breakfast food."

"Hergetova makes all food all the time. Find parking and come inside. You will see me. We will get your food and go to meet your friends and get this done. I am excited to see you, my friend." And Karel was gone.

Dev slid his phone back into his shirt pocket. "I must be hungry because even octopus sounds good to me right now."

"Turn here and follow this road. Be careful. Many traffic lights and much foot traffic, too. Pedestrians walking," Eliska said.

At this time of the morning there was not a lot of traffic on the road, but the sidewalks were lined with people walking to work. When Tara turned as she was directed, she saw a handful of police on both sides of the street. The officers were stopping random people, checking them for identification. This was obviously part of the all-out citywide search for Anezka and Jana Bucek. The trio in the car instinctively tensed up. And just then, the first flakes of snow began to fall.

Tara let out rigid sigh.

"Oh, and ladies," Kinley spoke up, "the man we're getting ready to meet up with – his name is Karel Josef – he knows me as Peter Krug. I'm an American businessman in the import-export business. We don't need to get into my back story too much, but just be sure to call me Peter. This guy's the only one who is going to be able to get us the proper paperwork to get the Buceks out of the country safely. We don't need to set off any red flags with him. I think there are enough of them already."

"So, if you're Peter, do we need to be anybody different?" Taralyn asked.

"No. You two just be yourselves."

"Does he realize who it is that he is helping out of the country?"

"Yes."

"And he doesn't find it odd that an American businessman is asking for his help to get the two most wanted people in Czechia new identities?"

"No, he doesn't," Kinley answered hesitantly.

"Really? Because – I don't know – I just think something like this would be a bit out of the ordinary."

"He doesn't find it odd because of the kind of business he knows me to be in."

"Importing and exporting?"

"In the past...when I've had dealings with Karel, he's known me as Peter Krug, an American businessman who rescues women and children from unspeakable situations and gets them safe passage to a better life."

"Well, that sounds very noble, but...I'm guessing there's more to this story?"

"Your guess is correct. I only worked with him one time. I was sent to Kiev on assignment to take out a very, very bad dude. Problem was, this bad dude must've gotten wind of something bad coming his way because he went into hiding, and I couldn't even get a whiff of where he was, so I had to resort to my baser instincts to draw this guy out. He had a wife and a teenage daughter. I made arrangements to have this guy's daughter kidnapped and brought to me. That's when I found Karel. I had him make papers for her: a new identity with all the necessary paperwork so that I could've sent this girl wherever I wanted to, and she would never be found. I took the paperwork, and I sent it to her mother. I knew she would be the one that would be able to get it to my mark. Along with the paperwork, I also sent a note letting my mark know that if he didn't make arrangements for a ransom drop, and if he did not show up himself – in person – that a new set of papers would be made for his daughter, and she would be taken far, far away, and he would never see her again."

"Did it work?" Taralyn asked.

"Well, *yeah*, it worked," Dev answered with an "as if" tone in his voice. "It worked perfectly. My mark showed up, I did what I do, and I had his daughter returned to her mother."

"You did what you had to do. So, what's the issue?"

"Yes, I *did* do what I had to do, but the thing is, Karel had no idea that I was using his services to draw some joker out into the open so that I could plant a stop sign into that guy's thought process."

"Well, at least, this time you're telling him the truth," Tara smiled.

"Ooo, T.T., turn here. Left!" Ellie interrupted. "Sorry."

Taralyn hit the brakes and made a sharp left turn, causing Ellie to topple onto Kinley in the back seat.

"Oh no." Ellie was embarrassed. "Am so sorry."

"You two okay back there?"

"I'm good," Kinley laughed. He looked at Eliska and asked, "Are you good?"

"Am good," Ellie confirmed, pulling herself upright. She then scooted up and pointed forward. "See Prague Castle? Is beautiful in the morning, yes?"

Prague Castle is, according to Guinness, the largest coherent castle complex in the world, with an area of about 70,000 square meters. This puts it just a few thousand meters smaller than Buckingham Palace, which is technically a palace, not a castle

Before either Taralyn or Kinley could answer, Ellie said, "Oh... park soon. Road ends."

"How far away are we from the restaurant?" Kin asked.

"A few blocks. About."

"Ellie, I thought you said we were still about ten minutes from being there," Tara was confused.

"*Promiň*," Eliska apologized. "I mean ten minutes to park. Then must walk," she explained. "Must park soon."

Kinley suddenly heard crackl.ng in the com in his ear which was soon followed by a familiar voice, "How you guys doin'?"

"Gimme a minute," Devereaux said quietly. He tapped his com to turn it off, then said aloud to Taralyn, "Why don't you just drop me here."

"What? Are you sure?"

"Hergetova Cihelna is just a block or two from here, right, Eliska?"

"Yes, will be ahead and on left."

"Drop me here, Tara. I'll go find Karel and call you when we are headed back. Find someplace to hole up in the meantime, but stay close. We'll meet you back here in just a few."

"But...what about the police? You can see that they're stopping people—"

"Don't worry about me. Worry about you and your friend. I'll see you soon, Tara."

Devereaux patted her on the shoulder, patted Lukasik on the knee, gave them both a confident wink and a smile, and quickly exited the vehicle.

Kin took a quick reconnaissance of the area before blending himself into the early morning throng of people lining Prague's sidewalks. He tapped his com nonchalantly and asked, "Still there, Harp?"

"Present and accounted for, sir. How's things on your end?"

"Some things got lost in translation, and it has set us back a bit timewise. Also, it's snowing here. Any white stuff where you are?"

"Precipitation free at my twenty," Harp answered in full cop lingo. "So, just how set back are you timewise? If it's snowing already where you are, then it wor.'t be long until the flakes are falling citywide. Which means...we are officially on the clock."

"My guy has me meeting him at a place that cars can't get to.

I'm on foot to him now. We'll meet and then make our way back to Taralyn. I mean, I'm going to move as fast as I can, both to him and with him, but the Prague police presence is pretty thick here on the streets where I am. If I go too fast, I'm going to draw some undesirable attention. Which means the pace at which I'm capable of moving is limited. Which also stinks because it's cold as ice, and I don't have a coat."

Soon enough, though, Kinley found that he was able to use the crowd density to his advantage. He waited for Harper's response, which seemed to be a long time in coming.

"Harp?"

"Yeah," Rowe replied, "I'm here. I'm just thinking."

"About what?"

"About waiting."

"Waiting for what?" Kin asked.

"We're rushing this as it is. If things were to go perfectly, we are still looking at, like, a two percent chance of success. You're rushing to get your guy and rushing to get him to the mother and daughter. Rushing him to get their documents done and in order. Rushing the mother and daughter to the airport. I'm rushing Constance to get everything together with her people and get them to the airport and meet up with the mother and daughter. Rushing them onto a flight and...we're going to end up rushing everyone right into a disaster. You're already behind schedule, and the snowstorm is already ahead of schedule. Why?" Harper hesitated for a moment before making his point. "We don't need to rush. Why are we rushing?"

"Why? Because you and I got someplace to be, buddy. Someplace that we should already be on our way to now."

"I get that, but we're here in Prague now. And like my old high school football coach used to tell us, 'Don't get caught looking ahead to tomorrow when what's right in front of you today is going to knock you down.' His words were true then, and they're true now. If we don't keep our focus on the here and now, we won't be around when it comes time to get back home. Whoever it is that Kelly Campbell has found that has information that can clear our names – it's not like they're going to evaporate into thin air over the next 24 hours. If they do, then they probably weren't a viable source of information anyway."

"Yeah, that's probably true," Kinley hated to admit. "So, what then? What are you thinking in that pea brain of yours?"

"Well, for one thing, I think we should embrace this snowstorm for what it can do for us. If it's as bad as they say it's going to be, then I'm betting there's a good chance that they'll be pulling some of the personnel that they have looking for our mom and kid and put them onto snow duty. That, in and of itself, will give us a little breathing room to move around more freely."

"Valid point."

"Plus...I have a gun now."

"Well, that was just a matter of time. What's your point?"

"I can probably get some more. and I don't feel like I'm going out onto too much of a limb here when I say that your friend, Karel Josef, could probably put us in touch with a few more weapons, as well."

"That may very well be true. but I'm still not getting the connectivity here."

"Okay, I get that my thoughts are a bit scattered, so let me walk you through what I'm thinking."

"This should be fun."

"The storm is already here. Just a matter of time until the airport shuts down. In the meantime, you get your guy and Anezka and Jana. All of you come to where I am at Constance's modeling agency. Your guy gets the mother and daughter documented so they can go with the modeling crew once the airport reopens. With me so far?"

"So far."

"It only makes sense to think that once the storm hits, all law enforcement personnel in the immediate Prague area will be assigned to either find the Buceks or to snowstorm-related issues. Thus giving you and me some time to get a few firearms together and go lay down some American justice on the sex trafficking ring that got our mother and daughter into this mess in the first place. I mean, you can't tell me that the thought of doing that hasn't crossed your mind a few times since we decided upon this adventure."

"I'd be lying if I said otherwise," Kinley smiled.

"Plus, you already know that Constance has some ties to people that might be able to take the kids in that children's home and relocate them to someplace better."

"Don't ya think we're already asking enough from her as it is?"

"Probably, but I know Constance, and I know that she would do anything to help out any destitute and forlorn children. Especially when said children are being taken advantage of. I know she has the means and wherewithal to do something about it."

"I hate changing plans in midstream, but when the initial plan seems to be failing like an ISIS fundraiser in Alabama...it may not be such a bad idea to reconsider things."

"I'm standing outside of the Ascending Angels Modeling Agency as we speak. I'll tarry hither for a few minutes if you need some time to think about all of this."

"No need to wait for me, kid. If I think about it for too long, I'm sure I'll find fourteen reasons why we shouldn't do it. No, I'm all in on this. Let me call Bairre to make sure that he's cool with riding the storm out here. Then I'll get up with Kelly to make sure we have the time you think we have to get back to the States. I'll call you back once I have Karel and we're on our way to the mother and daughter."

Harper laughed. "Never a dull moment with us, is there, Kin?"

Changing Plans in Midstream

Bairre did not care about riding out the storm in Prague as long as Bairre was getting paid to ride out the storm in Prague. "I don't mind ' ridin' duh storm out hayr, lad. I'll kape duh props and rudders dusted off forr ya."

Knowing that Bairre was good to go with the new plan of attack, Kinley's next call was not to Kelly Campbell. Instead, he called Taralyn.

"Are you on your way back already?" she answered.

"No. Not even. I haven't even gotten to the restaurant yet. What about you two? Have you found a place to lay low for a few?"

"We have...but I get the feeling that you checking up on our well-being isn't the reason you're calling."

"And you'd be correct."

"Then to what do I owe the privilege?"

"I was talking to Harper, and he brought a few things to my attention that were actually worth thinking about."

"Such as?"

"Such as: we might need to slow our roll a bit. The storm is already moving in, and if we try to beat it, we may end up making some irrevocable mistakes. Mistakes that could get all parties involved in this escapade killed or imprisoned."

"Sounds like he's on to something. I can get along with not getting killed or imprisoned. Did he give you an alternate plan, or are we winging it from here?"

"The plan as we know it is still the same. I'm about thirty seconds or so from meeting up with Karel. He and I are going to meet up with you just like we planned. I'll call you once we're on our way out...octopus and all."

"Then may I suggest something?" Tara asked.

"Yes, of course."

"Why don't you just take your time there. Meet up with your friend, bring him up to speed on what's going on, and, heck, maybe you can even eat your octopus at a real table with real chairs and silverware like a civilized human being. Ellie is going to take me to the Buceks. She said that where they are hiding out is a bit off the beaten path, and if this snow keeps falling at this rate, we may have an issue getting in and out of where they are."

"Then that's the plan. Call me when you're headed back this way...and be careful."

Out of The Wreckage

Jeb and Dave gingerly climbed out of the wreckage that was their blue rental car and began picking their way back to the dirt road in the dark.

Once in the open, they checked themselves for any major injuries. And ticks. All clear.

In the distance, they could hear the sirens of approaching emergency vehicles.

As they walked back to the dusty throughway, the two of them tried to figure out their next move.

"We're lucky to still be breathin'," Jeb started off the conversation. "I'd love to know who it was that sneaked up behind us and put us in this crappy predicament."

"I'm just glad to be alive," Baldwin admitted. "I think my entire life flashed before my eyes while we were bouncing around the trees."

"Oh, yeah? What did it look like?"

"Short."

Jeb laughed, "Well, I guess so if the entire thing passed before you in the seven seconds we were pinballing off these tree trunks. But I suppose that's the difference between you and me, Dave."

"And what difference is that?"

"While your short life was forming in your membrane, I was

trying to figure out where Big James was rushing off to...and if it had anything to do with who rear-ended us from behind."

"Did you come up with an answer? As far as our aggressor?"

"Some hunches, but they're long shots. Not that it matters, Dave," Jeb sighed, "because whoever it was...they be long gone by now."

Just about then, they saw the emergency vehicles skid to a stop and begin searching the woods. As soon as the spotlights were shined into the trees, Crool and Baldwin started waving their hands around and yelling, "We're fine! Come get us!"

A slight pause, then a voice came back from the rescuers, "Americans?"

"Yes. Americans," Jeb responded, and then said quietly to Dave, "Your life still passing before you now? Because I feel like we're still in 'probably gonna die' mode with these butt monkeys at the helm."

"Understandable, but getting back to what we were just talking about," Dave said, "even if it's one of your long-shot hunches that Big James was driving to, we still might be able to figure it out."

"Oh, yeah? And just how will we do that?"

"I may have slapped a tracker on Big James' vehicle when we left out of there."

Jeb looked at Baldwin incredulously. "Judas Priest, Dave, you're just telling me this now?"

"Well—"

"Well?" Jeb shook his shaven head furiously. "Well...we didn't even have to do what we just did – driving like maniacs on a barely visible dirt path." Jeb took a deep breath. "Although, you are one heck of a driver, Dave. Where did you learn to do that, anyway? I mean, they didn't teach anything like that at the Academy. At least, not the one I went to."

"Truth be told," Dave smiled, "I am good friends with a Hollywood stunt driver named Keith Jenkins. He wrote a book called

The Keith Jenkins Guide to Offensive Driving. I spent some time with him out in L.A. a few years ago, and he showed me some moves and taught me the kind of mindset you need to have to drive like that."

"Think you could show me sometime?"

"Next time we're in-between cases – if that ever happens – we can hit the agency driving track and I can show you and the boys a few things."

"Yeah, I'd like that," Crool answered, just as two members of the local rescue squad reached them and began leading them the rest of the way out of the woods.

"*Obrigado.*" The two of them were grateful for the help.

Once the NSA agents were back to safety, their rescuers started questioning them. Fortunately for Crool and Baldwin, Lieutenant Aline Rapido was on the scene.

"Fancy seeing you here, *Tenente,*" Crool said.

"Whoever it was that called this in was sure to drop your names to the police operator. When I heard them come over the radio, I volunteered to come out here and make sure you two were okay."

"We very much appreciate it."

"So, first of all, what happened, and, secondly, what the heck are you two doing out here at this time of the night?"

"When I questioned Palmeiro, the club owner, he dropped a name: James Gray."

"Ah, yes, Big James Gray. Gun runner extraordinaire."

"You're familiar with him then?"

"Our paths have crossed, yes."

"Well, we tracked him down out here and came to have a talk with him. He didn't give us what we were looking for, so we decided to follow him. Things got a little screwy from there."

"Is he the one that planted the two of you out there in the woods?"

"Not unless he has found a way to be in two places at one time. He was in front of us when we were smacked pretty good from behind."

"Think you were set up? Is it possible that he knew you were going to be tailing him, and he had an accomplice waiting in the wings to ambush you from behind?"

"I don't see how he would've known. The decision to tail him was very last minute. Even if he did know, how he would have been able to get a myrmidon in place in time is beyond me," Jeb shook his head.

The lieutenant gave Jeb a perplexed look. "I'm sorry. Did you say 'a mermaid'?"

"No, not a mermaid. A myrmi—" and then Jeb realized with whom he was speaking, and that while Rapido's knowledge of the English language was good, it may not have been that good. "An accomplice," he smiled.

"You using your Word of the Day calendar again, boss?" Dave snickered quietly.

"You two should probably get to a hospital and get looked at," Aline suggested.

"I think we're okay. We were able to walk out of the woods without too much trouble. Going to hospital would probably be a waste of time...time that we don't have."

"Then can I give you a ride somewhere? It'll give us time to go over what happened here. I am going to have to write up some sort of report on this. The rental car place will require something, I'm sure. Did you have the insurance on your car?"

"We did, yes. Government regulations," Dave replied.

"Yeah, and I'm sure that the rent-a-car people are going to be just thrilled to the gills when we ask to rent another one."

"So? To the airport then?"

"That sounds about right. My men should be there by now. Let's head there so I can get them on a plane back to D.C."

"Will the two of you be joining them?"

"In a hurry to get rid of us, *Tenente*?" Jeb laughed.

"By no means, Agent Crool," Rapido answered.

"Good. Because while it was my original plan to head back to the States because we have it on good authority that is where Harper Rowe is heading, I think Agent Baldwin and I will be sticking around just a little bit longer. Thanks to someone," and Jeb nodded toward Baldwin, "putting a tracker on James Gray's car, we will be finding him again before too long, and when we do, we'll be sure to let him know just how much we appreciate his hospitable treatment toward us tonight."

"On our way to the airport," Lieutenant Rapido began, "I will give you my contact number so that if and when you find Mr. Gray, I would gladly welcome a call from you so that I, too, might have a conversation with the big man."

"Oh? Got a few questions of your own to ask him? Is this about the club shooting? Or something else?" Agent Baldwin probed.

"A night ago the drug compound of a reputed Brazilian drug lord was raided, and the kind of firepower that was used...well...I only know of one man that could get an arsenal like that together, and that man is James Gray. Add that to the club shooting, and, yes, I most definitely have a few questions of my own to ask him."

OUTSIDE HELP

While Kinley was letting Kelly Campbell know that the snowstorm in Prague was going to delay his and Harper's return to the United States, Harper was reuniting with Constance Ondracek for the first time in four years. Before he even got in the door she gave him a bear hug.

"Harper, I am so glad you have made it safely to here," Constance said, releasing her embrace on the assassin. "Please come inside. It is so cold."

Harp gave a little shimmy to shake off the effect of the hug. "You been workin' out, Coni? You've got a lot of upper body strength," he said as he entered the modeling agency.

"I box."

"You box? Like punching boxing?"

"Yes, is good way to stay in shape while working out pinned up frustrations."

"You have a lot of frustrations, do ya?"

"I work with women models. Mother, friend, boss. Yes, have many frustrations," she laughed. "Please, sit."

The front reception area of the agency had several plush chairs, but it was the 96" Portofino Comfort sofa along the back wall that Rowe headed for. He took two quick steps, jumped in the air, and landed longways on it with his arms folded across his chest.

"Don't mind if I do."

"Easy, my friend. Other than me, the couch is most expensive thing in here." Constance took a seat across from Harper, smiled and sighed. "So glad to see you again, but sad it will be rushed."

"How's the plan coming along for the job in St. Thomas?"

"Is taking more time than I thought. Do not worry, Harper. I will not let you down."

"Well, I have good news and what a very few select people might consider great news," Harper informed her.

"Yes?" Ondracek asked.

"This storm has moved in much faster than anyone anticipated. With everything that is still left to do, my partner and I feel like it would be unwise and flat out dangerous to try to continue with the plan in the time frame for which we were hoping."

"Then what is plan now?"

"Basically, the plan is still the same," Harper explained, swinging his feet off the expensive couch and sitting up straight. "My partner, Kinley Devereaux, is picking up a man that will be able to make all the necessary travel documents for the mother and daughter—"

"The Buceks."

"The Buceks, yes," Rowe continued. "Kinley will get his documents guy – his name is Karel Josef – then they and the other two women that we are working with will get the Buceks and bring them here. Then we will get them all papered up and ready to go to St. Thomas."

"Yes, but you said that plan was basically same."

"And it is," he repeated.

"Yes, but why is basically same and is not altogether same?" Constance tried to make her point a little clearer. "What has changed?"

"Well, that's the part that I think you will find really great."

"Me and very select few people? Ha ha," she smiled her

million-dollar smile. "And what is this great news, my friend?"

"We – and by 'we' I mean me and Kinley – are going to wait out this snowstorm before we attempt to move the Buceks to the airport. We just think that right now there is too much of a risk for all of you to go and get stuck there in this snowstorm. I'm sure the airport is just crawling with security guards and airport police who have been given the strictest of orders to find the Buceks and bring them in. I don't think that any of these law enforcement types are in on what's going on in this town, but they have been given orders to pick up Jana and Anezka just the same. The last thing we want is them to be sitting ducks for hours on end, ya know?"

"Oh...is very good. Then I do not have to rush to get girls together and to airport in the next hour?"

"No, you don't," Harper smiled. "On top of that, Kinley and I are going to be sticking around here a little longer, too, but not for pleasure, I'm afraid."

"Then what is it you will be sticking around for?"

"We are going to make a play at the orphanage," Harper said very seriously, "and we will probably need your help to do it."

"Okay, " the leggy blond answered. "But what does make a play mean? I do not understand this."

"It means that Kin and I are going to try to get those responsible for all of this... this sex trafficking bullshit that has been taking place at that orphanage and bring them to justice for it." He looked at her beautiful gray eyes with as much intensity as he could before saying, "We *will* need your help, though, if we're going to do this."

"More help? Besides models and taking the Buceks out of the country?"

Harper tried to read her facial expressions, but she was rather stoic. He tried to read her eyes. Nothing. She was a blank page. He was about to say something else to try to convince her of how much he and Kinley would need her help when she surprised him.

"Yes. I will help you to make play on the orphanage. What they do is wrong. Wrong for them to do, and wrong for the children."

Harper sprung to his feet and punched at the ceiling in excitement. "Yes, yes, yes! Thank you so much, Constance. Thank you." He rushed over to her and shook her hand with the exuberance of a young televangelist.

"You are welcome." She pulled her hand away from Harper's iron grip. "What do you need for me to do?"

"Well, honestly...I don't know," was his anticlimactic answer. "I guess the first thing that we're going to need to do is find out just where this place is, and then from there we'll have to figure out what is going to be the safest and most effective way to get there."

" I know this orphanage. Is only few kilometers from here."

"A few kilometers?" Harper raised his eyebrows. "That's great. As long as we aren't getting belted by this snowstorm to the point that we can't see three feet in front of our faces, we should be able to hoof that on foot."

"What will you do when you get there?"

"At this point in time, I can say with one hundred percent certainty that I, lit'rally, have no idea. This whole thing has so many unknown variables. What do you know about the home? Any notion of how many children live there?"

"No. I do know that is small in comparison to Detský Domov which is largest children's home in all of Prague. It is in Prague 10 attached to Vinohrady Hospital. Contains more than 50 children and many workers. I have seen children from nearby home on outings in city, and there are much less of them."

"Ballpark figures on what that might be?"

"Ball...park?" Constance asked, unfamiliar with Harper's vernacular.

"Ballpark. It means an educated or estimated guess. Can you give me an estimated guess of how many children live in the home?"

"I would say that answer is less than twenty. Most are between eleven and seventeen years aged."

"So, not a lot of little kids, toddlers, babies, anything of that sort?"

"From what I have seen, no."

Good. That will make it easier..." Harper nodded as his sentence trailed off.

"Easier?"

Rowe was silent as he pondered different scenarios in his head. After several moments, he finally snapped back into the conversation. "I know that you have set up children's homes before by working closely with other like-minded individuals. My question to you is this: Is there anyone like that nearby that might be able to put these children in a safe environment temporarily until all of this gets sorted out?"

"I know you are man of morals and principles," Ondracek stated, "and because I know it, I already expect this to happen. I expect you to want to save children in home and not just the Buceks, and because I expect this to happen, I have made calls already. I have, as you say, put wheel in motion."

Harper smiled. "I like the way you work, lady."

"Is like you told me one day, 'A person does not change. Only our perception of that person changes,' and you are right."

"It really warms the cockles of my heart that you remember things that I told you years ago. If only more people would do that, this world would be such a wonderful place to live," Harper joked. "Seriously, though, how is that coming along? Have you heard from your people in regards to temporarily sheltering the children from this home?"

"Is coming along very good. I tell them once I have plan I will call them, and see what will work and not work."

"Really? Your people are really waiting on us to come up with a plan, and they will be ready to help out? Even in this kind of weather?"

"Ha, ha. Snow may seem very bad to you, but in Czechia, we know this weather well. Is not an issue. Yes, my people are waiting on us to tell them plan for moving children."

"Well, we should probably get cracking on a plan then," Harper shook his head in disbelief.

"Are you troubled, my friend?" Constance asked him.

"Troubled? No, not even a little bit."

"Then why shake head?"

"Let's just say that I was somewhat apprehensive to ask for your help with some of this stuff. You're already doing so much for us. I was just concerned that it might be too much. Now, not only have you agreed to help, but you're already two steps ahead of me."

Constance smiled warmly. "In past you and I have talked about necessity of faith in God. We live lives, you and I, Harper, that rely very much on our faith. We do dangerous things that we could not do on our own. People put faith in us to do these things. We put faith in God to help us do these things, yes?"

"Yes. Very much so."

"Then do not doubt your faith, Harper. In the eyes of God, all that needs to be done is already done."

Harp nodded in wholehearted agreement and, armed with this knowledge, did not hesitate to say, "In order for this hatchling plan of mine to really click its heels together and get on back to Kansas, we're going to need two more things."

Seeing the bewildered expression on her face, he realized that his colorful jargon had once again left Constance disoriented.

"Sorry," he apologized, "what I mean is that in order for us to get a solid base for this plan, we're going to need two more things: We're going to need some weapons for me and Kinley, and, even more importantly, we are going to need someone in a position of authority in this town that we can trust. Know anybody like that?"

"How much do we need to trust them?"

"A lot, Coni," Rowe answered. "Maybe more."

"Hmmm...then maybe we come back to that one," she decided. "As for guns, I have answer."

"Answers are good. What do you have?"

"The head of my security team when we travel. He is retired Russian Secret Police."

"Retired? You mean old?"

Ondracek tried to suppress a smile. "No, do not mean old. Mean retired. Very few Russian Secret Policemen make it to be old. Derek defected to Northern Ireland a few years ago before was too late."

"Your former Russian is named Derek?"

"Yes, Derek Cooke," Coni answered but was quick to specify, "Not his real name. Had to change when defected."

Before any more words could be exchanged, the agency's doorbell rang.

"Will be him now," Constance apprized Harp.

Awaiting del Fuento

Laurie Chase had called ahead to let Diego know that she and Big James were on their way back and ask him to get a light breakfast ready for the three of them. By the time she and James walked into the warehouse, the smell of bacon, toast and coffee filled the air.

"Snapdragons, lady," Big James grinned, "if you and that Devereaux fella weren't such a hot item, I'd be over here on a regular basis because you, without a doubt, know the way to this big man's heart: food and video games."

"Well, JFR, it is Diego that does all the cooking around here."

"Even better, my dear. That leaves us more time for games – video and any other kind we might find ourselves getting into." Gray put his arm around her shoulder and gave her a squeeze.

"Diego!" Laurie yelled. "We're back!"

Just a moment later, Diego came out from the kitchen to greet them. "Meess Laurie, Mees'er James, breakfast weell be ready een just a few meenutes. Coffee while you wait?"

"Perfect. You know how I like mine."

"An' for Mees'er James?"

"Do you have any Irish Crème creamer?"

"*Sim,*" Diego answered.

"I'll have that and three spoons of sugar in mine. Thank you, Diego."

"Diego, any changes to your cousin's flight plan since I've been gone?" Laurie asked.

"No, Meess Laurie, I jus' checked. Everything ees steell thee same," Diego answered on his way back to the kitchen.

Chase and Gray walked into the room containing her computer equipment and the diorama of del Fuento's compound that she had created to plan the attack.

"So, give me the rundown on what we know about Tito's return."

James pulled up a chair next to Laurie as she got to work on her computer. A moment later the printer produced Tito del Fuento's flight plan for his return trip from Amsterdam.

"Let's wait till Diego is back so I don't have to cover this twice," she said

"If it's okay, I've got a question for you in the interim."

"By all means."

"When this is over – when you've finally drained your last drop of revenge from this coffee pot – what's your next play? Got anything planned yet?"

Laurs shrugged. "My general plan is to finally take about two weeks to enjoy the paradise that is Rio de Janeiro. I'm praying that my boyfriend and his harebrained partner can get themselves reinstated as citizens of the United States without too much trouble, and that he can come back here to spend those two weeks with me." Laurie began to feel warm all over. "From there, I'm hoping that he and I can start making a life together."

"Do you think that will be here in Rio?"

"No, I would like to think that we'll be back in the States," she answered. "Why? What's with all the questions, bub?"

"Oh, I don't know. I guess I was just curious as to what your intentions were for this place." Big James waved his hand at the huge complex that Chase had turned into both her home and her headquarters. "You've put an unbelievable amount of work into this. Seems it would be a cryin' shame if you were to just walk away from it."

"I'm guessing you're interested in taking it off my hands?"

"Oh, I'd say that I'm far more than just interested, my dear. If you and I could come to a mutually beneficial deal for me to acquire this place from you, I'd be set like a cement pad."

Diego entered the room carrying a tray with three large cups of coffee. He lowered the tray and let Laurie and James take their drinks before removing his own mug of java. Laurie handed him a set of the papers she had pulled from the printer.

"All right, let's get started," Chase said, turning back to her computer monitor. "As you can see, Tito has arranged for his flight back to Rio to land at Galeao-Antonio. Which means that someone has gotten the word to him that the airstrip at his place is all shot to Swiss cheese. Why else would he be landing at the international airport instead of his own?"

"Is that where we're going to be, too? Or will we be waiting for them at their home?"

"The airport," was her quick answer. "Not that I've gone by to check or anything, but it seems almost certain that his compound is still crawling with several different branches of the law community and probably will be for a while."

"That makes sense," Big James agreed. "So, what's our strategic maneuver once he lands at the airport? I know we've taken out the majority of his protective detail, but we gotta figure that the ones that are left – the ones that he had with him on his own plane the whole time – are going to be his best guys."

"And he weell have hees fameely," Diego reminded the two.

"So, here's the plan: The three of us will arrive at the Galeao-Antonio well before Tito and his family do. We'll get in position so we can track them as soon as they deplane. In my opinion, he'll send his family away at this point. No way he'll be taking them back home. Just going to be way too dangerous there. He won't risk their safety."

"What did you have in mind for them then? I know you, at least, had plans for the Missus."

"I'll have you stay with Tito," Chase instructed. "He may have more men showing up to the airport for added protection for his family."

"No," Diego spoke up. "He weell not bring more protection for Mitra and thee children. He weell have thee men that are weeth heem go weeth them. When he travels weeth just one hundred men, he keeps thee best of them close. He has a handful – maybe eight, maybe ten – that he surrounds 'eemself weeth. Whenever there'ss danger to the fameely, he weell send them to a safe house een Santa Teresa, and these men, they go along to protect them. I remember thees from when I was weeth Tito. I took hees fameely to thees very safe house many times. When I work weeth Tito, only he and I know where thees house was."

"Diego, do they use that house for anything else? Does anyone live there when it's not being used as a safe haven for Tito's family?"

"No, eet's just a safe house. Nothing else."

"So, there ya go," Laurie said. "Diego and I will track the family from the airport, and you will—"

"I'm sorry," Gray interrupted. "Why?"

"Why what?"

"Why do you even need to track them from the airport? I mean, if we already know where they are going to end up, why don't you two just wait for them at this safe house? You might even be able to get a jump on them when they arrive."

Laurie was lost in thought for a few seconds, then shook her head slowly. "No. No, it's just too risky. I know that being able to get a jump on them would be a huge advantage, but what if this one time they use a different place? We wouldn't have a clue where they'd be and having Tito's family as a bargaining chip is a huge part of this plan."

"Okay, but not benefitting from an obvious advantage in our favor...we'd really be pissing away an opportunity to get the upper hand in this whole situation."

"No, I'm sorry, James, but I just don't think we can afford to take a risk like that right now. We've come too far."

Diego knew this was not his fight, so he quietly dismissed himself to go tend to the breakfast.

Gray was not happy, but he thought he might have a decent compromise up his sleeve. "Alright. Okay. Are you open for suggestions on the idea, at least?"

Chase hesitated, then let out a long sigh. "Sure."

"Let me run this by ya and see what you think."

"Fire when ready, my good man."

"Why don't we give ourselves enough time to swing by the safe house on our way to the airport and see if there's any movement at the place. Diego just said that they don't use this place for anything other than a temporary safe house from time to time, so maybe we get lucky and see something or someone moving around in preparation for the arrival of del Fuento's family. If we do, then we know that they are coming there."

Laurie Chase thought for a few seconds before finally giving in. "Stellar. Santa Teresa isn't that far off the beaten path. Let's eat some breakfast, and then we can be on our way."

"Just think, puddin' pop, after more than 500 days of waiting to exact your revenge, you're just a few hours away from finally getting your man." Then Big James looked in the direction that Diego had gone. "Both of yas are."

MEET ANATOLY VASNETSOV, DEREK COOKE, AND BRANISLAV SLOVACEK

Constance went to answer the door and allow a man named Derek Cooke to enter. Harper decided to wait patiently on the couch.

He sat for a bit, listening to Constance and Derek talk in the adjacent room. After a few seconds, he sat up straight. He knew that voice.

Harper stood up and carefully moved to where he could see Constance and Cooke talking. It only took one focused glance for Harper to realize who Derek Cooke really was.

"Well, pinch my cheeks and call me Darcy...Anatoly Vasnetsov, is that really you?"

Derek Cooke and Constance Ondracek turned and gave a synchronized scowl to Harper. "No names," Constance said sternly.

"Harper Rowe," Derek said, quickly moving from Constance to Harper. "I heard you were in town." The two embraced heartily, patting each other on the back.

"I don't believe it," Harper said. "It's been – what – ten years?"

"If you say so," Cooke agreed.

Constance stood confused. "You know each another?" she asked.

"By God's grace, we do."

"Yeah, Anatol...I mean, Derek...there was a potential uprising in Russia a while ago. A big one that could have led to the downfall of several world powers. It was all very hush-hush. My people sent me to do a job that would make sure this uprising never saw the light of day."

"And my people sent me to do the same job," Derek added. "I was about halfway through finding whoever it was that needed to be put down, and that's when this lovable *baystryuk* shows up from out of nowhere and is tasked to do the same thing."

"Anat...Derek... and I put our heads together, formulated a plan, and – together – we were able to put down the threat before there was even a whiff of danger to the public nose."

"Seems like forever ago," Derek said, shaking his head, "but when Constance said your name, I just had to come see for myself. Had to come see *the* Harper Rowe alive and in living color. After all these years."

Derek and Harper hugged again. "Daggone good to see you, old friend. Your English is as good as ever"

"Yeah. So is yours," Derek laughed.

"We need to focus on orphanage," Constance reminded the two men as she dusted the snow off Derek's coat. "We need to save children."

"The lady's right. We need to get a plan together. For every second we stand around reminiscing, it's another second that those kids are being abused," said Cooke.

Harper stood there for a second, thinking.

"How long have you known about the abuse?"

Derek was silent. He looked at Constance as if he were waiting for her approval.

She answered Harper, "We have known."

"We have known for a little bit, but...there was nothing that we could do," Cooke said. "Not alone, at least. The corruption runs deep."

"How deep?"

"Deep enough that we knew it was going on and did nothing because we were too afraid that whatever we would do wouldn't be enough to get to the root of it all."

"That's pretty deep."

"Truth is we do not know how deep corruption is. We know some but not full extent," Constance added.

"I'm going to come on in and take a seat," Derek said. He walked past Harper and Constance and into the main parlor, sat down and kicked off his shoes.

"I appreciate you asking me here," Cooke continued. "Working with you again, Harper...tops, baby." He ran his hand across his unshaven face. "Fixing that children's home and righting the wrong that has been going on there for so long...it's been a long time coming."

"So, you have known about what's going on with these kids."

"I, sadly, have known...well...for some time."

"Then why do nothing about it?" Harper asked.

"Like the lady said, we know some of the depth of the corruption – local business people, local law enforcement, and two local politicians that we know of: the *Větší* and a city *Radní*."

"The mayor and a councilman? The local police, too? That is deep," Harper shook his head. "What about Interpol? Have you barked up that tree yet?"

"I have."

"And?"

"They sent some officers to check it out, but there wasn't enough evidence to warrant an official investigation. I do have a guy at Interpol that has been keeping an open investigation into this place. He has been waiting for any sort of screw-up on their part that would give him an opening that might allow him to go in there and bust the place wide open, but, so far, he's gotten nothing. Whoever's running the show there knows how to keep it clean and evidence-free. Heck,

I've gone to that place several times to see for myself, and, frankly, there's just no evidence at all."

"So, this place goes through the effort and is able to keep up a clean appearance to experienced Interpol agents, but a random mother and daughter accidentally see enough to bring down the whole process including local polit cos and law enforcement? My gosh, those people must be pissed. No wonder there's an all-out dragnet for the Buceks."

"They're why you're here in the first place, right?"

"They are. The initial plan was to work with Coni, get in, get the Buceks some new IDs, get them out of town, and my partner and I would head back to the States. But with this storm coming in as fast as it did...well, we've got a little more time on our hands. Figured we might as well put it to some good use. We're going to go pull those kids out of the nightmare that they've been living and get them somewhere safe where they can start experiencing a real life." Harper made a wry face. "Those poor kids. I mean, isn't it enough that they've lost their parents? Living in an orphanage...it's the only place they know as home. Home. Where you're supposed to feel safe and secure. Judas Priest, I can't think about this anymore. It's tearing me up."

"Good. It should," Derek said. "Now...tell me...what I can do for you?"

"We'll need some weapons. I have a gun that I got off a cabbie on my way over here."

Derek laughed. "Oh my. Some of our mass transit locals showing off their public service hospitality, were they?"

Derek Cooke was silent for a few moments. He once again stroked his face as he stared at the floor.

"How many of you will be storming the castle?"

"It'll just be me and my partner, Kinley Devereaux."

"Umm, and where is this partner of yours?"

Harper took a deep breath before saying, "He's picking up a guy who will be putting together the paperwork for the Buceks' new identities. Then he'll be bringing him and the Buceks here. Along with them, my friend Tara Tharp, and her friend...whose name I can't remember right now...will also be on that chuckwagon."

"But it's just you and your partner that are coming to the orphanage. Did I understand that correctly?"

"Yes."

"Coni, where are we with getting the children evacuated to someplace safe?" Derek asked her.

"My people are ready. Standing by. Waiting for time frame to pick up children."

Rowe and Cooke nodded in understanding. Harper stood to his feet and walked over to the plate-glass window that made up the front wall of the reception area. He looked outside at the wintry scene and back to Ondracek.

"And you're sure that your people going to be able to get where they'll need to be in this weather?"

Constance tried to hide a slight smile. "When live in Prague, people are used to this weather. This," she pointed out the window, "is just a dusting. Have seen much worse. Do not worry, friend. All will be well."

"You do realize that it's only been snowing for about an hour, and there's already three inches on the roads, right?"

"Yes, and in next hour there will be more snow. In Prague, this is frequent occurrence." She looked at Cooke and said, "Tell him, Derek."

"Yes, tell me, Derek."

Cooke furrowed his brow and slowly said, "Well, this"—he pointed at the snow—"might be a little more than the average snow event, but yeah, Coni's right. I mean, as long as her people aren't from Boca Raton or the Congo, they'll be fine. People that live here know their way around the white stuff."

"All right then. Color me convinced." Harper walked back over to the couch and sat down. "Next point of business. Derek, you said you've been inside this orphanage before. How well did you get to see the layout of the place? And more importantly, how well do you remember it?"

"Oh, I think you will appreciate this, my friend. Using a rather brilliant disguise and telling some believable lies, I have gained access to the place more than just a couple of times as Branislav Slovacek, the helpful Hungarian handyman who is always willing to do pro bono work 'for the kids.' So they give me a call from time to time when they need something fixed immediately and don't have time to wait for all the governmental red tape that goes along with pretty much any work order from a government-run facility like that one. Of course, from the moment I walk through the door, there's always one or more persons with me anywhere I go inside the place. So what I've seen has been very censored. Also, I'm sure it's no surprise to you that they haven't had me in to do any work while they are having one of their little perverted pecker parties, either."

"But you've seen enough to have a general layout of the place?"

"Absolutely. I just thought it prudent to wait until your partner got here before going over the arrangement of the building."

"That makes sense."

"Till then...I'm parked about a block and a half away. Care to brave the elements with me and go get a few things out of the back of my car?"

"I'm down for that. But since my previous stop before here was in Rio de Janeiro, I don't have much in the way of winter weather attire." Harper turned to Constance and asked, "Do you have anything around here that might be applicable for the task at hand?"

"Yes, in storage area. I have some winter coats from last year's Paris show. What size for you to wear?"

"Do you have anything in an extra medium?"

Constance gave Harper a pitiful look and shook her head. "You look like size 42. Will grab some gloves and a muffler also."

Cooke and Rowe watched Constance leave the reception area.

"What were you doing in Rio, if you don't mind me asking," Derek inquired.

"I was down there working with a crew to, for all intents and purposes, annihilate the drug compound and estate of a Brazilian drug kingpin named Tito del Fuento."

"The attack on the drug czar's place in Rio...was you?"

"Well," Harper shrugged modestly, "it wasn't all me. I did have some help, but, yeah, that was us. All nine of us. And I think the word 'czar' might be giving the guy a little more cre—"

"I'm sorry. Did you just say nine? As in the number that precedes ten?"

"I know, right? That's crazy," Harper gave a goofy look to his friend. "What kind of complete mental incompetence are we dealing with when nine people think they can take on hundreds of soldiers that are in the employ of one of the biggest names in the South American drug world?"

"Have you seen the news story? Have you heard what they're saying?"

"I don't have to see the story. I made the story," Harp pointed out, trying his best to be humble. "But just for argument's sake, what're they saying?"

"They're estimating and guesstimating what and who was responsible for what happened. Throwing around numbers like damages to the place are just short of a billion dollars, the number of casualties are, just like you said, in the hundreds. The experts are figuring this was some kind of well-organized army that one of the other drug cartels assembled to put del Fuento out of the picture and out of business for good. They're blindly throwing around numbers like Stevie Wonder at a roulette table, but I can tell you that absolutely no one has mentioned the number nine."

"I'm sure they'll be trying to figure that one out for a while. The way I see it, once they realize that none of the other cartels are taking responsibility for it, one of the cartels will eventually step up and say that they did it. And why not? It'll be a huge feather in whomever's cap it is that says they were the ones that put Tito out of the game. And they won't ever have to worry about getting in trouble for it, because there's no evidence to actually prove that they did do it. The focus of the probe will turn to the confessing cartel for a while. But ultimately, it'll just fizzle out for lack of evidence. Game – and investigation – over."

"Wow." Derek gave Harper a much-deserved pat on the back. "I wish we had more time. I would love to hear how you guys pulled that off."

"Eh, ya never know. Maybe one day I'll make it to being old, and I'll write a book about it. Put some coloring book pictures in it, some games, some stickers. Make it real interactive so that the book that tells all the details about all the people I killed to keep this world safe for democracy and soccer hooligans can be something the whole family can enjoy."

"So, I just want to make sure that I have this straight: Two days ago you were in Rio destroying the empire of a major drug lord, and today you are in Prague and will be attempting to bring down a pretty sizable sex-trafficking ring?"

"And if we get through this, Kinley and I will immediately head back to the States to try to clear our names in the matter of the assassination of Secretary of Defense Paul Michaels."

"My friend," Derek grinned, "reality TV has got nothing on you."

"I know. I really think I need my own video game. I wonder who I need to call to make that happen."

SITUATION RESET

Karel Josef was Kinley Devereaux's ace in the hole. His escape plan. His safety net if all else went belly up.

Kinley had gotten used to living in the shadows and off the grid over the last year and a half. He was used to it, but by no means did he like it. He always kept hope that things would eventually work themselves out and he could set the record straight about what had happened in Mexico City. And what it had to do with the assassination of United States Secretary of Defense Paul Michaels.

He had hope, and he had faith, but he also had a timeframe.

Kinley had set himself a deadline for living life as he currently knew it. A time when Kinley Devereaux would disappear for good, and a new man would come into existence. A man with a fresh start in a new place with new opportunities. A man that would no longer have to live life looking over his shoulder.

A man that would be made possible through the deft and proficient work of Karel Josef, forgery expert.

However, Kinley did not want to be a new man in a new place with new opportunities. He wanted to be Kinley Devereaux back in his native USA doing all the things he was good at, all the things he enjoyed, all the things that made him who he was.

As of yesterday, the opportunity for Kinley to keep being Kinley had finally shown up. Kelly Campbell – whom herself had been in hiding for some time – had reached out to Kinley with the news he had been waiting so long to hear: someone with information about what had happened a year and a half ago in Mexico City, in Washington, D.C., had come forward and was willing to help. Now all he needed to do was to get home and make everything right.

Except for this unscheduled rescue operation in Prague.

To give the rescue plan its best chance to succeed, the Buceks needed new identities and clean papers. Kinley knew he had the best guy for the job right here in Prague. Karel Josef. Kinley Devereaux's safety blanket.

Granted, Kin was not all that keen on bringing the one man that could protect his future this close to the action. But then again, if it meant expediting the whole process so he and Harper could get out of Prague sooner rather than later, he was all for it. Besides, once the two assassins were back to the States, back to Kelly Campbell and to whomever it was that was stepping up with the evidence needed to clear their names, Kinley's need for a back-up plan would no longer be necessary.

Feeling good about the whole process and the way it was headed, Kinley had called Karel Josef and brought him into the mix.

But now the once free-flowing plan to extract the Buceks out of Prague was beginning to back up a bit. First came the unexpected snowstorm. And now Harper wanted to bring justice to all the people responsible for this whole ordeal. Goodness only knew what he had in mind there.

Still, the one thing that really weighed on Kinley's mind was that Karel Josef, the man sitting right across from Kinley at the moment, did not know him to be Kinley Devereaux. Instead, he knew him to be Peter Krug, a specialist in relocating embattled souls to a safer, less embattled setting. As it turned out, Kinley's reason for being in Prague today really was to do just that. So no explanation to the contrary was necessary.

No, what was really troubling Kin was that at any moment he would be receiving a phone call from Taralyn Tharp saying that she was there to pick him and Karel Josef up. And Devereaux and Karel would be getting into a SUV with four women that Kinley had never worked with before – three of whom would be scared out of their minds and not thinking straight. Hopefully Taralyn would have really driven home the point that he was to be called Peter Krug. Because Kinley was not sure how Karel Josef would react if he were to find out that Kin had been lying to him the whole time about who he was. Devereaux knew how he would react if the situation was reversed. Not well. Not well at all.

"Was I right about the octopus, Peter?" Karel asked.

"Spot on, Karel. I may have to stop back in here before I leave and get a 'to go' order for my flight back to the States."

"I can tell you like it, my friend. You have been shoveling it into your mouth since you got here and have barely said five words to me. Is it just because the octopus is so good, or does my friend have something on his mind?"

Devereaux smiled. "You read me well, Karel. First of all, please, let me just say how grateful I am that you are on board with all of this. We would not be able to pull this operation off without your help."

Karel gave a hearty laugh, which was somewhat disconcerting to Kinley. But then Karel said something insightful.

"I see these two on the news. I hear about the search effort that is being put into finding them. I have lived here long enough to know that when this happens"—Karel shook his head sadly—"it means that you either have committed a heinous crime against the state, or you are being set up to be caught for something that you have not done but someone important needs a patsy.

"When I saw the pictures of the mother and daughter that they were looking for, I knew which of the two scenarios was going on. I've never seen two more innocent-looking creatures in my life. So, I know why you are here and why you have asked for my help. I am more than happy to help you and your people, Peter."

Kinley scarfed down the rest of the octopus entrée and looked at Karel. "I know people all over this globe we live on, but the number of them that I trust...I can count them on one hand. You, Karel, I count twice. I thank you for being here for me when I need you."

"You have proven yourself to be a hero to the people that need you. You have proven yourself to me. Of course I am here for you. There are so few like you. True men."

And with every word that Karel said, Kinley felt even worse.

The phone in his pocket rang. It was Taralyn. It was time.

"Taralyn, I take it you are close?" he answered.

"Closer than your worst dream. Just a couple blocks up and to the left."

"Your left or my left?"

"Your left."

Kinley hung up without so much as a goodbye and then looked at Karel. "Time to go. Our ride awaits." As soon as he said it, he remembered Harper's line about a chariot. "The octopus was good. Thank you, Karel. Time to go. Better bundle up. It's wintry outside."

Karel did as he was told, and he and Kinley left the restaurant.

As they walked up the street toward the car and Taralyn, Karel realized that Devereaux was only wearing a long-sleeved Henley shirt. "You must be freezing," he said, pulling off his coat and wrapping it around Kinley. "I am used to this cold. I can walk to the car without a coat."

Kinley *was* cold. He took the coat. And he felt even worse about what might be awaiting them both.

They walked briskly through the falling snow until they saw

Taralyn's Mazda SUV. Kinley approached it first. "Hop on in, Karel."

The SUV had seating for only five. Taralyn and Eliska were in the front, Anezka and Jana Bucek were in the back. There was just enough room for Karel Josef. Kinley stuck his head in and asked Taralyn to open the hatch.

"You're good, Peter. It's open."

Kinley breathed a sigh of relief. Taralyn had called him Peter, giving him confidence that everyone in the vehicle was good to go. He walked around to the back of the SUV and climbed in. "You good, Karel?"

"Crowded car, yes, my friend?" Karel laughed.

"*Relaxovat*," Eliska told Anezka and Jana. "*Ti muži jsou tu, aby ti pomohli.*" Ellie was trying to calm the Buceks' fears.

Kinley wasted no time making it known that he was Peter Krug. "*Dobrý den. Já jsem* Peter Krug," he introduced himself, using what little of the Czech language he knew.

Kinley could tell immediately that the Buceks were very uncomfortable. They had every reason in the world to be. But he figured that having Karel sitting next to them was the better seating arrangement since Karel spoke Czech as his native tongue. It seemed to be working because, even though Devereaux did not know what Karel Josef was saying to the ladies Bucek, the distressed look on Anezka's face appeared to be dissipating.

"Tell them who we are, and that we're going to get them new IDs and get them to where it's safe," instructed Kinley.

"*Já jsem Karel. To je můj přítel, Petře. Pomůžeme vám. Dostaneme vám nové identifikace. Chystám se dostat vás oba na nové, bezpečné místo,*" Karel said calmly. "*Pochopit?*"

Anezka and Jana smiled and nodded that they understood.

While Karel and Kinley were doing their best to keep the Buceks calm and up to speed, Taralyn had given the address for the Ascending Angels Modeling Agency to Eliska. Eliska was pointing out to her where to go and where to turn – a task becoming increasingly difficult because of intermittent squalls and whiteouts from the dense snow.

"Is turn left ahead on *Ostrovní*." Ellie instructed.

The Prague sidewalks were still filled with pedestrians, even in the current weather conditions. "Look at these people," Tara remarked. "You'd think it was the middle of summer the way they're walking around out here. Like they don't have a care in the world."

"It is Saturday. Many are going to shop at market and to trade shows. Charles Square always busy on weekends. It is largest square in Prague. Be careful, Taralyn, coming up to Vodičkova Street. Very many people walk here all the time, at day and night."

"You know, I remember one time you told me that you had a car, but you never drove it. At the time I thought that sounded absolutely crazy. Why would someone have a car but never drive it? But now... it's the most sensible thing I've ever heard in my life."

Tharp's nerves were becoming more frazzled by the second. She was using every mental relaxation and stress-relieving technique she knew to keep it together. The snow. The cramped quarters inside the vehicle. Ellie's directions in broken English. Karel's calming of the Buceks in Czech. Not being able to see out the back window because Kinley was crammed into the back of the SUV. The dense foot traffic.

Add it all up and it was making an already-tense situation practically untenable.

"Turn up here to right," Ellie pointed.

"You mean in between the guy with the white shirt and the woman with the blue coat?" Taralyn joked.

Eliska's literal Eastern European mind did not understand the joke. Eyes opened wide, she responded in a panic. "No. No. Do not drive through people, Taralyn. Put on turn signal and go slow. They will let you through."

"I think she knows that, Eliska," Kin piped up from the back of the Mazda. "You do know not to run over the pedestrians, right, Tara? I mean, I'm not a hundred percent familiar with the customs and laws of Prague, but I'm pretty sure you can't use its citizens as human speed bumps."

Tara signaled to turn and slowly inched the SUV along as she waited for the pedestrians to separate. While she did, she looked into the rearview mirror and shot Kinley a dirty look. "Do you want to come up here and drive? Peter?"

Just at that moment, Kin's cell phone rang. It was Harper. Before he answered the phone, he looked up and caught Tharp's eyes in the rearview. "I would, but I'm being beckoned...Tara."

She squinted her eyes and gave him a bratty smile as he answered his phone.

"Harp? That you?" Devereaux asked quietly.

"Well, I haven't fingerprinted myself lately, but, yes, I still feel relatively sure that it's me. Are you guys on your way here?"

"We are."

"Your guy and the Buceks in tow?"

"They are."

"Did you talk to Kelly?"

"Yeah. She wasn't real pleased, but I talked to her. Told her where you and I were and what we were doing, and that what you and I were doing was both noble and necessary. Did I use her attraction for me to our favor? Yes, I did. Do I feel bad about it? No, I don't."

"Do I like it when you ask me questions and then answer them yourself? No, I don't."

"Do I care?"

"No, ya don't."

"So, what's going on there?" Kin continued in a hushed tone.

"A lot, actually. I ran into an old friend."

"Well, there's a shocker. Imagine that. You knowing someone in a foreign land."

"Be nice. He's arming us," Harper laughed. "Speaking of which, where's your rifle?"

"I left it with Laurie. I wasn't exactly sure where we would be traipsing over the next few days so I left it where I knew it would be safe. I still fully intend to meet up with her very soon, regardless of the outcome when we get to the States."

"Have you heard from her since we parted ways?"

"I have not," Kin sighed. "What about you? Have you heard from your girl? The doctor?"

"Not yet, but I'm sure it won't be long now."

"So we're"—Kinley spoke even quieter—"really going to go take the orphanage?"

"Yes. Yes, we are. And the sooner you get here, the sooner we can sure up the plan to do that."

"Sure up? Do I take that to mean that you've already got a strong outline going as we speak?"

"I've got things well under way here. Here's my thought. Upon your arrival, we'll get your guy to paper you and me first. Make us someone besides who we are so that if we do get caught during this operation, they won't know who they've got. Not that I'm planning on getting caught."

"What about your old friend that you ran into there?" Devereaux asked. "What can you tell me about him?"

"His name is...Derek Cooke. I've worked with him before. He's solid. Couldn't ask for or get a better guy for this job. He'll make us a better unit."

"So, three of us to take the orphanage? Is that doable? I mean, what are we going to do once we get there?"

"Well, that's the part of the plan that we'll have to sure up once you get here."

Kinley growled, then looked up to see that everyone in the car was looking at him. Even Taralyn was flashing him a concerned look. He smiled conspicuously and said, "I'm good. Just got a little something caught in my throat."

He then turned to look out the back window of the vehicle. "Umm," he whispered, "I hate to be the one to bring this up, but that part of the plan *is* the plan, Harper."

"Yes, of course, it is. And like I said, we'll get it sured up when you get here. Till then, here's what I was thinking. Like you said, as far as an outline. The three of us will be able to walk to the orphanage from here. It's that close. Derek's got a layout of the building so that's something else that we can go over once you get here. Anyway, do you remember how Black Ice pulled off her heist at the Undersecretary's house?"

"Um," Kinley shut his eyes in thought for a few moments before his recall kicked in. "Yeah, she made a big commotion at the front of the place – got everyone to move up there – and then she sneaked in through an upstairs window when she thought no one was looking."

"Right. Absolutely right," Harper acknowledged. "So, I was thinking about employing the same kind of strategy to our attack on the orphanage. The two of you will hit the front door of the place and get anyone who's important to come running to see what's going on. While they're doing that, I'll sneak into the back and get the kids ready to go. I mean, I figure that I'm the one that should do that. I speak the language, and I'm good with kids."

"What about your friend? Did you say his name was Derek?"

"I did say that."

"Well, doesn't he speak the language, too?"

"Yes, he does, but let me give you a quick background lesson on Derek: former member of the Russian secret police."

"Oh," Kinley said with sudden understanding. "Well, like you said before, you're good with kids."

"Exactly."

"And your friend Derek – given his particular background – is probably quite good with the whole intimidation process. Which may very well come in handy at the front of the building."

"We should be playing rummy, buddy, because you are definitely picking up what I am putting down."

"Okay. Okay. Cool, but here's my next question: Where do we go from there? I mean, if Derek and I are up front puttin' the screws to the hired help, and you're back getting the orphans calmed down, what's our next move?"

"Well, now that's the one part of the plan that is already taken care of. Constance has people that will be in place to take the children out of the orphanage and get them someplace safe."

Just then, Devereaux felt the automobile come to a stop. He looked out the back window, then turned toward the front to see why they had stopped. But the SUV was just too crowded.

"Hey, why are we stopped?" he asked.

"We're not stopped," Taralyn turned around to say to him. "We're parked."

Karel Josef reached back and patted Kinley's arm and said in his raspy voice, "I think we have reached our destination, my friend."

"Oh." Kin put his cell phone back up to his ear. "We're here."

"Cool. I'll come out to meet you and your party...which should be right about—"

When the rear hatch of the Mazda SUV sprung open, the first thing Kinley saw was Harper Rowe garbed in a ridiculous-looking fur coat.

"Good Lord, Harper. What are you wearing?"

"Constance assures me that this is the biggest thing in the Paris winter line of fashion." Harper ran his hands up and down the luxurious fur coat. "It sure is warm. What do you think, buddy?"

"It makes me think that I'm glad I'm not French."

A Worrisome Kelly Campbell

She was not very pleased with hearing from Kinley and what he had to say, but she knew that she loved him enough to await his eventual return. She also knew that it would be sooner rather than later.

She knew that what he was doing – saving a forlorn mother and daughter from certain death – was the most noble of causes. That was her Kinley. That was her man.

She did not like his terms. But nonetheless, she listened and accepted what he had to say. Who was she to stop them?

She was Kelly Campbell. And she was worried. And, well, she should have been.

She worried about Kinley being sucked into another one of Harper's schemes like she had seen so many times before.

She wanted to tell him that very thing when she was on the phone with him. And that she loved him. Nevertheless, she had things to get done before their arrival.

One of those things was to get with Senator Brenda Cobb-Schmidt and inform her of the pushed-back timeline of the appearance of Kinley Devereaux and Harper Rowe.

Kelly called her on the private cell number that the senator had given to her at the Capital Grille the day before.

Cobb-Schmidt answered after only one ring.

"Kelly?"

"Good morning, Senator. I do apologize for the early morning call."

"No, it's fine. Is everything okay?"

"I'm pretty certain that I'm not supposed to tell you this," Kelly admitted, "but considering the bed that we are about to get into together, I'm sure that it's not going to matter much."

"What's going on? Are Kinley and Harper okay?"

"Well...as far as I know, yes. I got a call from Kinley a couple of hours ago. He and Harper are currently in Prague on a humanitarian mission."

"Prague? Why? Do you know what's going on there?" The senator's concern was obvious.

Not wanting to give away the purpose of Kinley and Harper's mission, Kelley played dumb. "I'm not sure what you mean?"

"There's a manhunt citywide in Prague for a woman and her kid. Some kind of capital murder case. At this moment in time, Prague is not someplace I would want to be. You said your boys were there on some sort of humanitarian mission. May I ask the specifics?"

"No." She took a second before continuing. "Senator Cobb-Schmidt, you obviously know the nature of me and my 'boys', so I won't pretend to even guess as to what their mission is. Kinley Devereaux called me a little while ago, like I said, and he told me exactly what I'm telling you. "I could have asked for specifics myself, but I knew better. I will tell you this Devereaux did assure me that the two of them would be back in the States within the next 36 hours."

"Do you trust him and what he says?"

"There are few men on this planet that are more trustworthy than Kinley Devereaux. So yes, Senator, I trust him implicitly."

"Let me ask you this then. Are he and Mr. Rowe into something illegal? Because I don't want you calling me sometime in the next several hours asking for my help to get them out of some

Czech prison because of something they've gotten into and can't get themselves out of."

"No, Senator Cobb-Schmidt, I'm sure it's nothing like that. And even if for some out-of-this-world reason something like that were to happen, I have my own resources to get them out and here to meet you, like I said before, in the next 36 hours."

"A resourceful woman, I like that," the senator smiled. "All right, Ms. Campbell, I'm not real happy with this time change, but I'll hold you to your word. I do hope you will do me the kindness of notifying me when Rowe and Devereaux are on their way here from Prague."

"I surely will. Until then, Madam Senator," Campbell said as she disconnected the call.

She was glad to be off the line. It felt like there was a baseball-sized lump in her throat from all of her nervousness. She bit her lower lip with worry and said under her breath, "Oh, Kinley Devereaux, do not let me down on this one."

Senator Brenda Cobb-Schmidt hung up the phone on her end and shook her head in disbelief. She let out a long sigh and said, "Unbelievable. Just totally unbelievable." She began to hit the intercom button on her office phone to page her secretary, Madeline Sparks, but she realized that it was only 6:15 a.m. Madeline wouldn't be in for another hour, at least. Instead, she began searching frantically for the phone number that needed to be called immediately. As soon as she came across it, she put in the call.

The voice on the other end answered after just one ring. "Madam Senator, I'm surprised to hear from you. I didn't think that—"

"Listen, Kent," the senator interrupted, "there's been a change in plans. Rowe and Devereaux won't be arriving as scheduled."

"What? Well, how long until they do arrive? And what's the holdup?"

"Well, according to their former handler – the one who's delivering them to us – they are in the Czech Republic doing some sort of humanitarian work. It will be another 24 – 36 hours before they are here."

"Wait. So you're seriously telling me that this guy, Harper Rowe, has been on the run from the U.S. government for the last year and a half, and his buddy...Kenny...Kevin—"

"Kinley...Devereaux," she corrected him.

"Right. Kinley Devereaux has been playing dead for the last 18 months, and you're telling me that they fully understand that you can clear their names and restore their citizenship to good standing, and yet they've still chosen to go do some sort of charity work in Czechia instead of coming here straightaway?"

"Yes, Mr. McCleary, that is precisely what I am telling you."

Senator Cobb-Schmidt could hear Kent McCleary laughing on the other end of the line. He finally said, "I have to admit, Senator, when you first told me that you would be using two former government assassins to be the fall guys for this plan that you've put together, I was more than a little bit concerned about it. But hearing this now, I must admit that you were a hundred percent right in your choice of patsies."

"Well, it's good to know that you approve," Brenda said sarcastically. "As for the plan, just sit tight and don't make a move until you hear from me."

PLAN OF ATTACK

Harper and Kinley were back together. At the moment they, along with Anezka and Jana Bucek, Karel Josef, Taralyn Tharp, Eliska Lukasik, Derek Cooke, and Constance Ondracek, had all crowded into the welcoming parlor of the modeling agency. Since Harper knew the highest percentage of the people in this particular gathering, he took it upon himself to do the introductions. He even remembered to introduce Kinley as Peter Krug and hoped that, at this point, everyone else was in on the dupe. He even did a version of everyone's names in Czech for the benefit of Anezka and Jana.

"*Prosím, sedněte si a cítit se pohodlně,*" Harper invited the Buceks to have a seat and get comfortable. "Let's all take a seat," he said to everyone else. Harper took off the big furry coat that he was wearing and handed it to Constance. "Think you might be able to find me something a little less garish for when we head to the orphanage?"

Constance took the coat and gave Harper a sideways look. "I'm sure I can find something more suitable to you."

"Thank you," Harper acknowledged. He turned back to Derek. "So, what do you have for us, brother?"

Cooke looked around the room. "There doesn't seem to be an available table, so I will use the floor, if that's okay, Constance?"

"Of course, friend. Do you need paper?"

He walked over to one of the bags that he and Harper had retrieved from his car and removed a large scroll of construction paper.

"I'm just going to sprawl it out here on your parlor floor," Cooke said, sliding the rubber bands off of each end. He got down on all fours and unrolled the five-by-four-foot square piece of thick white paper. On it, he drew a cursory blueprint of the orphanage and highlighted the points of entry, all points of escape, and everything in between. He then began to talk out his plan of attack.

"Okay, Ki—", and he stopped just in time as he remembered to call Kinley by his alias. "...Kirug, right?"

"Just Krug," Kin corrected him.

"Right. Just Krug. Like I was saying, you and I will go in the front door, get their attention as much as we can. The idea being that we get as many of the adults that are in the place to be up front and distracted. If we can do that, then Harper's job of sneaking into the back of the place will be substantially easier." Derek stopped long enough to give Kin a good look. "You understand so far?"

"So far, yes. Sounds like you and I need to be enough of a distraction to the point that we get a fair amount of attention so Harper can sneak in the back door and start getting the kids up and ready for the extraction."

"Yes, for the most part you're on point."

"So, what am I missing?"

"Me," Taralyn spoke up. "I want to go with Harper."

Everyone in the room looked at her in surprise.

"What? Why?" asked Devereaux.

"Because there are boys and girls in that place. I am sure that they are scared to hell and back, and I'm sure Harper's more than capable of getting them all up and ready to leave, but the friendly face of a woman will do wonders to calm them down. Especially the girls."

Derek looked at Harper. "It's your call, boss. Whaddya think?"

"Absolutely," Rowe said without hesitation. "She can handle herself, and I could use the company."

"How's your Czech?'

"Not fluent like Harper, but I know enough to do this."

"In that case," Derek nodded enthusiastically, "welcome to the team."

"Thank you. I just figured that you two are putting your necks on the line because of my asking for your help, so I feel that it's only right that I do the same. Not out of obligation, but out of gratefulness. Besides, who wouldn't want to be a part of an operation that's going to save a bunch of helpless kids? I know I do."

"Thank you, Taralyn," Harper said, "but if you hadn't taken the chance to reach out to us, none of this would even be happening. You're the real hero here."

"Very true," agreed Derek, "but what else is true is that we are on a time crunch here. So let's get back to our entrance strategy. Agreed?"

"Agreed," responded Kinley.

"So, Kinley, you'll be with me. We'll go in up front, whether they want us to or not. My Czech is good enough that we shouldn't have any issues with getting in. Plus, I'm a pretty smooth talker... in seven different languages. The important thing to remember is, number one, to make sure we have each other's backs. You can never tell where danger might be lurking in a place like this. As you can see here," and Derek pointed to his drawing of the orphanage layout, "there are a lot of access points to this front area. You or me loses focus for just a second, Krug, and it could spell curtains for one or both of us."

"You don't need to worry about that," Kinley assured. "If you're worried about that, then just go ahead and stop. Focus is my middle name."

"I thought it was Pan," Harper smiled at his friend. "Peter Pan Krug? No?"

"No, oddly enough, it's not," Kinley said, "but if you want me to send you to Never Never Land, I'd be more than happy to oblige."

"And that's why you and Derek are the muscle on this mission, and Taralyn and I are the humane part. So, let me see if I've got this straight: You boys go bustin' in up front and bust a few heads, if necessary, and Taralyn and I sneak in the back, round up the kids, and get them safely to Coni's people. On paper, this whole plan is kinda thin...kinda sketchy." Harp motioned to Derek's rough blueprint of the children's home. "This is a plan that most people would shy away from. Not me. I wholeheartedly embrace it. I just have one question: Can we shoot any of these jackasses? I won't lie to ya, gang...I really enjoy putting evildoers to rest. Eternally. What happens after they die is between them and their maker, but up to that point...I am very eloquent in the language of kill."

"We could sit here for hours and theorize all the different ways this plan won't work," Derek pondered, "but, in the end, this is what we're going to do and this is how we're going to do it. If jackasses get shot? Then jackasses get shot...no sleep lost here."

Kin looked at Harper and gave him a head nod. "Can I talk to you? For a minute? Not here?"

Harper was more than obliging. "Sure."

"Be right back," Kin said to Derek.

Harper and Kinley distanced themselves from the group enough for Kinley to quietly ask, "What do I need to know about your guy Derek Cooke?"

"Whaddaya mean?"

"I mean...I don't want to be here, and now that it's go time, I'm going in with someone that isn't you. How much do you trust this guy?"

"Derek? I trust him a lot. If I could go in the front with him and let you come in the back, I would...but you don't speak Czech, and Taralyn's Czech isn't good enough to explain exactly what's going on. It is good enough to tell them that everything's going to be okay, though."

"Derek's Czech is good. Why can't he go in the back with Tara and rescue the kids?"

Harper laughed a little. "You've seen Derek, right?"

"Yeah."

"I mean, look at him. The five o'clock shadow, the wavy hair pulled back into a ponytail. He looks like a hipster version of Charles Manson."

"True."

"If you were a scared thirteen-year-old kid, who would you rather see sneaking in through the back door of your home to save you from a life of debauchery. Me? Or Derek?"

Kinley was quiet for more than a moment before he answered, "So, I can trust your friend to have my back?"

"Of course. Why else would I have you with him?"

"I don't want to be here," Kinley finally said. "Can't we just go?"

"Now you know how the kids we're getting ready to rescue feel...every day."

Kin sighed. "Ugh, I absolutely hate it when you're on point."

"Yeah, but I know how diabolically opposed you are to my being wrong. So, I thought I'd try something different this time."

Kin patted his partner on the back. "Then let's go make this right."

IT WAS HARPER'S IDEA

Once Kinley and Harper rejoined the group and they sharpened up the plan, the collective broke off into smaller groups. Taralyn, Ellie, and the Buceks were one unit; Derek, Kinley, and Karel Josef were another crew; and Harper and Constance were the remaining duo.

"The snow isn't showing any signs of letting up. Maybe we should go look for a coat for me. Kinley and Taralyn, too," Harper said.

"Oh, have just the perfect thing for you. Want to come with me to look for it?" Constance invited him upstairs.

"I don't believe I've gotten a better offer all day. Besides, I have something I want to run by you."

"Run by me?"

"I have an idea. I want to see what you think of it," Harp explained as the two of them began walking.

"What is your idea?"

"You have video equipment here, yes?"

"Yes."

"Do you know how to use it?"

"Yes," Coni confirmed, "I use it for to make promotion video for advertisement agency few months ago. Why do you ask?"

Ondracek led Harper around a corner into a long hallway with periwinkle blue walls. It made him think of Dr. Mercedes Lara, a woman with whom he had made a very strong connection during their takedown of Tito del Fuento just a few days before.

At first Harper couldn't pinpoint why he was suddenly flooded with memories of Mercedes. But then it hit him – the color of the walls was almost the exact color of her eyes. Eyes that he had looked into just a few days ago. Eyes that he was mesmerized by. He smiled and began feeling warm all over, momentarily lost in his thoughts.

"Harper? You are okay?" Constance asked.

"Oh...yeah...sorry."

"Answer question then. Why want to know about video equipment?"

"I've been thinking, and I may have an idea."

"Okay."

Constance stopped and opened a door on their right. The pair entered a room filled with racks of designer garments of every sort: dresses, slacks, skirts, shirts, lingerie, blouses, and, of course, coats.

"Holy crap," Rowe blurted out. "What's the dollar value of everything in here?"

"I say close to half of million dollars U.S." Constance answered. "We will find what you need in a minute. Please tell idea about video equipment."

Harper perused the racks of designer clothing as he divulged his plan to Constance.

"Derek said he has a guy at Interpol. I was thinking about asking Derek if he could get that guy to come here. My idea being that even though the four of us are going to get those kids out of that godforsaken orphanage and to someplace safe, it's not like we're going to be able to keep the place shut down. As long as they're allowed to operate, they'll just bring more innocent kids in off the street and keep committing the same vile, heinous atrocities.

"However, if we could get the Buceks to give a sworn testimony in front of the Interpol agent about what they've seen, we could videotape it and have it on record to be used at a later date to close that place down, once and for all, in a court of law. By the time the video comes to light, the Buceks will be living a new life in a new place where no one can find them."

"Is good plan. I like it," Ondracek nodded enthusiastically. "They are only ones to witness bad things that happen there. If we can find way to use what they see to shut down orphanage, and keep Buceks safe at same time, then I say we should do it."

Coni had made her way past several racks of clothes to a shelf on the back wall. She pulled down a white garment in a clear zippered bag.

"This should be perfect," she said, pulling a snowsuit from the garment bag and presenting it to Harper. "Please try this on while I go find suits for Derek, Kinley, and Taralyn."

As instructed, Harper put the snowsuit on, zipped it up, pulled the hood over his head, and wriggled around in it until he was comfortable. "Wow," he said, "this is really quite warm. Comfortable, though." He started exploring the outfit for pockets and other places that he might stash weapons. "How much does this cost?"

"Is close to $2,500 U.S.," she answered upon returning with three more bunglesome packages. She set them on the floor and retrieved a pair of sunglasses from her jacket pocket. "These are Glacier sunglasses. They sell for another $600 U.S."

"So, what you're saying is that, all told, the suit and the shades are coming in at just over three large each?"

"Yes, is what I am saying," the golden-haired beauty smiled.

"Well, I hope you take travelers checks because I'm not sure that I'm carrying twelve grand in cash inside my jeans."

"I make deal with you, Harper Rowe. You wear it to orphanage today. You come back alive and no bullet holes in it, I give to you for free. Is good arrangement?"

"Ya got yourself a deal, little lady," Harper said.

"You will need that in snow," Coni stated the obvious. "Is warm in here. Is cold out there."

"Indeed. Now that we've got all this sorted out, let's go find Derek and see if we can't get this idea of mine in motion."

"Yes. Let's do."

Jaw-Dropping Surprise

Diego del Fuento was heading back to Rio for the first time in a long time. Ever since he had met Laurie Chase over a year ago – except for the rare occasions when he accompanied her on recon missions – the diminutive Portuguese man had stayed out of sight.

He had been holed up with Chase in the abandoned warehouse that was her headquarters for the operation against Diego's cousin, Brazilian drug kingpin Tito del Fuento. Diego used to be Tito's second-in-command. Then Tito wiped out Diego's entire family.

Laurie had gotten Diego to turn on Tito after Diego grew a conscience over all the evil crap he and his cousin had been doing for the last decade. The drugs. The kidnapping. The extortion. The killing. And that was just a typical Monday.

Chase was able to lock up Diego's services with the simple promise that when she finally brought his cousin to his knees, Diego could be the one to give the kill shot.

It had been a long time coming, but Diego and Laurie were finally going to get their revenge. For the last day and a half, they had been waiting for Tito and his family to fly back to Rio. Thanks to intel from Diego, they knew the location of the safe house where Tito would probably stash his family, and they hoped that getting to Tito's family would be the key to getting Tito.

Now Laurie, Diego, and Big James Gray were heading to the safe house in one of Big James' minivans. It was an isolated, sprawling neighborhood, with each residence separated by two acres or more on either side.

"Thee house ees up here on thee right. We should be there een less than a keelometer or so," Diego instructed. You'll see a yellow spleet level home. Eet seets back off thee road about 45 meters and has a big, metal fence that surrounds thee property."

"I'll do a quick drive by," said Big James. "Laurie, get your camera ready and snap off as many pics as you can. I'm not going to be able to slow down much without looking conspicuous. Just not enough cars on the road. We'd be spotted like a leopard if I tried."

"I'm ready to go. Not sure how many useful shots I'm going to get if there's a security fence though."

"See what you can do. I'll drive by and then circle back around to a spot where we can park that's, hopefully, out of sight but can give us a decent enough view of the place to see what's going on."

"Sounds good," Chase answered.

"Oh, thees ees eet!" Diego pointed excitedly. "Right there, Meess Laurie."

"Got it," she said, snapping pictures rapidly with her digital camera.

James Gray slowed the vehicle to let Laurie get a few last shots. Glancing to his right, he noted a few cars in the driveway and the structure of the security fence. It was wrought iron, with spear-topped spires spaced about six inches apart. This allowed Laurie to get a pretty clear line to the house.

Suddenly Diego burst out, "Oh, holy cheet!"

"What? What's wrong?" Big James asked.

Diego turned to him in wide-eyed astonishment. "Ees Tito!"

"Tito? Where?" Gray looked in the rearview mirror at Chase, sitting in the rear bench. "Laurie, did you see—?"

"Hang on, I'm checking." The woman yanked her laptop out of her briefcase, flung it open and powered it up. She fumbled around for the cord to connect her camera to the computer and hooked it into both devices.

"I tell you, Meess Laurie, Mees'er James...it was heem," contended Diego.

"Laurie, whaddya got back there?" Gray asked.

Ignoring him, Chase fidgeted nervously for the twenty seconds it took her to start dumping her pictures into a folder on her laptop.

Big James kept driving, spending more time looking in his rearview mirror to see what was going on with Laurie than at the road.

"Sonofabitch...he's right. That's Tito...getting out of a car...a car that appears to have a woman and two kids inside of it."

"How...how is that even possible? He and his family aren't even supposed to be here for another three plus hours."

"If you don't believe me then pull the van over and come back here and see for yourself. I can't explain it either. But the pictures don't lie, my friend."

"No, I believe you. It's just...it's just...crazy."

"Well, if you think that's crazy, then you're gonna love this: We're going to have to take him now."

"What? That's crazy."

"Pretty sure that's what I just said," she mumbled. "Yes, we're going to have to take him now. Our plan to pick him up at the airport is obviously out, so we'll have to take him now."

"And just how are we going to do that? We don't even have a plan. We can't just go bustin' in there, guns a-blazin'."

"These pictures show three cars in the driveway, what appears to be two bodyguards standing next to Tito and, from what I can see, three to four more guys inside the house."

"From what you can see? And pray tell, exactly just how much is that? How far inside the house can you see?" Big James asked, pulling the minivan off the road and into a parking area.

"Just inside the front door."

"So, if you can see five or six of Tito's henchmen out there in plain sight, then let me assure you, you can probably bet that it's more than double that number for your grand total." Gray shook his head. "If I'm doing my math correctly, that puts us down 12 to 3. Not to mention, we have to get past the security gate. Look, Laurie, things have gone awry here. I hate like Hitler to be the one to say this, but maybe we should cut our losses. I mean, we've destroyed the guy's home, his drug army, his crops, his plantation buildings... we've put a mighty big hurting on this guy."

"I don't want to put a hurting on him, James. I want him dead, and that's just what I'm going to do. With or without you."

Big James gave her a look of disapproval. "How? Suicide mission?"

"If that's what it has to be, yes."

"Good Lord, you're stubborn as a stump. You mean to tell me that you're this devoted to your cause that you're willing to die for it? What...what would Kinley say if he were here?"

"Guys?" Diego spoke up.

"He'd tell me to do it because he knows what this means to me!" Chase yelled.

"Oh, you don't know that!" James hollered back.

"Yes, I do!"

"Uh, guys?" Diego said again.

"You're just being childish now, Laurie."

"Oh, *I'm* being childish? Well, that is a fine—"

Diego had had enough of being ignored. He leaned over and laid on the horn and yelled, "Hey, you guys!"

"What?" Big James and Laurie shouted together.

Diego sat back in his seat. "I have a plan. Eet's not great, but I think eet could work."

DIEGO'S PLAN

The squabble ceased. Big James and Laurie Chase focused all their attention on Diego and his plan.

"Thee fence ees electreefied , plus there are spear teeps at thee top. But, I do know that, when thee front gate ees opened, the fence electreeceety shuts off for a moment unteel thee gates are shut once again."

"Well, that's super information to know, Diego," Gray sassed, "but just how the heck are we supposed to get them to open the gates at the front of the fence without setting off about twelve different alarms?"

"I can get them to do eet, Mees'er James," Diego came back.

"And just how do you intend to do that?"

Silence.

"We're all ears," Chase said from the back of the van.

Diego thought before answering. "Thee cameras at thee front gate record everyone going een and out of thee place. Eef I go up to thee front gate and tell Tito that I have heard of his meesfortune, and that I have come to offer my hand een helping rebeeld hees home and plantation. I know he'll open the front gates for me...even eef eet's to keell me...he'll open those front gates. That's when thee two of you weell be able to get over that fence."

"No." Chase was the first one to object.

"She's right, little buddy. We can't let you just give yourself up like that," James Gray seconded. "Gotta be another way."

"What other way?" Diego asked. "Tito weell be gone soon. We need to get heem now."

"Can we take, at least, three minutes to formulate some shell of a plan?" Big James asked.

"Drop me off a block or so from thee safe house. I'll walk up slowly. They'll see me. I weell signal you once I know that they are focused on me. Eet weell be the only time for the two of you to gain access to thee groun's."

"Here's an ear com so that we know where you are and what you're saying. You'll be able to hear what is going on with us, too. We'll all be looped in to one another." Gray handed the com to Diego.

"Thank you, my buddy, Diego said, inserting the earpiece. "I feel like part of thee team now."

"Alright," Big James said as he pulled the minivan out of the parking area and back toward the safe house.

Halfway to the destination, Diego said solemnly, "I won't let you two die. You are my family."

"Diego, I need you not to die," Laurie said sincerely, "because when the time comes, I'm going to need you to put the final bullet in Tito's brain. I really need you to be around for that."

The trio rode on in silence until the safe house came into view.

"Getting ready to drop you, chief," Big James pulled to a stop and looked over at Diego. "You ready? You want a gun or something?"

"No, Mees'er James. If I tell Tito that I am showing up een peace, and then hees men freesk me and find a gun on me," Diego shook his head, "We'll all die. Best to go een peace than to show up carrying a piece."

"Alright, *mi amigo*," James reached out and shook Diego's hand, "I'd say *be safe*, but if you were going to do that, you wouldn't even be doing this in the first place. So instead, I will just say *see ya inside*."

"*Ir com Deus*," Laurie said from the back of the van.

Diego turned and gave her a big smile. "I'll see you soon, Meess Laurie!"

As the little man hopped out of Big James' minivan and shut the door behind him, Big James looked at Laurie in the rearview mirror.

"That dude is gonna get killed and killed bad. Sadly, his only hope is us, and our only hope is him."

"Then let's not let the little dude down."

"Diego, you reading me?" Gray did a com check.

"Yes, Mees'er James."

"Walk slow. We're going to need some time to get into place." Big James pulled the com out of his ear and turned to Chase, "You got your life insurance policies all paid up, Laurs? Because this might be the day they end up getting cashed in."

STRAIGHT

Karel Josef was in the process of breaking out his materials to make new identities for Anezka and Jana Bucek.

"Where can I set up?" he asked Ondracek.

"Follow me, please," she said, leading him to one of the studio's photography rooms. "Will be more private and easy to work in here. We have cameras all ready to take pictures." No sooner had Ondracek left Karel to work in peace then in walked Kinley. "You good here, Karel?" he asked.

"Peter, my friend, yes. I am so very excited to be a part of this. Knowing you are saving this mother and daughter from a fate worse than hell itself, I am grateful to do what I can to help both you and them. Plus, this area is complete with cameras ready to go, thus saving time and effort."

"Well," Kinley said, hesitating for a moment to make sure he had Karel's full attention, "before you take care of the Buceks...might need you to do some paperwork for me and my partner."

"For certain, my friend. Whatever it is that you need, please, tell me."

"Well, my partner, Harper Rowe, and I are going to be trekking it to the orphanage along with Taralyn Tharp. I hope that it won't

come to this, but...if we were to get stopped and asked for ID, we'd
be in a bad way with no papers. Do you understand?"

"I can make you papers. This is no problem, my buddy."

"Derek, quick question," Harper approached his friend.

"What's up?"

"You said you had a friend at Interpol. How close a friend
is that?"

"Pretty close. Why?"

"Think he would come here...today?"

"Right now? In this snowstorm?"

"Yeah, that's what I'm asking."

"Whatever for?"

"You said that he was looking for some sort of opening to take
the orphanage down. I don't think he's going to get a much bigger
opening than the Buceks. I have an idea," Harp began to explain.
"Good God willing, by the end of this day the Buceks will be out of
Czechia for good, and once they're gone...they won't be coming back.
I was thinking that while the four of us are taking care of business
at the children's home, your Interpol friend might be able to come
here. He could record the Buceks giving a videotaped testimony of
just what it was that they saw that day at the orphanage. Once this
case *does* make it to court, your Interpol friend will have it to use
as evidence to put these scumbags away once and for all.

What do you think? I mean, he works for Interpol. They've
got to have some way to get him over here, right? Especially for
something of this nature. Wouldn't you think?"

Derek pondered Harper's proposition. After a good ten count,
he finally answered.

"I will give him a call."

"While you do that, I'm gonna go let Anezka and Jana know
what's going on."

However, before he could take the first step toward that plan, Constance Ondracek called for everyone to reassemble in the building's welcoming parlor. Once they were all in the room, Constance – who was seated behind the receptionist's desk – stood to her feet.

"I just hear from my people picking up children from orphanage. They will be ready and in position within half of the hour." She looked at Derek and Harper. "Very soon is time to go."

PLAYING CATCH UP

Jeb Crool and David Baldwin were within striking distance. They had been tracking the signal from the beacon Dave had put on James Gray's van a day ago, before they had gone careening out of control late last night while in hot pursuit of the big man.

"He's back on the move again," Baldwin said from the passenger's seat.

"How far away is he?"

"Two, maybe three miles. Take a right up here," he instructed Crool.

"Wonder what we're gonna find him doing all the way out here. Looks pretty upscale. Even the low-end houses look like a million bucks."

They had not the first clue of the significance of the yellow house surrounded by the wrought iron fence ahead, or of the little Portuguese man walking along side of the road when they drove past.

"He's a gunrunner, Jeb. Whaddya think he's going to be doing out here? Selling Girl Scout cookies?"

"Do ya think the Girl Scouts in Brazil sell cookies?" Crool queried. "And if so, do you think they sell the same flavors?"

"If the Brazilian Girl Scouts aren't selling Samoa macaroons, then they're missing out on what could possibly be the largest source of income they may ever have."

Jeb laughed. "Ya like the macaroons, do ya?"

"Let me put it this way: You know that game people play where the scenario is that you're stranded on a deserted island for a year and you can only have one food item for that entire time? Mine would be Samoa macaroons, *and* when I returned to civilization... the first thing I would do is buy another box of Samoa macaroons."

"Wow. Does your wife know about this passionate affair that you have with these cookies? Or do I need to keep this dirty little secret just between you and me and the Girl Scouts of America?"

"Not only does she know...she approves. I guess you could say that we have an open relationship," Baldwin snickered.

"And I guess you could say I'm old because I still think an open relationship means not lying to your spouse."

"Sadly, Jeb, the goofy kids of today would tell you that *is* what an open relationship is. Each person knows the other one is out banging other people, ergo, they're not lying about it."

Jeb shook his head. "I wouldn't ever say that, as Americans, we have too much freedom. But daggone, we sure do know how to abuse the privilege."

"Hey," Baldwin said suddenly. "Pull over here."

"What? Is he here?" Jeb pulled over, scanning the area.

"According to this, his vehicle should be right here. It says we're right on top of him – his vehicle, at least."

"Is that it up there? A minivan, right?"

Baldwin looked to where Jeb was pointing. Directly in front of them, on the shoulder of the road, was a light blue Dodge Caravan.

"It was dark when I put the tracker on it last night, but that definitely looks like it."

Baldwin and Crool unbuckled their safety belts and exited the vehicle. Both men pulled their sidearms from their shoulder holsters and began a cautious approach toward the rear of the minivan, Jeb on the driver's side and Dave on the passenger's side.

"Looks empty from here," Jeb noted.

"Same," Dave answered from his side. He checked the doors. "Locked up over here."

"Windows are too tinted to see anything inside."

Crool walked around to the front of the vehicle and tried unsuccessfully to look in. Baldwin joined him, and the two agents began scanning for any sign of Big James Gray.

On their side of the road were two large houses that sat several hundred feet back from the street. Each house was surrounded by several acres of plush grass peppered with large trees and well-groomed shrubs. On the opposite side of the street was a very similar scene, the only difference being that there were three homes instead of two.

"Call me judgmental, Dave, but this just doesn't look like the kind of neighborhood where a big-time gunrunner would be conducting business. The lawns are pristine. The driveways are long, paved, clean, and filled with nice cars. The only cars parked out here on the street are his and ours."

"You don't think the criminal element can live in nice houses?"

Jeb laughed. "I know we're in South America, Dave, but I'm pretty sure the saying, 'Don't squat where you eat.' is a global mantra."

"Meaning?"

"*Meaning* that even if there are some ne'er-do-wells residing in these abodes, I'm pretty sure they're not going to invite the guy they buy guns from to come over for a pool party."

Dave flashed his partner a quizzical look. "Who do you think they would invite then?"

"Well, their accountants, if they're the intelligent kind of criminal element."

The sudden sound of dogs barking in the distance broke the serenity of the neighborhood.

"So," Jeb smiled, "how much ya wanna wager that those hounds are barking at a jolly fat man that's carrying a gold membership card to the NRA in his wallet?"

"I'd wager my entire year's salary," Dave answered as he and Jeb took off into a full sprint. "And my Christmas bonus!"

LOVE BEFORE THE STORMS

Chase and Gray had parked the minivan about a half mile away from the rear of the del Fuento safe house property. Which meant they would have to cut through the neighborhood behind the house. But since most of the land between them and their destination was shrouded with large trees and extensive, complex shrubbery that they could use as cover, they felt confident they would be able to do this undetected.

Laurie Chase had her phone on movie theater mode. So when he called, her phone did not ring. It vibrated. She was practically running at top speed, therefore very much out of breath. But it was *him*. So she answered it anyway.

"Kinley?" she panted.

Big James, who was struggling to keep up with Chase, asked in complete befuddlement, "Why in the heck are you answering your phone at a time like this?"

Kinley, who could hear Laurie's breathlessness and Big James' question, said slowly, "Laurs...is there something going on you need to tell me about? Why are you so out of breath?"

"Big James and I are on foot. We're headed to get Tito and his family now." Laurie stopped running so she could talk a little more coherently. Which also gave Big James time to catch up to her. "Tito and his family are back in Rio already, and we've tracked them to a safe house that Diego knew about."

James, out of shape and equally out of breath, stood bent over with his hands on his knees. It did not help his cause that he was toting a large duffel of weapons on his back. "Who's...who's that on the phone?" he wheezed. "Is that Kinley?"

Chase nodded to her chubby buddy and resumed her conversation. "Diego's gone up to the safe house now to use himself as bait. He's hoping to cause a big enough distraction that James and I can get over the security fence when it goes down for just a few seconds when they, hopefully, open the front gate to let him inside. So, that's us. What's going on where you are?"

"Harper and I and two others are headed to an orphanage to rescue some kids from what seems to be a pretty decent-sized sex trafficking ring."

"Are you serious?" Chase asked.

"As a heart attack."

"That sounds potentially dangerous."

"Potentially, yes," he answered. "But enough about me. I'm so proud of you, baby. Getting ready to take out the big-time bad guy. Finally, you'll be bringing to fruition your ultimate plan."

"You're proud of me?" she blushed. "Look at you – going to rescue children from a life that must be just the other side of hell for them. I'm proud of *you*."

Big James shook his head and began to mimic her. "I'm proud of you...no, I'm proud of you...no, I'm more proud of you, space pants...no, I'm more proud of you, puddin' sickle." He laughed at his own folly. "Hey, you two lovebirds wanna wrap this up sometime today? We are on a bit of a schedule."

"Alright, alright," Chase said to Gray. Then to Kinley she asked, "Before I go, what's next for you after you rescue the orphans?"

"Harper and I are going to be flying back to the States. Our former boss-lady has us meeting up with a senator from Minnesota, Senator Brenda Cobb-Schmidt."

"She sounds important. Are you sure you should be taking Harper along?"

"Apparently, she has what we need to clear our names – and yours – from all the wrongdoing with Paul Michaels."

"Do me a favor and call or text me when you're finally safe and headed back home."

"Copy that, beautiful. You guys be safe and watch each other's backs. I love you."

"I love you, too, Kinley. Talk to you on the other side."

She disconnected the call, shoved the phone back in her pants, and said to Big James, "You ready?"

The big man gave her a hurt puppy dog look and feigned sniffing and tears.

"Oh for cripes sake...I love you, too, big guy."

"Great," he beamed. "In that case, would you mind carrying the bag of guns until we get to where we're going?"

"Sure," she said taking the bag from him. "I couldn't help but notice how much they seem to be slowing you down."

THE RIGHT APPROACH

One more round of goodbyes and good lucks, and Kinley, Harper, Tara, and Derek exited the modeling agency in their matching $3,000 white snowsuits.

For a moment, Harper thought that the quartet might stand out from the crowd wearing such pricey garb. But the truth was that it was snowing so hard there really was not much of a crowd to stand out from. Plus, the early afternoon Prague air was frigid, and these snowsuits were warm like a log cabin fire. An added bonus was that each snowsuit offered several deep pockets; pockets that made it possible to conceal the kind of hardware that would be necessary to pull off a job like this.

The four of them made their way toward the orphanage through the blitz of snow. Each had an in-ear com and multiple weapons, and each had their wits on high alert.

"Com check," said Derek.

"Check," came back Kinley.

"Check," responded Taralyn.

"Ya know," Harper started up, "I was looking up 'How to Rescue Children From a Sex Trafficking Ring' on Pinterest earlier, and I found some really great ideas. Wish I had printed them out. Probably could've used those right about now."

"Com check, clear," Derek laughed. "Streets looking deserted."

"Do you know where you're going, Rudolph?" Harper asked Derek. "This snow is blinding."

"I know where to go, and I can see where we're going. Let's stay together."

"When we get close, I have something that might give us a bit of a leg up," Kinley said.

"Did you get whatever it is from a Cracker Jack box?"

"No, Harp, but I did get it from a police evidence locker...thanks to you."

"Oh," said Harper dismissively until it clicked in his mind what his partner was referring to. "Oh. That."

"Yeah, that."

"Mind if I ask what *that* is?" Taralyn wondered.

"*That*, m'dear, would be a very expensive, very effective infrared scope," Kin answered. "And when we get close enough, it should allow us to see – to a point – what's going on inside the orphanage building itself."

"Really?" she looked at Harper for some sort of confirmation.

He gave it. "Yes, for realsies."

"Even in this kind of weather?"

"Well," Kinley said as he pulled the hood of his snowsuit tight around his head, "that remains to be seen. Hopefully, though."

"Ugh, I've never been so excited and so cold at the same time," Harper complained. "I'm thinking this must be how Santa Claus feels on Christmas Eve."

"Or a snowman attending his first dance," Kin smirked.

"We can double time it, if you want," Derek suggested.

"You mean...*run*?"

"We're not playing the drums here, Harp. We can run, get where we need to get, and settle in...see if the infrared scope your partner's going on about will work in this kind of cold. However, it's been my experience that they don't."

"Why ya gotta be so negative, Derek?"

Cooke did not answer immediately. Instead, he broke into a run before saying, "Let's get to this. Harper's right. It's crazy cold out, and the sooner we can get to these kids, the sooner their waking nightmare will be over."

"That sounds proper."

So, they ran. And the snow fell. And the air was cold.

"Great Scott, it feels like someone is pouring gasoline down my lungs," commented Harper. "I'm starting to question if this whole running thing was really that splendid of an idea."

"Well, at least you're not thinking about how you can't feel the tip of your nose anymore, right?"

"Yeah, I get that, but...it's not helping."

It was not long before they were within a hundred yards of the orphanage. In spite of the snow, they could tell it had a large yard with playground gear out back.

"That's it there?" Taralyn asked.

"That's it."

"It's huge."

"It used to be a hotel, but then about five years ago the state bought it and turned it into a very nice children's home. When and where it all went horribly wrong...who's to say."

"We should dig in here," Kin said. "If this scope is going to work, it should work from here."

Harper did a faceplant right into the drifting snow. "I'm good. Tell me what you see when you see it."

"Stop screwing around," Kinley said, hitting the snow and pulling out his scope. He popped open the lens caps on either end and held it up to his right eye.

"Judas Priest."

"What?"

Harper snatched the scope away from Kin and took a look for himself.

"Judas Priest."

"My words exactly," Kin said.

"What's going on?" Tara asked.

"Seems like the adults have decided to make company on a snowy day."

"Oh, man. I am so ready to kill these bastards. I just..." Harper got choked up on his own feelings. "I just want to pull the spine out of these people. It's not like they're using it anyway."

"Geez, what in the world are we walking into?" Kin asked.

"We're going to do what we talked about. We're going to liberate these kids," Cooke reminded them.

"So let's go," Kinley was mad and ready to do something about it. He did not even look at the other three that were with him. He just stood up and took off on a sprint toward the orphanage.

Harper, Derek, and Taralyn took off after him.

"It's blitzkrieg time!" Harper yelled.

"Good gosh, we're so outnumbered."

"I can't help but recall how we were, not so long ago, outnumbered by seriously outrageous numbers – like 200 to 1 – and we got by," Harper noted.

The four of them were on the run again. But once they were within some 65 yards of the building, Cooke held up his hand to signal everyone to stop. "This is where we split up."

They all took deep breaths as the snow showered down upon them.

"Do we know where Constance's people are?" Taralyn asked.

"They're in play and close," replied Derek. "Once we have the situation under control, I'm supposed to call her, and she will contact them and get instructions about what to do with the orphans. Other than that, we won't see them."

"I'm down with that," Kinley said, "because to me it looks like once we get in here, it's going to be a crowded house. I would hate for any innocent blood to get shed."

"Nobody wants that," Derek affirmed. "So, you and me, brother," he slapped Kin on the back, "we'll head up front. Harper, you and Tara head that way. You shouldn't have any trouble finding the rear entrance to this place. We'll see the two of you on the inside."

Harp walked over to Kinley and gave him a quick hug and said, "Let's do this and go home, brother."

From there, the quartet went their separate ways: Derek and Kinley headed toward the front door while Harper and Taralyn went in search of the back entrance to the building.

Harper reached up to his ear and turned off his com. He motioned to Taralyn to do the same thing.

"What's up?" she asked him.

"You ready for this?"

"I've been through worse with you," she smiled.

"And we'll be through worse again," Harp pulled out two handguns from his snowsuit and feigned modeling them like he was in Gun GQ. "Let's go make a better life for these kids, shall we?"

"Sure," Taralyn agreed as she pulled two handguns from the pockets of her snowsuit, as well. "I've got nothing else to do today."

"Try not to shoot the children," Harper said, reaching up to turn on his com. "I see the back door into this place. We'll be heading in as soon as we get the okay from you."

"We're going to go in soft before we start getting things stirred up in here," came back Derek. "Like I told you earlier, they know me here as a handyman. I'm going to go in under that guise just to get us inside the door. We'll be doing that in the next ten seconds. Wait for us before you enter."

"Wouldn't have it any other way," Harper replied as he and Taralyn crept in close to the back door. "They want us to wait for them," he told her.

"Yeah, I heard."

"Harper," Kinley said, "this isn't a baseball game. We don't need play-by-play."

"It's not play-by-play, buddy. It's communication."

He gripped the doorknob and turned it slowly.

Locked.

Harper reached up to his ear and turned his com off. He motioned to Taralyn to do the same once again.

"What's wrong?" she asked.

"You know how to pick a lock?"

"No, not really. Do you?"

"I do. I learned by watching YouTube videos. However, with all the gear that I have stuffed into this snowsuit, I forgot to bring any sort of lock picking device with me. You have a hair pin or a barrette or even a bobby pin on your person?"

Tara reached up and pulled the hood of her suit back far enough to unclasp a barrette. She pulled it free from her hair before shaking her head to free her long brown locks from their tight bun.

"You didn't have to do that," Harper smirked as he took the barrette from her. "I was going to give it back to you."

"Shut up," she said, and playfully kicked the back of his hamstring. "By the time you do what you do, I'm pretty sure I'm not going to want that back in my hair."

Harper took the barrette and manipulated it just so before carefully sticking it into the doorknob lock. He maneuvered it effectively enough to be able to turn the knob. He pushed the door ever so slightly to make sure that it would, indeed, open.

It did.

Rowe looked back at Taralyn. "We're in."

"Wow. Nice. That took you – what? – ten seconds?"

"After this is over and we're both back in the States, we'll get together. I'll give you a tutorial. For now, I want to go over our entrance approach."

"Okay."

"Those guys," Harper began, referring to Derek and Kinley, "are going to eventually start making a scene. You and me, we're going to go in quiet as church mice. Not exactly sure what we're going to find on the other side of this door, so we don't want to go busting in like the Kool-Aid pitcher. Know what I'm saying?"

"Okay. I will follow your lead. But I think we should turn our coms back on. It's been a minute."

"Oh, crap. Yeah," Harp hastily tapped his com back on. Tara did the same. Both of them heard the same thing, "Harper? Taralyn? Do you read? Come back."

"Depends," Harper said carefully. "How long have you been trying to reach us?"

"Dude, stop screwing around and DO NOT turn your coms off again."

"You said you didn't want to hear my play-by-play so...I muted me...and Tara."

"Okay. Okay," Kinley was trying to keep his cool. "We're all set here. It's just about *go time*, so...be cool, buddy. You, too, Tara."

Derek Cooke looked at Kinley Devereaux and nodded. Each man knew the plan of entrance: stay calm and watch each other's back. Kinley would follow Derek's lead.

"Let's do this," Kinley said.

"Just stay behind me, keep your hands where they can see them and keep your eyes open for anything else that might be going on around us."

"Got it."

Cooke knocked on the front door and opened it partially before saying loudly, "Hey, anybody home?"

He saw a woman that he recognized as Luckinka Dvorsky. He had met her several times before when he had come to the orphanage in the guise of a handyman. He quickly explained to her that he was stopping by to be sure that everything was okay in this storm.

"*Ahoj, Luckinka! Byl jsem v této oblasti, a myslel jsem, že pokles o, aby zjistili, zda jste něco potřebovali.*"

She looked surprised and unnerved by his presence. He could hear it in her voice. "*Branislav, co tady děláš dneska? Všechno je v pořádku.*"

She asked him why he was here and told him in a very cold tone that everything was fine. This was out of character for Luckinka. On a normal visit by Derek Cooke, aka Branislav Slovacek, she was always very warm and welcoming.

Luckinka's demeanor did not matter to Derek. He knew exactly why she was acting the way she was.

Derek explained to her that he wanted to make sure the antiquated boiler in the basement was holding up in these bitter temperatures. She assured him that it was fine and tried to hurry him away. But Derek was having none of it.

"*Klídek, Luckinka. Půjdu zkontrolovat kotel. Mezitím,*" Cooke told her he was going to check the boiler. But in the meantime, "*To je můj přítel, Petr Krug, a má zájem o adopci,*" Derek told Luckinka that his friend, Peter Krug, was interested in adoption. He went on to explain that Peter was an American, and he asked her if she would mind speaking in English.

"Mr. Peter and Mr. Branislav, you must go now," Luckinka urged.

"Is everything okay, Lu? You seem a little bit nervous."

"The two of you must go. I will call police," she threatened.

Derek felt that now was the right time to pull a weapon. It was a Glock 19, and he put it right in her face.

"And why is that, Lu? Something going on here that you don't want anyone to know about?"

Dvorsky rushed over to a nearby desk and tried to hit a button – a button that would alert everyone in the building that there was trouble. But Kinley grabbed her by the arm and spun her around.

"I don't think so, lady." He pulled a Beretta 92FS and stuck it right to her throat. It was at that point that Derek said loud enough for Harper and Taralyn to hear through their coms, "I think now's as good a time as any for the two of you to come in."

The Go-Ahead for Diego

Laurie Chase and Big James Gray finally arrived at the back of the security fence – the exact spot that Diego del Fuento had told them about.

This fence was not made for climbing. The only way to scale it was to grab onto the upper horizontal bar, swing their legs up over the top and let the momentum of their bodies carry them to the other side. To make it even more difficult, each vertical bar was spear-tipped. So a heavy-duty mat of some sort had to be thrown across the top to avoid having various and sundry body parts punctured.

For the athletic Laurie Chase, this feat would be easily accomplished. For Big James Gray, not so much.

"How am I supposed to get over *that*?" were Big James's first words upon seeing the fence.

"I'll give you a boost and flip you over."

"You're aware that I'm well over three hundred pounds, and you are – what – about a buck thirty, soaking wet?"

"I'm a buck thirty bone dry. Never weighed myself soaking wet. I have an electric scale, and it doesn't take a Chernobyl scientist to figure out those two things don't go together."

"C'mon, Laurie," James said. "How are you going to toss me

up over the top of that fence? Don't know if you've taken a real good look up there or not, but if I don't clear the top of this gate on my first attempt, I'm going to be shish kabob James Gray instead of Big James Gray, and I kinda like the current nickname."

"It'll be fine," Chase assured the big man. "Look, we can throw the gun bag up on top of the fence before we toss you over. It should keep you from getting gutted on your way to the other side."

"I would just like to point out a couple of words and key phrases that bother me about that last statement you made: First of all, *gun bag on top of the fence*, which seems very, very much like a bad idea. And then there's that word *should*. I'm no English major, Chase, but I'm pretty sure that word – *should* – means that it may or may not work. Which, correct me if I'm wrong, that whole statement means that you want to use a bag of armaments to – maybe or maybe not – protect me from getting impaled while you, a woman about a third of my size, tries to flip me over that fence."

"That sounds right, yes."

"I thought of a hundred and twenty-eight different ways that I was going to die, and I'm ninety-nine and forty-four one-hundredths percent sure that this was not one of them."

"That's because you're not going to die. You'll be fine," Chase said. "We'll be fine."

"'Ey, guys?" Diego came through their coms. "How are we doing?"

"Great, Diego," answered Chase. "We are right where you told us to be. Just need for you to get them to open the front gate so that the security wall will go down around the perimeter fence. That's all on you, though."

"I am ready," Diego said.

"As soon as the gate opens and the fence is down, clear your throat. That will be our signal to go."

"Okay, Meess Laurie. Now remember, thee gate weell only be open for about twenty seconds. Once eet ees closed again, thee fence weell be back on."

"Then be prompt with your throat clearing, Diego."

APPALLING DISCOVERY

Harper silently opened the back door the rest of the way. Weapons down to their sides, Harp and Tara entered the back of the orphanage.

"The words for 'everything will be okay' are '*všechno bude v pořádku*'," Harper said. "Just say that to any kids we run into. I'll tell them the rest."

"Um...okay," Tara said.

"Okay, just practice real quick."

"Can you say it again?"

"*Všechno...bude...v pořádku*," Harper said slowly.

Taralyn carefully repeated it to him.

"Close enough. Just say it with some compassion, okay?"

"Okay," she said. Taralyn repeated it to herself, trying to sound compassionate. She followed close behind Harper as they came upon the first bedroom.

In it, they found two boys, ages nine and twelve, playing a board game called *Laborigines*, the Czech equivalent to the American game Jumanji. The kids looked up at Harper and recoiled in fear.

"*To je v pořádku. Neboj se*," he told them it was going to be okay, and that they should not be afraid.

Taralyn repeated the line Harper had told her to say in the most sympathetic voice she could muster, "*Všechno bude v pořádku*."

Harper and Taralyn slowly dropped down to their knees to be at the same level as the boys. It was a proven way to help ease initial tensions between both children and dogs.

"*Ahoj, jmenuji se Harper Rowe*," he said, then pointed to Tara and introduced her. "*To je můj přítel, Taralyn.*"

Tara smiled at the two frightened boys and slowly extended her hands toward them. They initially recoiled with fear, but the kind look in Tara's eyes told them she was not there to do them any harm – unlike almost every other time an adult had come into their room.

"Tell me again how you say 'friend'?" she asked Harp.

"*Pritel*," he answered quietly.

Tara looked at both boys and calmly said, "*Pritel.*"

Each boy cautiously reached out and took one of Tara's hands. Fearing that they were in some sort of trouble, the first boy asked why Tara and Harper were there, "*Proč... Proč jsi tady? Jsme v průšvihu?*"

Harper told them why he and Tara were there, and what was getting ready to happen. He was careful to speak patiently and kindly, being sure to ask the boys if they understood what he was saying or if they had any questions.

The lads understood perfectly. They even began to smile as Harper instructed them to quickly and quietly get a bag or a box and start packing their belongings. He told them that when they were finished, they should go help their friends get packed up, too.

Harper and Tara stood up and began to leave the boys to their packing. But before they got to the doorway, they heard a door to another room open in the corridor. Harper looked at Tharp and gave her a hand gesture to stop. He silently moved to the door, crouched down and peeked out into the hallway. There stood a man with a panicked look on his face – and not because he had seen Harper and Tara.

"*Pomoz mi!*" the man yelled for help. "*Pomoz mi!*"

Harper motioned for Tara to pull her weapons and join him in the hall. The two were quickly on the distressed man.

"Harper." Kin's voice crepitated through Rowe's com. "What's going on down there?"

"I got it. I got it," Harp assured his friend.

"*Ztichni! Ztichni!*" Harper told the man to shut up. One look into his eyes let Harper know this guy was coked out of his gourd.

Hallway man spoke something unintelligible in Czech while pointing frantically toward the bedroom from which he had just emerged. The last thing that Harper wanted was for him to bring a bunch of people into the hallway right in the middle of what was supposed to be a stealth mission. He grabbed the man's arm and hurried him back inside the bedroom.

"Oh, Lord, Harper." Tara was completely repulsed. "There." She pointed to a girl laying face-up on a mattress. The girl's mostly-naked body was convulsing, and a white, foamy substance was oozing out of her mouth while blood streamed out of her nose.

"She's OD'ing."

Tara took a step toward the girl, but had to peel back into a corner of the bedroom as she was unable to control the contents of her stomach.

Sadly, Harper had seen more than his fair share of drug overdoses, and he knew that there was nothing he could do for this girl. She was just a kid, no more than fourteen years old.

Knowing he could not help her, Harper turned his attention to the man who had done this to her. With his right hand, Harper grabbed the man's collar. With his left hand, Harper proceeded to pummel his face.

"You maggot-infested"—he punched his face—"piece of stink-filled"—he punched his face again—"dog dung"—he punched his face again. "I'm going to"—he popped him good again—"cut off your dick"—yet another punch—"and make you choke on it." He let go of the man's collar and with a big wind-up, landed a haymaker to the man's right temple which sent him crashing into the wall behind him. The pervert's unconscious body slid down the wall into a motionless clump on the floor.

He looked over to Tara, "You okay?"

"Yeah," she answered in complete disgust. "Kinda got caught up in the moment. I was *not* expecting to see that. I'm good now."

She walked over to the Czech man that was out cold, pulled one of her handguns from the pocket of her snowsuit and checked the silencer to make sure that it was on tight.

"Hey, what are you doing?"

"He doesn't deserve to live," she said flatly. She held the handgun about a foot away from the man's head and pulled the trigger.

Tara looked at her partner, not sure if he approved of what she had just done.

"Well," Harper shrugged, "I sure wasn't going to try to talk you out of it."

Without a word, Taralyn bent over the man's corpse and spat on him, then kicked him in the groin.

"Ya finished?"

"No." Tara walked over and looked at the lifeless girl. She pulled up a sheet and gently covered her with it. "Now I'm finished."

"Then let's move."

TIMING IS EVERYTHING

"Okay, you guys, I am really counting on you," Diego said as he took his final few steps up to the gate of the safe house. "I'm sure Tito weell open thee gate for me to go een, but once I am eenside, there ees no telling what he weell do. Ees a fine line between joy an' rage sometimes."

From where they were, behind the western corner of the fence line at the back of the property, Laurie and James could only see the very top of the safe house roof.

"Don't worry, little buddy. You can count on us," James said.

"Let's get ready," Laurie said to Big James. She put her hands together and held them about knee-high.

"Are you sure about this?"

"Stand over there so you can get a bit of a running start," Chase suggested.

"Do you think a running start is going to help?"

"Yes. Absolutely. It's Newton's third law of gravitational resistance...or something like that."

"Is that a real thing or are you just making stuff up as we go along?"

"Don't worry about that now. Just make sure that when your foot hits my hand, you push off with your other leg for all you're worth. Between your momentum and my strength, we'll flip you right over the fence. All ya gotta do is have a little faith."

Just then they heard Diego through their coms. He had reached the front gate and was talking in his native tongue to whomever it was that had answered his call. The exchange was relatively low key, which told James Gray that the person Diego was talking to did not know who Diego was. It had been nearly two years since Diego had been part of Tito's entourage, and was entirely possible that some of Tito's newer recruits did not know him.

Eventually, though, someone that *did* know who Diego was realized it was him standing outside the front gate, asking permission to enter the premises.

Being fluent in Portuguese, both James Gray and Laurie Chase knew that if Tito and his people were going to let Diego in, it was going to be very soon. They listened attentively for Diego to clear his throat.

They listened...and they waited. And waited. Come on already... somebody let him in! Laurie and Big James made eye contact and nodded. They were tingling with expectation.

Then they heard it: Tito was allowing Diego entrance. Now it was just up to Diego to give them the signal.

"Mmm-hmm," Diego cleared his throat. Go time.

Laurie wasted no time in taking the bag of munitions and tossing it onto the top of the fence. It landed perfectly.

A fraction of a second later and Big James was on his way. He took three long running strides toward Chase, put his left foot into Chase's cupped hands, pushed up and off the ground with his right leg, and was surprised past the point of sheer reason as Chase tossed him through the air like a basketball.

He was so sure that he was going to have to navigate the *top* of the fence that he completely forgot about how he was going to land on the other side. So the big man flew through the air with the uncoordinated grace of a hatchling on its first flight, and landed with all the deftness of an awkward octopus.

Chase turned just in time to see him hit the ground. "Ew, shit," she winced. "Dude, are you okay?"

Much to her amazement, the big man quickly bounded back to his feet. "I'm fine," he said brushing himself off. "Just come on already, will ya? The clock's a-tickin'."

"Coming on," she answered, and began the athletic challenge of climbing and clearing the fence. She was almost to the top when she accidentally knocked the weapons bag to the other side. Then she heard Diego whisper almost inaudibly, "Thee gate ees closing."

All Chase could do was grimace. As much as she wanted to hurry, she knew that one careless move could lead to her being impaled – not to mention that she and Big James would almost certainly be caught and killed.

With both hands on the crossbar of the soon-to-be electrified fence, she pulled herself all the way up. Now her arms were straight, her torso was above the top of the fence, and she placed each of her feet upon two side-by-side spires. She bent her knees and prepared to spring up and over the top. But just when she pushed, her right shoe slid off the post. She clambered frantically to maintain her position on the fence, but she knew she was running out of time.

"Tito's men are just about here to meet me," Diego said discreetly. "Are you guys een yet?"

James Gray knew the situation was bleak. He also knew that Laurie was hanging high and dry on that fence. In desperation, he moved as fast as he could toward her, reached through the fence, placed his huge hand on Chase's rear end, and with all of his mass and might, pushed her upwards.

The former DEA agent felt a slight tingle go through her fingertips as her slight frame was suddenly launched into the air.

James Gray recoiled from the jolt, took two steps back, and

held out his big, burly arms just in time to catch the descending frame of Laurie Chase.

The two exchanged exasperated looks as he set her upright on the ground.

"Yeah, we're in, Diego," Big James confirmed with a big sigh of relief.

Hidden Cameras

"How many people besides the residents are here, Lu?" Derek asked.

"Mr. Branislav, what are you doing?" Luckinka was nervous. "You do not know who you are dealing with. There are people...very powerful people...coming here. They will not hesitate to kill you. To kill all of us."

"Why don't you take a seat there behind your desk, Lu, and my friend and I will tell you what's getting ready to happen."

"No."

Kin leveled his weapon at her head. "Do what the man asks and sit down, lady."

Derek and Kin heard Harper through their coms, "Kneecap the broad if she doesn't wanna play ball. Show 'er who's in charge."

"We got this, boss. You just do what you need to do where you are."

"Who...who are you talking to?" Dvorsky resentfully took a seat behind her desk.

"We've got people in and around this building already," Derek informed her. "Ya see, Lu, we know what's been going on here. The sex ring operation that you've had going on at this place for who knows how long, we know all about that."

"You know nothing," she hissed.

"We do, actually...know something." Kinley walked over to the desk and leaned down toward Dvorsky. "You know that mother and daughter that everybody and their labradoodle are out there looking for? Well, we've got them, and we know what they saw, and we know what ya did. And soon," he leaned in a little closer to the woman, "everyone's going to know. As we speak, those two are giving a sworn testimony on video as to everything that they saw taking place here. And that video is going straight to Interpol. You and all your friends are going down, lady."

"I do not believe it," Luckinka said.

"It doesn't matter if you believe it or not. Believe *this*," and Kin stood back from the desk. "Mr. Branislav and I and the rest of our people are here to liberate these children from this nightmare that you've created for them. We're going to get them out of here to someplace safe. And if you or any of your creepy deviant cronies try to stand in our way, we're going to put you all down."

Kinley turned to Derek for support, but Derek was nowhere to be seen. Kin swiveled his head back and forth, scanning the room for Cooke.

"You stay put," he pointed his gun at Dvorsky, then turned his back to her and said quietly, "Derek, where are you?"

"I've found something. You need to come see this."

"Where are you?"

"To your right – out in the hall. I need you to grab Dvorsky and bring her out here. I need the two of you to see what I'm seeing."

Devereaux looked out into the hallway where he could see Derek looking back at him. Derek, who was as pale as an albino ghost.

"Get up, wench. We're going for a walk."

"Screw you. I'm going nowhere."

Kinley walked behind the desk and gave Luckinka his patented piercing stare. "Your taking another breath means nothing to me. If it means anything to you, you'll get up and walk."

Dvorsky let out a long sigh as she stood up and started walking with Kinley.

"Derek, Kinley, what's going on up there?" Harper came through their coms.

"Harper, did you and Tara take your snowsuits off?" Cooke asked.

"Yeah, it's kinda warm down here, plus they were very cumbersome. Not to mention that they...Wait. How did you know we took our suits off?"

"Because I can see you," Derek said.

With Dvorsky in tow, Kinley walked down the hall to where Derek was standing. It took Kin only a second to realize that a panel in the hallway concealed a security room full of monitors. They saw feeds from cameras peppered throughout the building: hallways, common areas, stairways, and, yes, the bathrooms and the bedrooms had cameras, too. Seventeen in all. Each monitor was labeled according to the location and room of its corresponding camera: LL, GF, and UL denoting lower level, ground floor, and upper level.

Besides being able to see Harper and Taralyn, Derek and Kinley could witness the sexual perversion taking place inside various other rooms at that very moment. Their eyes eventually came to one particular monitor that showed a room with a sheet-covered body lying on a mattress, and a bloodied man lying in a clump on the floor.

"Harper, what happened in that room that's about two doors behind you on your right?"

"Guy OD'd a girl while, apparently, doing heinous things to her."

"So, the girl – is she—?"

"Dead? Yes," Harper said. "So is the dude."

"Well, I kinda figured that from the bullet hole in his head."

"For the record, that's Tara's handiwork. Not mine."

"It's okay. I don't think anyone is keeping score today," Derek said.

Silence.

"Are we?"

"No, of course not," Harper scoffed. "Well...maybe subliminally, but that's it."

"Hey," Kinley barked. "We're wasting time. We need to stop all this yapple-dapplin' and get back to why we came here. I say it's time to start kicking in doors and busting some heads."

"Absolutely," Derek agreed. "Harper, are there numbers on the doors down there? I can't quite tell from this vantage point."

"Yeah, this place is older than the hills, but the doors still have numbers on them."

"Then you need to get to rooms 4, 7, and 9. You will find some horribly egregious crap taking place. I want you to— "

Derek's last few words fell on deaf ears as Harper and Taralyn did not wait around to hear the rest. With the ferocity of two wild boars, they moved to the next room in the corridor – Room 4 – kicked in the door, and busted in on the occupants.

The scene was despicable. A naked gray-haired man was having his way with a young boy that seemed barely conscious. Despite Rowe and Tharp's presence, the man continued his evil actions. Taralyn grabbed his hair and flung him to the floor. Coked out of his mind, he flailed wildly trying to get his bearings. Just as he gained some equilibrium, Tara landed a roundhouse kick to his left temple, laying him flat on his back. From there, she jumped as high as she could and landed with both feet on his testicles. The man screamed in agony, writhing in unspeakable pain.

Meanwhile, Harper found a robe and wrapped the young boy in it. He was smacking the youth's face, attempting to bring him to reality long enough to find out if he was going to be okay.

"Hej, chlapče, slyšíš mě? Vrať se do reality pro mě, kámo?" He asked the kid if he could hear him, and said that he needed him to come back to reality. After several attempts, Harper finally brought

him around. The youngster started coughing profusely, yakking up bile and mucus. Harper rolled him onto his side to keep him from choking to death. He brushed the kid's hair back out of his face, repeatedly assuring the frail youngster that he was going to be okay.

Harper looked over at Tara, who was still tuning up the silver-haired perv, and said to them all, "We're going to need more people. This is a mess."

"Well, now is not the time to be realizing that," Kinley came back. "It's not like we can hit the pause button and wait for reinforcements. We probably should have planned this a little better."

"This kid's going to be alright," Harper said, and he looked over to the man that Tara was standing over, "and that guy isn't going anywhere any time soon. So...we're moving to the next room. Mind giving us a heads up as to what we're walking into, Derek?"

"You have a quartet of people in the next room: a man and a woman and a boy and a girl. Get in there and get this stopped." Derek shook his head. "Good Lord, what is wrong with these people?" He turned to Luckinka. "How long has this been going on, Lu?"

She turned away from him in shame.

He grabbed her chin and made her look at him. "How long, Lu? How long...how long have you been making these kids go through this?"

"I don't know," she muttered, then swore at him in Czech.

Through their coms, Kinley and Derek could hear Harper and Taralyn taking the next bedroom. It was loud. And brutal. And justified.

"That's what we need to be doing," Kinley shouted, "instead of standing here with this demented witch."

Derek looked back at the monitors and saw that on their floor, the ground floor, there were two rooms that needed their immediate attention. "GF-2 and GF-7. Take us to these rooms now," Cooke barked at Luckinka.

"You do not understand, Branislav. It does not matter—"

"No, you don't understand, lady. We're asking you to help us as a courtesy," Kin grabbed her arm firmly. "My boy, here, and I are smart enough to figure out where rooms 2 and 7 are on our own. So if you don't want to cooperate with us, we've no need for you. Now...come on."

"No, it is *you* who do not understand. There are men coming here today to take three of our girls to Dubai in the UAE. It is these men that make us do this. Those cameras are not just for viewing. They also record. The men from Dubai come here and watch the videos and decide which of our children they will take next. They are ruthless. They do not just threaten us but also our families. If it were just me, I would have gladly given my life to end this long ago, but I have a family, and these men, they will kill all of them. A policeman in Prague tried to stand up to them and shut all of this down, and they took him and his wife and three children, and they slaughtered them. They tell us if we do not comply, the same will happen to us and our families, too."

In a steely cold tone, Devereaux said to her, "You make me sick. You take the fear that you have for yourself and your family, and use it to justify what is happening to these children?" He shook his head. "I hope you burn, lady."

"Me, too, Lu," Derek said without sympathy, "but we'll deal with those men when the time comes. Right now, let's deal with the issue at hand. Rooms 2 and 7, Lu."

She hesitated, then led Kinley and Derek to the designated rooms.

On the way, Kinley talked to Harper and Taralyn. "How are you guys doing down there? Did you hear everything that this woman was saying up here?"

"I did, for the most part. Sounds like we picked a heck of a day to show up here, Kin."

"When it comes to me and you, Harp, is that any real surprise?"

"God brought us here when we could do the most good, of this I am sure," Harper testified. "One thing that we *do* need to find out is when these men from Dubai are supposed to be showing up."

"True," Kinley concurred. "Hey, lady—"

"My name is Luckinka."

"Hey, *lady*, how much time do we have before the guys from Dubai show up here?"

"Why should I tell you anything?"

"Because I listened to your sob story about the bad, bad men from Dubai that have your family in their sights and how concerned you are for your family's well-being, and I can help you with this situation. But I'm going to need a little cooperation from your end."

"You cannot help," Lu squawked. "No one can help."

"Well, then how 'bout this, lady." Kinley put his Beretta up to her nose. "You can either tell me when they're going to be here, or I can permanently clean out your nasal passages. Either way, I'm good."

Luckinka looked at Derek for some sympathy. "Mr. Branislav, please? You know I am a very good person."

"If you are a very good person, Lu, then you'll tell us what we want to know."

"Fine." She gave Derek a betrayed look. "They'll be here," and she looked at her watch, "in less than two hours."

She pushed past the two of them and pointed to a door. "This is GF-2. Do what you must."

Cooke looked at Kinley. "You ready for this?"

"No, not even. You could give me an entire week to prepare for what we're about to do and see, and I still wouldn't be ready."

"Well," Cooke shrugged, "let's go then."

Kinley stepped up and busted through the door. He fired his gun into the wall to stop whatever action was taking place in the room. He saw an older man on top of a young girl. He took the butt of his gun and furiously slammed it across the base of the man's skull, instantly rendering him unconscious.

"Help her." Kin directed Derek.

Derek moved to the aid of the girl, and Kin threw the man onto the floor. He knelt over him and checked for a pulse. "He's fine," he said, then punched the unconscious man in the nose for good measure. Devereaux looked over at Derek and the abused girl. Derek was speaking Czech to her in a comforting tone.

"What do you think?" he asked Cooke. "How is she?"

"I don't know. Battered and bruised pretty badly," a look of concern was etched in Derek's face. "She's going to need medical attention and fast." He looked at Lu. "Go get me whatever medical supplies you have."

"You have any medical training?" Kin asked him.

"Not the kind that this girl needs." Derek looked up from the helpless girl and toward Kinley. "I'll do what I can for her, but you need to keep going."

"Yeah," the assassin nodded in agreement. "I'm on to the next room."

40

UNEXPECTED GUESTS

Laurie Chase and James Gray were on their bellies foraging through the sack of weapons, gearing up for the impending foray.

Diego's plan to walk right through the front gates in hopes of getting everyone's attention had worked flawlessly. Whether it was perfect design or Divine intervention, Laurie Chase and James Gray had been able to scale the security fence and gain access to the grounds of Tito del Fuento's safe house without being detected. Now the duo was perfectly positioned behind a small grade in the back yard, out of sight of Tito's sentries and security cameras.

Shotguns and shells, handguns and clips, submachine guns, grenades, smoke canisters, even a few knives were among the items they were arming themselves with. As they finished gearing up, Laurie and James strained to hear as much as they could through their coms. Diego's voice was clear, but the others were harder to discern.

Big James wriggled himself over to Chase and put his head up against hers. In the quietest of whispers, he said, "I can't believe we've made it this far. When you were flying over the fence, did you happen to see any guards at the back of the house?"

"I did – just briefly, of course – it was two of them," she answered in an equally quiet voice. "But they didn't seem to be guarding anything. They were standing right next to each other with their backs turned toward us."

"Well, I figured when my sack o' bones went flying through the air and didn't draw any kind of gunfire that we were in good shape," James smiled. "Plus, I really gotta hand it to whoever it is that does the grounds at this place. It was like landing in a fluffy bed."

"Oh, yeah?"

"Oh, yeah. The word *plush* comes to mind." Gray ran his hands across the opulent lawn. "And at the risk of sounding sacrilegious, I have to say that we, more than likely, owe our successful entrance into this place to the second coming of Diego del Fuento. We could not have gotten a better distraction from Lazarus, himself."

Chase smiled as she and Big James continued listening to their coms. Hearing only a third of what was being said made it hard to judge how the situation was going.

"Is he inside the house yet?" Gray asked.

Chase shrugged. "Diego, if you're in the house, give a quick cough. If you're still outside...um...sniff twice real quick."

They both heard Diego sniff twice.

"We need to get ready to move," Big James whispered.

"Alright. Stay here," Chase said. Using her elbows, she maneuvered to the top of the rise and lifted her head long enough to see if any more of Tito's men had been disbursed to the back of the safe house. Satisfied with what she saw, she ducked down and slithered back to Big James.

"And?"

"And...I think if we stay close to the fence there"—she pointed to the fence that ran along the west side of the property—"we could avoid most of the security cams. Plus there's a small tree line that we can use as cover. It will get us close enough to the house that, by the time we start shooting, I like our chances of getting in."

"Still just two of them out back?"

"A few more."

"How much more is a *few*?"

"Five, but they're all on the other side of the property. Seems like they're all trying to get a good look at what's going on out front. None of them are even looking this way, which is why we need to go and go now."

"Okay. Alight." Big James nodded fervently, psyching himself up for the attack. "Are you weapons ready, Laurie Chase?"

"I *am* weapons ready, big boy."

"Then let's go do this thing."

Chase and Gray got off their bellies and onto all fours.

"Diego," Chase said, "we are advancing toward the safe house."

But then, as if someone had hit the pause button on a DVR, James Gray and Laurie Chase were stopped dead in their tracks by a voice from behind them.

"I'm going to need the two of you to stay right where you are."

Laurie and James slowly turned their heads. On the other side of the fence, there stood Jeb Crool and David Baldwin, guns drawn.

"Make a move," Jeb hissed, "and I will see to it that the both of ya end up in the obits section of tomorrow morning's newspaper... and that ain't a threat, boys and girls."

A Cry for Help

Harper and Taralyn progressed through the rooms that Derek had alerted them to and did what had to be done. The scenes they were privy to made their blood boil and their stomachs turn – disgusting things so enraging that the two of them had to fight with all their might to not bludgeon the evildoers into a bloody pulp. Instead, they subdued them into unconsciousness and made sure the children that were being brutalized were awake and alive.

Unfortunately, the physical damage to some of the children was critical. Harper had his cell phone in his hand and was dialing a number.

"Who are you calling?"

"We need help. Some of these kids can't be moved In their current state. I'm calling Constance to see where her people are and if they have any medical supplies and people that know how to use them."

Taralyn reached out her hand. "Let me talk to her. We don't have a lot of time, and you need to get around to the rest of these rooms and help the children get packed up and ready to leave."

Harper handed his phone to Tara. "Have her people call that phone. If you need me, holler."

No sooner had Tharp put the phone to her ear then Constance

answered, "Hello? Harper?"

"No, Constance, it's Taralyn. I'm—"

"Oh, no...is Harper all right?"

"Yes, yes. He is fine. We're all fine," Tara replied, "but things here...we tragically underestimated the situation. Constance, we need your help."

"What can I do?"

"Harper wanted me to ask you if you can contact your people. We need medical help – supplies and people that know how to use them."

"Can you not take children to them? I told them I would keep them at safe distance. Was part of terms for their help."

"I understand that, but that was before we got here. When we got here, Constance, there were...there were people here...people brutalizing these children in just unspeakable ways, and...and now we have been told that there are men from...from…" Tara tried to recall where Luckinka had said the men were coming from, "men from...Dubai!" she shouted as if she were on a TV game show. "There are men coming from Dubai—"

"Dubai?" Ondracek asked. "Why men come from Dubai?"

"They are coming here to take some of the children. They will be here in less than two hours. We need to move the children now, but without medical help, some of these boys and girls will not be able to be moved. Without immediate medical attention, some of them *will* die. Please, Constance," Tara pleaded, "we won't be able to save all of these children without some help."

"I will call to see. I cannot make promise."

"Harper said to have them call this phone."

"I will try. Goodbye, Taralyn."

The disconnect was sudden. Taralyn worried that she had irritated Constance. All at once, she was feeling out of sorts and unsure if she had gotten her point across to Ondracek just how badly the four of them – Derek, Kinley, Harper and herself – were in need of some serious help if the rescue of these children was to be successful.

Taralyn felt like she had dropped the proverbial ball. She had specifically asked Harper to let her talk to Constance, to relay to her the urgency of the situation at hand. And all she could hear was *I will try. Goodbye, Taralyn.*

Her head was spinning as she stepped out of the room and into the hallway to look for Harper, to give him the news that she may have messed up badly just when she was needed the most.

That is when she saw them, the two little boys that she and Harper had first encountered upon entering this godforsaken place. There they were – along with several other children and their belongings that the two boys had helped pack – looking up at her like she was St. Jerome and St. Rita of Cascia all rolled into one. The two little boys pointed to the other children and said, "*Přítel.*"

Tara was taken by the display of affection and ready to return in kind, but her actions were cut short when Harper stepped out of one of the bedrooms.

He walked up to her and held out his hand for his phone. "What did she say?"

"Umm, well, she said she would try," explained Tharp as she handed his phone back.

"Okay."

"Okay? That's it?"

"If she said she would try, she will try."

Harper's phone rang. He answered it and walked away from Tara and the children.

Tara did not know who he was talking to – it sounded for all the world like a FedEx guy, as she overheard Harper talking about packages, pick-up times, delivery options, etc. – but she breathed a huge sigh of relief when Harper pointed to his cell phone, then to her, then gave her a thumbs up.

The phone call was not from FedEx. Harper had answered it, even though he did not recognize the number on the readout screen.

"This is Harper Rowe."

"Hello, Harper Rowe. My name is Dr. Ian McCoy," the voice on the other end said. "I was given your number by a mutual lady friend of ours and told that it was of utmost importance that I contact you immediately. I trust this is a secure line?"

"Secure as a car seat. Thank you for your expediency, Dr. McCoy," Harp answered. "Since time is of the essence, let me get right to it. Do you know the address that I am calling you from?"

"Yes."

"I do understand that the initial arrangement with our mutual friend was that my team would be delivering parcels to you from this address, but some of the packages here are severely damaged which greatly hinders our delivery options. They require outside assistance before they can be moved. Is there someone on your end that could come here and make the necessary repairs?"

"We do have people that can fix the packages. If I may ask, how many of them are in need of repair?"

"About four or five total."

"My team and I can be there within the half hour. Any special instructions we need to know before their arrival?"

"Yes," Harper answered, "it is very cold here. So it would behoove your repair team to wear ski masks and hooded jackets to keep themselves warm. I'll meet them out at the street and bring them in. Once your repair team is in the building, we will begin transporting the packages that are in good working order to your location. We're on a time frame of about 90 minutes to have everything out of here and to you. That 90 minutes will begin as soon as this conversation is over and you hang up the phone. Any questions?"

"Seems pretty cut-and-dried on this end. We'll see you shortly, Harper Rowe."

FENCE LINE AGREEMENT

"You're going to want to do yourself a favor, guys," Chase said to the two armed men on the other side of the security fence, "and get down before you get shot at."

"It's Agent Crool and Baldwin, right? With the NSA, was it?" Big James asked them.

"Right."

"Yeah, she ain't kiddin'," Gray stressed. "This is a Brazilian drug cartel safe house."

"What are you two doing here then?" Crool asked as he signaled to Baldwin to get down.

"Well, we're here to kill a drug dealer and his family," James said matter-of-factly. "What are *you* two doing here?"

"We're here because we have a few questions for the two of you."

"Questions about what?"

"About a car accident that Agent Crool and I were in last night," Baldwin answered.

"What?" Big James feigned surprise. "Car accident? Are you guys okay?"

"We're here, aren't we?" Jeb muttered. "And is it just the two of you that are here to take out this supposed drug dealer guy?"

"Look, boys," Chase said quietly as she crawled closer to the security fence, "ya kinda got us at a bad time. Things are getting ready to get a little hairy around here."

"Whose house is this, anyway?" Crool asked.

"Ever hear of Tito del Fuento?"

"Del Fuento? Wait, isn't he the one that just had all his crap blown up the other night?"

Again, James Gray bluffed his knowledge of the given topic. "Is that right? Wow." He looked at Laurie. "Did you know anything about that?"

She looked at James, then looked at the two NSA agents who were looking at *her* with anticipation. She immediately used this to her advantage.

"Tell ya what, fellas, I'm willing to play ball. The two of you give me and the big guy here some help with our current situation, and we'll be more than happy to tell you everything we know about whatever you want to ask us."

"No way, lady," Baldwin was quick to answer. "We're not going—"

"Okay, yeah," Jeb overruled. "You're former DEA Agent Laurie Chase, right? Harper Rowe and Kinley Devereaux's girl?"

"I am, and you're Jeb Crool, the agent that's in charge of finding them," Chase stated. "Are those handguns the only weapons that the two of you have on ya?"

"Yes."

Chase looked over to James. "Give them some of your stuff... and hurry. We're on the clock here. Very much so."

Chase began to disarm and hand some of her own weapons through the fence, as well. "Be careful," she was quick to warn. "This fence is electrified."

"Then how did the two of you get where you are?" Baldwin asked as he scooched closer to the fence and cautiously took what appeared to be an Uzi from James Gray.

"Oh, you wouldn't believe us if we told you," the big man said, shaking his head. "I'm still having a tough time wrapping my brain around it, and I'm the one that did it."

While the guns were being quickly and carefully passed through the security fence, Jeb asked, "Do you two have any sort of plan here? Or were you just going in guns a-blazin'?"

"We have a guy inside...sort of." That was when Laurie and James both realized that they had completely lost track of Diego.

They stopped momentarily to listen to their coms. Unintelligible voices could be heard, but none of them were Diego.

And then they heard him. They heard him loud and clear. He was talking to Tito.

"We need to get going," James said to Chase, slowly lifting his head to see where the guards at the rear of the house were currently positioned.

While he did that, Chase finished passing the rest of the weapons through the fence and described the plan to Crool and Baldwin. "We're going to head up the side fence there. You two head along the back fence here. Try to stay out of sight."

"The rear guards are still distracted," Big James said as he ducked back down, "so we need to get while the gettin's good."

"Chase," Jeb said as he and Dave finished strapping on the weapons they had been given, "I know what this is. I know *who* this is. I know enough to know that this is Tito del Fuento, the man responsible for wiping out your DEA team in Mexico City." Crool locked eyes with her. "We're going to help you, but I need you to swear on the souls of your fallen comrades that you're not going to screw me on this. I'll help you get what you want, but when this is over, you're mine, and you will give me what I want."

Laurie let out a long, pensive sigh before finally answering, "I swear, Agent Crool. I swear."

FINDING TRANSPORT

The total number of children requiring medical attention was four. The number would have been higher, but, tragically, two of the children had died before the necessary help could be administered.

The total number of able children that could be transported to Ondracek's people was seventeen.

"Not sure who has heard what, but I've been in contact with Coni's people, and they are sending medical personnel of some sort," Harper said loud enough for Kin, Derek, and Taralyn to hear him through their coms. "We have a lot of work to do and not a lot of time in which to do it. Kin, you're in charge of the staff members, the perverts, and any other adults on the premises. Round them up and get them to the basement by whatever means necessary."

"I can do that. I may not speak Czech, but I definitely speak the international language of 'whatever means necessary'."

"Derek," Rowe continued, "going to need you to get Luckinka, and the two of you are going to have to track down a vehicle of some sort so that we can start moving these kids to Coni's people before the guys from the UAE show up."

"May I also employ whatever means necessary?" the Russian quipped.

"I'd be disappointed if ya didn't," Rowe came back. He was

now standing face-to-face with Taralyn in front of an anxious throng of orphans that nearly filled the basement hallway. "Which leaves Tara and me to get the rest of these lovable lads and lasses up to the ground level and ready for transport."

Harper looked at the children and gleefully asked them who was ready to get out of there and go someplace fun. "*Kdo je připraven se odsud dostat někam jinam?*"

To which all the children boisterously answered, "*Měěěě!*"

Harper clapped his hands and began jumping up and down. Taralyn took his cue and began to do the same. Then Harper motioned for the kids to follow Tara up the stairs as he brought up the rear of the group. Kinley was waiting for them at the top of the steps. He pointed toward the front of the home

"Head that way," Kin said to Tara. "There are two decent-sized rooms near the front entrance. Plenty of space for all these kids. Derek and I have the ones from this floor and upstairs in there already. Get 'em in there, settled, and out of the way. Once you do, I'll take the adults downstairs and lock them up."

Tara led the kids to the front of the house à la the Pied Piper while Harper hung behind to talk to Kin.

"I'm going to go outside to meet the medical personnel that are coming this way."

"You want my snowsuit?"

"Nah, mine's right downstairs."

"Take mine," Kinley said as he started to strip himself of the heavy outfit. "I'll grab yours when I go downstairs. Things are getting heated enough around here as it is."

"I told whoever it was that I was talking to on the phone to make sure that his people were wearing ski masks and hoodies when they came here. I'm not sure who has access to these camera feeds. Could be anyone, I guess. Right now, our number one priority is to make sure we get the healthy kids out of here, and the medical people in and out of here with the kids that are in a bad way."

"I'm guessing Constance knows what we're doing?"

"I talked to her, yeah."

"She didn't happen to say whether or not your buddy's Interpol friend had shown up to talk to the Buceks, did she?" Kinley asked.

"Well...when I said I talked to her what I really meant to say is that Taralyn talked to her on my behalf because I thought that Taralyn – being a woman – might be able to express our situation to Constance a little more convincingly than I would be able to do. So, that being the case, I'm pretty sure that the Buceks never actually came up."

Kinley gave his friend a doubtful look. "Wait, you mean to tell me that you were being sexist in hopes that it would get you a better chance at your desired results?"

"Well...when you put it that way…"

"You're going to make a great politician once we get back home," Devereaux grinned, "and I, for one, can't wait to see it." He patted his friend on the shoulder and laughed. "I'm off to go migrate some already-irritated adults to the basement of this place. It's probably not going to make them any happier."

Having been given his specific task, Derek Cooke had taken Luckinka Dvorsky by gunpoint. He had allowed her to get her coat, gloves, and cap before compelling her to accompany him outside to show him the location of the vehicles that the home used to transport the children on public outings.

The air outside was numbingly frigid, but, for now, the snow had stopped falling.

That was the good news.

The bad news was that the snow was nearly waist deep in many places.

"I don't know what good you think will come of this. We have two big vans that we use to carry the children, but look," she scoffed as she pointed up and down the road that ran in front of the orphanage, "everything is buried. You will never be able to use these in the time you have been given. This is a pointless effort."

"Just take me to the vans, Lu."

She trudged through the deep snow, stumbling and grumbling, making every step that Derek took with her as much of a nuisance as she possibly could until they reached the two vans.

The vehicles were parallel parked about two blocks away. They, along with every other car on the street, were buried in snow – both from what had fallen from the sky and what the snowplows had deposited.

"See? Buried."

"I do," Cooke said without expression. "Stay right there. Don't move."

Derek looked up and down the road. The street itself was quite driveable, under the circumstances. He traipsed through the snow to get a closer look. Unfortunately, both vans really were...buried.

He looked at Luckinska, who scowled right back. She threw her hands up in the air and shook her head mockingly. "Well?"

"Kinley, can you hear me okay?" Cooke asked through the com.

"Sure," came his reply. "What's up?"

"I was just contemplating," Cooke answered slowly. "Since all the adults you're taking to the basement are already going to be in a bad mood..."

Do Some Good

Crool and Baldwin kept their heads down as they moved along the fence line. This was by no means how they had seen their day going. But nevertheless, here they were.

"You sure this is the right play? With those two?"

"I know there were other options, but this seemed like the best one to me."

"Really? The *best* one?"

"Just keep your head down and be ready to start shooting."

"Are we supposed to start shooting first or are they?"

"Umm...not really sure. Did we cover that with them?"

"I thought we had...oh, no...oh, crap...I think we've been spotted," Baldwin said.

He and Jeb had, indeed, been spotted.

"*Zastavit!*" one of Tito's guys was yelling at them. "*Zastavit přímo tam!*"

"I guess it's too much to hope that there's a really short man between us and them that only they can see that they're yelling at?"

"Doubtful. What do you think we should do, Jeb?"

Jeb Crool looked to his left to see how far along the east fence line Laurie Chase and James Gray had progressed. "Let's keep going. There are a couple of trees straight ahead. Take cover there."

"Should we start shooting?"

"They haven't shot at—"

Agent Crool's sentence was interrupted by del Fuento's men shooting at him and Baldwin. The bullets landed in the ground in front of the agents, kicking up dirt and soil onto their pants. The closeness of the projectiles caused both men to dive into shoulder rolls and come up on their knees, firing at del Fuento's guards.

There were five of them. Were. With tactical acuity, Crool and Baldwin dispensed of the quintet of henchman with minimal effort.

"See there, Dave? That's U.S. government training versus Brazilian drug lord training. Good old American ingenuity wins out in the end again."

"What do we do now?"

Jeb stood up and brushed the dirt off of his pants. "Now that they know we're here, I'm sure we can expect more in the way of opposition." No sooner had Jeb finished talking than did his prophecy come true in the form of another ten of Tito's goons appearing in the back yard.

As Jeb and Dave retreated to cover behind some large trees, Jeb pulled out his cell phone.

"Who are you calling?" Baldwin asked, reloading the clip in his handgun.

"I'm calling Rapido to let her know we found James Gray and get her to send some officers out here."

Del Fuento's men had started firing an onslaught of bullets as they moved toward the corner of the backyard fence.

Baldwin stuck his head out from behind one of the trees to see what kind of attack formation their assailants were employing. "The bunch of idiots are just walking in a spread-out configuration. The dumb dopes aren't even taking cover."

"In that case, we...hang on," Crool held up one finger. "*Tenente* Rapido? It's Special Agent Crool," Jeb said loudly into his phone as bullets and gunfire filled the air around him.

"Agent Crool...where are you calling from? What's all that noise in the background?" Rapido asked.

"I'm calling to let you know that—" Jeb's sentence was interrupted by Dave returning fire.

"Agent Crool, are you still there?"

"Yes, yes, I am. Look, *Tenente* Rapido, I'm in a bit of a spot here. I've found Gray, and right now Agent Baldwin and I are involved in a shootout. Thing is, I don't actually know where we are. I know we're west of the city, but that's about it. Do you have the ability to triangulate my cell phone to see where I am?"

"Yes, I can get—"

"Find us and bring some officers – as many as you can. Gotta scooch." Crool disconnected the call, put the phone in his back pocket, then removed the AK-47 strapped over his shoulder. He moved to the other end of the tree line and prepared to fire.

Prepping for One Last Move

Once the shooting started, Laurie and Big James decided to take cover behind a small tree line close to the safe house. It may not have been the best of places to hide, since Big James' trunk was actually wider than the trunk of most of the trees. But he and Chase would not be there long. They watched as Crool and Baldwin took out the five men in the back yard.

"Perfect. Those two have the attention of del Fuento's guys. They will focus their assault on Crool and his partner, and you and I should be able to sneak right in the back."

They saw the next crew of del Fuento's men come onto the scene and fan out toward the left corner of the property. Chase and Gray paused a moment before making their next move.

"Before we enter the house, do you think we should flank and chip those guys? Level the playing field a bit for our party crashers?"

"I'll take care of it. Let's move to the house."

Chase led the way as she and Gray moved from the tree line to the nearest corner of the house. Stopping to do a quick recon, they saw that the ten gunmen had Crool and Baldwin pretty well pinned down. Chase reached down and pulled a grenade from the weapons utility belt around her waist. She took a moment to try to hear what was going on with Diego. Most of what she heard was a lot of loud, garbled voices.

"Diego," she said, "what's going on inside the house? Are you okay?" While she waited for Diego, Laurie looked at Big James. "Can you make out what's being said?"

"Not really," Big Time shrugged and shook his head. "Sounds like utter chaos to me. I'm just hoping they don't have a gun to my little buddy's head. I think—"

"Ees panic," Diego's voice finally broke through the coms. "Ees very much confusion."

"We are getting ready to enter the back of the house through the basement. Any idea what it looks like down there?"

"Tito has hees wife and keeds down there. Maybe seven or eight men weeth them."

"Where are you?"

"Upstairs. Een the bathroom," Diego answered.

"Does Tito have any suspicions about you yet?"

"Eef he does, he has not let onto eet yet. He has more pressing matters right now, eef you know what I mean."

"Okay. When I say so, count to ten. Just before we enter the house, I'm going to toss a grenade at the crew Tito has in the back yard. That should be enough of a distraction for us to get in undetected. How many men are upstairs with you right now?"

"I theenk there are eleven plus Tito. So, twelve."

"All right, then," Laurie took a deep breath, "start that ten count."

The duo moved out and began creeping along the wall until they reached the back entrance. Big James readied himself with an Uzi in one hand and a TEC-9 in the other. "Let's rock and roll these muttonheads," he said as he cocked both weapons.

Chase gave him a look out of the corner of her eye. "Yeah, okay, Leonidas. Stick close." Laurie pulled the pin on the grenade and launched it on a beeline into the back yard toward del Fuento's men. They were so focused on their targets that they never saw the explosive projectile roll to a stop right in front of them.

Laurie and James waited for the grenade to go off – creating the necessary distraction – before they sneaked in the back door of the home.

Crool and Baldwin saw Chase throw the grenade and dove for cover. After it detonated, they waited a few seconds before coming back up to survey the scene. Most of the shooters were dead from the blast, but a few of them were still squirming on the ground in pain-filled bewilderment. However, the squirming was only momentary as the two NSA agents, still holding their cover, fired a few well-placed bullets to finish off the job.

"I do believe that puts us up on them, fifteen-love," Crool smiled.

He and Baldwin looked through the fence toward the safe house just in time to see their counterparts enter the building through the basement.

"We're in, buddy," Gray informed Diego.

A View from the Basement

Laurie and Big James entered the basement through a cramped utility room replete with coats, shoes, boots, a washer and dryer, detergents, fabric softeners, and various and sundry tools and supplies. The utility room led into a large open rec area off to the right.

Chase and Gray's entrance had gone completely unnoticed as the attention of most of the guardians had been drawn to the rear basement windows as they took in the devastation that was their fallen comrades. Mitra del Fuento and the del Fuento children were huddled together in fear on a very expensive-looking couch on the far side of the room.

James gave a quick whistle to get the attention of the startled guards.

"*Fique quieto.*" He ordered them to be quiet as he brandished his guns. He then directed them to put their weapons on the floor and step away from them.

Between his intimidating size and his intimidating weaponry, Big James' demands were met quickly and without incident. Laurie Chase made short work of gathering up the weapons and placing them on a billiards table in the center of the large room. She then walked over to Mitra.

"*Fala inglês?*"

"Yes," the Portuguese woman answered with much trepidation. "Do your children?"

"No, they are only very young – 8, 5, and 2."

"I don't care," Chase said, taking a handgun from one of her hip holsters and pressing it to the temple of the oldest child. "Do as I say or I will not hesitate to kill all of your children right in front of you. Do you understand?"

Mitra's eyes opened wide. "Yes, yes, I understand. Please, I beg of you," she began to weep, "do not hurt my children."

"Well, now," Chase pulled her gun away from the head of the petrified child, "that is entirely up to you." She looked over at James, who was busily tying up del Fuento's men with some rope and tape he had found in the utility room. Then she refocused her attention back on Tito's wife.

"Tell your husband to come down here...by himself. Tell him that your children are scared, and they want their papa. Oh, and don't try anything stupid because the big man over there and I speak perfectly fluent Portuguese. Is that clear?"

"Yes. I will do as you say."

"Get on with it then."

Mitra was trembling so badly that she could barely stand up from the sofa. She looked at her three children and assured them that everything was going to be okay. "*Tudo vai ficar bem,*" she said softly, trying to cover the dread in her voice. She looked at Laurie as she moved to the stairs. Then she called out, "*Tito! Tito! Por favor, desça aqui. As crianças estão assustadas. Eles precisam ver você. Por favor, Tito!*"

"Diego," Big James said to him through the com, "make sure you're the only one that comes down with him."

Diego cleared his throat to let Big James know that he understood. He looked over at his cousin and nodded, "*Está tudo bem, Tito?*" He checked to see if everything was all right.

"*Diego, meu irmão, você voltou e minha casa está cheia mais uma vez.*" Tito walked over to Diego and wrapped his arms around him and kissed his cheek. He welcomed him back and told him that it felt like he was being attacked on all sides—"*mas estamos sendo atacados por todos os lados*"—and that he was glad for the miracle of his return—"*Agradeço a Deus por este milagre de seu retorno*"— and that he needed him now more than ever—"*Eu preciso de você agora mais do que nunca.*"

Diego asked Tito if he knew who his attackers were.

Tito shook his head. He was getting ready to say something, but before he could, Mitra yelled from downstairs, "*Tito! Agora! Sozinho!*" She wanted him now...and alone.

Tito motioned toward his men to stay put as he hurried down to the lower level of the house. He saw Mitra waiting on him at the foot of the stairs.

Laurie Chase had moved out of sight and was standing stowed away underneath the stairs. Big James had successfully bound and gagged the members of Tito's basement crew and moved them into the utility room.

"*Qual é o problema, minha rosa?*" Tito asked his wife what she needed.

Chase stepped out from behind the stairs and aimed her gun right at the back of Tito's head and whistled a cat call. "Yoo-hoo. Over here."

Tito's wife moved aside as Chase took her place at the bottom of the stairs. She waved her gun at Tito, inviting him down the rest of the stairs. "Come on. Don't be afraid. Come on down, Tito."

Del Fuento looked at Chase for a moment before he started laughing. "Welcome to one of my many homes, American. To what do I owe the pleasure?"

"The pleasure of *me* killing *you*."

"Oh, is that right?" the drug lord asked in flawless English.

"Oh...that's right."

Tito cleared his throat before saying, "Many a man – better than you, I assure you – has tried to do what you are trying to do now. But just when they thought they had the upper hand," and again he cleared his throat, "they fell to a disgraceful defeat."

"Did they?" Chase laughed. "Well, did any of them do this?" She fired two bullets into Tito's right kneecap.

"Diego!" Tito yelled up to his cousin.

Upstairs, Diego looked at Tito's men and asked for a weapon. "*Preciso de uma arma.*"

One of the thugs tossed Diego his pump shotgun. Diego asked him, "*É este carregado?* – if the gun was loaded.

"*Sim,*" he acknowledged.

"*Quantos tiros?*" Diego asked how many shots the shotgun held. "*Quatro.*"

"*Oh, muito bom, de fato,*" Diego said happily. "*Obrigado,*" he thanked them...and then pumped the shotgun and fired it at them, pumped it again and fired it, and, one more time, pumped it and fired it. The trio of blasts felled the group of men, but just for good measure Diego pumped the shotgun one last time and fired it into the lifeless pile of flesh. "*Isso foi para a minha Mary e meus meninos.*" That was for my Mary and my boys.

Diego walked over to the man that had tossed him the shotgun. He knelt down and fished through the dude's pockets to find more shotgun shells. He loaded four shells into the shotgun, then shoved a handful into his pants pockets. He propped the gun against his shoulder and slowly descended the stairs. "Deed you call for me, Tito?"

Saving the Orphans

Kinley had done a great job of getting the adults all dressed and ready for their outdoor activity. Then he and Derek Cooke did an even better job of getting them outdoors and in position to shovel the snow from around the two vans. And shovel they did. Both vans were excavated in no time. As soon as the task was completed, Kinley and Derek moved everyone back inside.

Harper was pacing impatiently in the road, keeping lookout for the medical personnel's arrival. He knew that if the medics did not show up soon, it would be too late for some of the children inside.

He finally spotted a van about five blocks away. It slowed to a stop and dropped off three people. Each person carried what appeared to be a medical bag. Rowe began running toward them and was soon relieved to see that all three of them had their faces covered. Once he was close enough, he identified himself.

"You are an American?" one of them, a woman, asked.

"Yes," Harper answered. "You speak English?"

"We all do," she replied, "I'm from Toronto. Dr. Mary Clements," she introduced herself as she reached out a gloved hand to Harper.

"Dr. Michael Riddle," said the second member of the group. "Bakersfield, California."

"Dr. Ian McCoy," came the third. "Galway, in the Republic of Ireland. We spoke on the phone earlier."

"Thank you all for coming. We need to hurry though," Harp urged them, "because the situation is critical for some of the kids. And besides that, we are on a timetable to get the children out before some really bad dudes show up."

The trio of medics picked up the pace to a quick jog.

"What about the other children that do not need medical attention? Are they all ready to go?"

"They're all ready to go. Absolutely. We've just been waiting to hear from your end."

"Our group is five blocks up and three blocks over," Riddle said, "on the first floor of a parking area at the *Alfa Tourist Service Hostel Svehlova* on the corner of Slavikova and Krizkovskeho. Are you familiar with that?"

"Derek," Harper said loud enough for Derek Cooke to be able to hear him through the com. "Do you know the *Alfa Tourist Service Hostel Svehlova?*"

"I do indeed," Cooke came back.

"We're good to go there," Harper confirmed to Dr. Riddle.

"I've got to tell you," Dr. McCoy said, "given the circumstances surrounding these kids, this isn't something that we usually get involved with. I don't know how much you know about the children's home situation in Czechia, but the state runs things with an iron fist. For us to provide the help that we do, we have to keep a very, *very*, low profile."

"Truth is," Dr. Clements added, "Miss Ondracek's donations to our cause are the only reason that we are able to stay afloat financially. So when she contacted us and asked us to help out with you guys and these kids...saying no just wasn't an option, regardless of the risk of exposure."

"Yeah, I get that," Harper breathed heavily from the cold air in his lungs. "Well, just let me say that you and every member of your organization has our utmost respect and unending gratitude for all that you're doing. Especially today. I don't know what kind of butchery you've come across with the work you do, but I need to warn you that what you're getting ready to see is not for the faint of heart. I'm sure being doctors – by the way, what kind of doctors are you exactly?"

"We are all general surgeons," answered Dr. McCoy.

"Righto. Well, like I was saying: I'm not sure what you may have experienced in your previous encounters, but what you will be walking into is a critical situation. I will tell you that some of these children have been, for lack of a better term, physically shredded." Harper paused to catch his breath, then continued.

"I mean, I think that me and my people were able to get the kids stabilized as best we could. We were able to stop the bleeding that we could see, but I'm almost certain that there's some internal bleeding going on."

"My Lord. What kind of savages are we saving these kids from?" Dr. Michael Riddle contemplated aloud. "It's one thing to treat children in such a manner for nothing more than intrinsically perverse reasons, but then to be so depraved morally that they don't even have the basest of decency to get them some sort of help for the damage that they've caused?"

Before anyone could comment on what Riddle had just said, the group arrived at the orphanage. Cognizant of the ubiquitous cameras, all three doctors instinctively adjusted their ski masks and hoods to ensure maximum coverage of their identities before stepping inside the orphanage.

"Let's do some good," Dr. Riddle said.

Harper opened the front door and led the team of doctors in. Derek and Kinley were ready and waiting for them.

"If one of you will follow me upstairs," Derek said.

"And I will have one of you follow me downstairs," Harper invited.

Dr. Michael Riddle followed Derek up to the second floor.

Dr. Ian McCoy went down to the lower level with Harper.

"I guess you are with me," Kinley smiled to Dr. Mary Clements. "My name is Peter Krug." They shook hands, and she followed him through the ground floor hallway to a bedroom on the right.

Upon entering the room, Clements saw a barely conscious girl laying atop a twin bed. The girl was covered with a dark bedspread and had two ragged-looking pillows under her head. The doctor placed her medical bag at the foot of the bed and removed a penlight from one of the bag's outer pockets.

"Have you spoken to her at all, Mr. Krug?"

"I have not, but one of the other members of my team that speaks Czech was trying to talk to her. But I don't think he had too much success. Do you speak Czech?"

"I do, yes," Mary answered as she shined the penlight into the girl's eyes. "Is this how you found her?"

"Um, no," he said slowly. "Not at all."

Dr. Clements pulled the bedspread back to reveal that the girl's clothes, from her abdomen down to her knees, were covered in blood. "Dear Lord."

Kinley came closer to the injured girl and gasped, "Whoa. Now *that* is not how we found her either. I thought Derek had gotten her to stop bleeding."

The doctor lifted the girl's bloody shirt and moved to examine her more closely. "She's ruptured. She's getting ready to bleed out," Mary Clements said, trying to keep an air of composure.

"Is there anything I can do to help you, Doc?"

"Towels. Dampen about half of them with warm water. The rest leave dry. Hurry."

Kinley bolted out of the room and said through his com, "Derek, where can I find towels in this place? Any idea?"

"Check the bathroom. I seem to remember seeing a linen closet in there. What's going on down there?"

"The girl that you were looking at – the one that we had to pull the guy off – she's bleeding out," Kin explained.

He found the bathroom and the linen closet therein. The closet was a complete mess, but he was able to extract six towels. He tossed three of them into the sink and turned on the hot water, then rushed the other three back to Dr. Clements. "I'm warming three more for you. Is there anything else I can do?"

"I'm going to need some cold rags, too. This child is burning up with fever."

Kinley looked at the ailing girl and shook his head in anger. "I got more than half a mind to go downstairs and put a bullet in the brain of every one of these sickos."

"What?" Dr. Clements seemed surprised by the statement. "You mean the people that did this are still here?"

"Yes, they are. We are holding them in a room downstairs. Gonna go get those towels and rags for you." When Kin walked out of the room, he saw Derek Cooke descending the staircase.

"My guy's good to go up there. Let's move these kids."

Derek followed Kin into the bathroom. Devereaux turned off the spigot and started ringing out the towels. "If what Lu said about the people from Dubai is accurate, we've got about 30-45 minutes to get this place cleared out." He handed Derek the wet towels. "Take these into Dr. Clements, and then you and Taralyn go ahead and start loading the kids into the vans. Get them the heck on outta here."

"Roger that."

"My guy is good down here," Harper said through the coms. "I'm coming up."

Kinley grabbed some clean rags, ran cold water over them, and hustled them back to Dr. Clements. He was surprised at how much of the blood she had already cleaned up.

"Put them on her head and face, and then I need you to hold pressure right here for a moment," she said.

Kinley placed the rags on the girl's sweat-covered face as he looked to see where the doctor was needing him to put pressure. "Right there?"

"Yes."

"That's...um...well..."

"Yes. Now, come on already. I've got to do surgery on her right here, and I need you to keep the blood flow cut off while I do."

A bit squeamish, Kinley did as he was told. He moved his fingers right to where Dr. Mary Clements had hers. As soon as she released pressure, blood began to surge rapidly from the area. Kin felt his gag reflex kick in, but he nevertheless pressed to stop the bleeding.

Dr. Clements placed the penlight into her mouth and frantically removed from her medical bag everything necessary for the surgical procedure she was about to perform. She heard Kinley gag again.

"Are you going to be okay to do this?" she asked, her teeth clenched down on the pen light.

"Yeah, yeah. I'm fine."

Harper had entered the room unnoticed. "Anything I can do to help?"

"Yes, actually," the doctor answered. "It would be a very great thing if you could come over here and hold my penlight for me."

"Of course."

"There are certain jobs that I like to perform with something in my mouth, but this isn't one of them."

Harp took the pen light out of her mouth and gave a quizzical look to his partner.

Devereaux was giving him the same look back.

"Well...yes," Harper began to stammer, "I mean... there's always—"

"I'm kidding," she said to Harp. "It's just that your friend is so pale, I was trying to make him blush to get some of the blood to return to his face."

"Oh," Harper said as he forced a nervous laugh. "Well... it worked."

Derek made his way to the front of the orphanage to join Taralyn and the children. She was trying to break the language barrier by singing Christmas carols. It was oddly effective.

He watched for a moment, but finally had to interrupt the festivities because of the time crunch they were under. "*Dobrý den, děti!*" he said loudly to get their attention.

Everyone stopped singing and turned to see him in the doorway. Having their attention, he began to explain what would soon happen. He told them they were going to go for a ride to meet some people who would take them to a new home – a home where they would be cared for in a much better way, where they would be safe and no longer have to worry about bad people coming to do bad things to them.

Cooke was having a hard time staying composed. Tough guy soldier and big time mercenary that he was, seeing the pain and fear in their faces, but also the hope in their eyes, caused him to get a bit choked up.

When he finished talking to the children, he clapped his hands, pointed to Taralyn and said, "You lead the way, my dear."

Derek watched her walk to the front door, and watched the orphans close in around her. Each kid had nothing more than a backpack of belongings. Even for the orphans who were sixteen years old, everything they had to show for life so far fit inside that one bag.

"*Svázaný, Gang, venku je zima!*" he shouted to them. This was to remind them to bundle up because it was cold outside.

They zipped their coats all the way up, buttoned the top buttons, pulled up their hoods or pulled down their hats. They were ready to go.

And when Taralyn opened the front door, go they did.

Derek said through the coms, "Taralyn and I have the kids, and we are out. You two hold down the fort, and, hopefully, the good doctors will have the rest of the troops in good enough shape to move out by the time we get back."

"Godspeed, you two," Harper replied. "Oh, and don't forget to turn your cell phones back on. Your coms may not work when you get a certain ways away."

PAINFUL INTERROGATION

"Diego?" Tito asked as he watched his cousin come down the stairs. "What just happened upstairs? What is going on?"

"What jus' happened upstairs ees that I shot and keelled all your men."

"You mean...you mean that you are with *these* people?"

"You know, Tito," and Diego walked right up to his cousin, "you make a lot of stupeed meestakes when you are scared."

In less than a minute the look on Tito's face had gone from smug to confounded to painful and, now, into the complete and utter realization that he was, indeed, screwed.

Laurie looked over to Big James. "Let's get him over to the couch."

The big man walked over to Tito and yanked him up by his arm. The drug lord cried out from the pain in his leg where Laurie had shot him.

Mitra jumped in and put Tito's arm around her shoulder. "Please, let me," she begged.

"Fine by me," Big James let the man go. "I didn't want to get blood on my pants anyway. That stuff takes forever to bleach out."

"You know what's good for that?" Laurie piped up. "Soft soap."

"Really? Because I would've sworn that you were gonna say apple vinegar."

"Apple vinegar? Eh, maybe, but for me it's soft soap. I have yet to find a stain that it can't remove."

"Well, I am gonna have to remember that. Honestly, I can't stand the smell of apple vinegar. The only thing vinegar is good for are boardwalk fries."

Mitra had gotten Tito to the couch where the two of them now sat with their three children.

"You know, Laurs, since this is kinda yours and Diego's scene, you want me to take the kids somewhere else so...you know," Big James suggested.

"Oh, I don't know, actually. Why don't we ask Diego what he thinks?" Chase gave a hard, cold look at Tito. "What do you think, Tito? Want to ask Diego what he wants to do with your kids? You know, since you saw fit to have *his* kids and *his* wife put down like useless horses, I really think that he might have something to say about this."

Tito looked at Diego for compassion and said, "Diego, these are lies that this woman has told you. I would never do that to you. We are family. Like brothers."

"Thee only one lyin' here, *Irmão*, ees you. You think I don't know what you deed? You keelled my family, and you wanted to keell me." Diego moved close to Mitra and put the muzzle of his shotgun to her chest.

"Diego, please," she shook her head with frantic fear and burst into tears.

"Deed you know thees, Mitra? Deed you know that your husband murdered my wife and my lee'le babies?!"

She buried her face in her hands, crying, "No, Diego. No."

"Liar!" Diego roared. His rage took even Laurie and Big James by surprise. "He ees your husband. You share a bed. And you expect me to think that you knew nothing about any of eet?" Diego pumped a shell into the chamber of his shotgun. "Thees woman," Diego pointed to Chase, "she took me een. She gave me shelter and a reason to leeve. She ees my family."

"*Espero que morra, filho da puta!*" Tito cursed his cousin and spit at him.

"Oh, now there's a brilliant move," Big James said. "Cuss and spit at the guy you betrayed to the depths of hell and back, and who now holds the lives of you and your family in his gun-totin' hands. Undoubtedly brilliant."

"You know why I am here, Tito, but now eet's time for you to find out why *she* is here."

"And why would I care about some stupid *puta*?"

"Oh, maybe because she ees thee one that ees responseeble for thee complete destruction of your estate and plantation and all thee men you had there."

It took a second for Diego's statement to sink in, but when it did, Tito was visibly shocked. He tried to hide it, but, in reality, ever since he had received the news that someone had destroyed his home and his property, a hundred possibilities of who was behind it all had run through his mind. Now, to find out that it was a woman that, to the best of his knowledge, he had never met or even seen before, caught him completely off guard.

He then asked Laurie the wrong question. "So, tell me, miss, who was it that hired you to do this to me?"

"I'm sorry. Did you just ask me who hired me?" She gave Tito a steely cold glare.

Tito returned in kind.

The two were so locked in on each other that Big James was afraid to walk between them for fear of getting cut in half by the sheer force of their stares.

After a long silence, Chase opened up on Tito. "You wanna know who hired me? I'll be more than happy to tell you who hired me. The DEA team that you slaughtered two summers ago in Mexico City is who hired me. You decimated ten men and women, and you didn't give a monkey's ass about any of them. I'm sure you haven't even thought about them since. But as you are finding out the hard way, I've kept their memories alive, and I've been thinking about you...and I've been thinking about *this* – right here, right now."

Tito was trying to recall the particular incident about which Laurie was talking. Two summers ago. Mexico City. A United States DEA team. And then...he remembered. And remembered it well.

He started to laugh out loud. "Oh, I should have known that making a deal with the Americans would eventually be the cause of my undoing." He smiled at her and shrugged. "I can appreciate your level of preparation and determination, and I can see that you have your mind made up to kill me, but – and I hate to tell you this – you're bringing down the wrong guy."

"Am I really? And pray tell, you lying sack of crap, just who is the *right* guy?"

"Two U.S. government people set up that particular transaction. Me and my men were to take out the DEA team, and in return, I was given certain fringe benefits as far as the flow of drug shipments from North America into my country."

"And I'm guessing that you don't happen to have any paperwork that can authenticate this particular transaction?"

"I do." Tito sat up and his eyes widened. "Oh, wait," he sighed. "It was in my house...which you destroyed the other night so...no."

He started laughing again.

"Oh, you stupid *puta*," he cackled. "You got the wrong guy."

Laurie did not bother giving Tito a warning. She just raised her handgun and fired it at his head. The bullet grazed his ear and landed in the wall behind him.

If the desired effect was to get Tito to stop laughing and start swearing like a sailor, then the maneuver was completely effective. However, it also served to frighten the three children who had, up to this point, done a commendable job of sitting still and being quiet. The gun shot sent the three tykes sprawling onto the floor in hysterics. Mitra went to move off of the sofa and console her children, but Diego put the shotgun right in her face.

"Uh-uh. You stay. They weell be alright."

Laurie shouted to Tito, "You've got about five seconds to remember the names of those two U.S. officials that supposedly put you up to killing my team. Or else the next bullet goes right through your brain. I am done fooling around with you, man."

"Okay, okay," Tito cried. He was doubled up in pain on his left side, holding his ear.

"Sit up."

The wounded man sat up. The blood loss from the gunshots to his leg was causing his equilibrium to be off-kilter, and he was having trouble focusing.

"Look," he said, "I will tell you the names, but you must promise me that you will let my wife and my children live. Please."

Laurie Chase backhanded him across the nose. "Oh, I'm sorry, Tito, but you seem to have lost so much blood that you think I'm freakin' Monty Hall and you're a contestant on *Let's Make a Friggin' Deal*." She grabbed him by the hair and pulled his head back so that he was looking straight up at her. She pushed the business end of her handgun up tight underneath his chin, bent down to his non-bleeding ear and whispered, "The names."

There was a sudden commotion from up upstairs.

Chase looked at Tito and put her index finger up to her mouth. "Quiet."

"You want me to go check that out?" Big James asked softly.

"Keep an eye on them," Chase whispered to Diego and James.

"I'll go check it out. If either one of them makes a sound...pop 'em."

Laurie backed away from Tito and made her way over to the stairs. She listened for a moment to footsteps and hushed voices. Male voices. She could not make out what they were saying. She carefully began her ascent until she got to the landing halfway up. She listened again. The voices had stopped, but the footsteps had not, and now they were headed right for the top of the stairs.

She readied her weapon and waited for the men to come into sight.

Time's Up

It was painfully obvious that the situation was getting worse. Kinley was keeping as much pressure on the area as he could, but blood was now coming from other places. Dr. Clements said that excessive bleeding is quite often the aftermath in cases of sexual assault of girls.

"I'm not going to be able to do this on my own," Clements finally admitted. "Harper, can you go see if Dr. McCoy or Dr. Riddle can come help me? Please, hurry."

Rowe spun on his heels and was about to dash out the door when she requested one more thing. "Also, if you could find a turkey baster, that would really be great."

Harper furrowed his brow, shrugged his shoulders, and was out the door like a shot.

"Dr. McCoy. Dr. Riddle. Dr. Clements needs you. Either one of you. So...if you can, come help. Thank you," he shouted into the hallways.

From there, Harper began to roam the ground floor in search of a kitchen. *Gotta be here somewh—* he was saying to himself when he finally happened upon it. *Bingo.* He smiled to himself. *Now to find a turkey baster.*

Dr. Michael Riddle's patient on the upstairs floor was a 12-year-old boy, and while the lad had been atrociously brutalized, his physical injuries were minor. He was not bleeding. He had no broken bones. He was conscious and, all things considered, the boy was in a decent mood. So, when Harper Rowe came calling for some assistance, Dr. Riddle was able to accommodate.

"What do we have, Mary?" he asked upon entering the room and seeing Clements and Devereaux performing some sort of medical procedure on the young girl's body.

"This poor thing's been torn up something awful, Mike. Massive hemorrhaging. We've been trying like heck to stem the bleeding, but it's more than we can keep up with. On top of that, the girl's pupils are constricted to the size of BBs which means they've drugged her with some sort of opiate which has her blood thinner than water, and it just won't clot."

Riddle assumed the spot where Harper had been standing and set his own medical bag down next to Mary's. He did a quick once-over of the affected area. "Geez, that's a lot of blood." The first thing he did was to grab one of the towels and carefully sop up some of the blood that had pooled up around where Mary Clements was suturing.

"Hey, where are you guys?" came a voice from out in the hall. It was Dr. Ian McCoy.

"Ian, we're in here."

McCoy made his way over to the girl's bed, then walked around to the far side and stood next to Kinley. "Good Lord, that's a lot of blood."

"You know what we could use?" Riddle asked.

"One of these?" Harper answered as he bounced back into the room and held up the turkey baster he had found.

"Yes, perfect," Dr. Clements smiled. "If you don't mind handing that to Dr. McCoy."

Rowe handed the baster to McCoy, and the doctor immediately

placed the tip of it into the bloodied area and began sucking the blood away.

"Oh," Kinley finally comprehended. "Well, ain't that swift."

Dr. Riddle pulled his suture kit out and began to stitch one rupture. Dr. Clements finished closing off another and moved to the area that Kinley had been holding shut. She looked up at him and nodded. "You're quite the trooper," she grinned. "I think the three of us can take it from here."

Kinley let out a sigh of relief as he removed his blood-soaked hands from the operation, grabbed a towel, and wrapped them up. He walked out from behind the bed and headed toward the door. "I'm going to go wash up, and then we can go check on the other kids and start getting them ready to get out of here," he said to Harper.

"Doctors McCoy and Riddle, the kids you were tending – are they stable enough to prepare to move?"

"The boy upstairs is stable. Banged up pretty good and plenty sore, but I gave him something for the pain, and he's resting," Michael Riddle answered.

"The boy downstairs is unconscious, but I think that's more from whatever drugs they gave him than it is from the actual physical abuse. I checked him as best I could, but I did not find anything that would physically keep him from being moved," Dr. McCoy explained. "The girl that is downstairs – my God, they did a number on her. She's not bleeding like this one, but her body is just covered in contusions and abrasions, not to mention how malnourished she is. The boy, too. In my opinion, we're getting them out of here just in the nick of time. These kids are virtually at death's doorstep."

"We need to hurry," Kinley said as he headed toward the bathroom, "because we are running out of time."

"I'll meet you upstairs." Harper turned back to the doctors. "Holler if you need anything."

He made his way up to the second floor of the orphanage. It

looked very much like the lower level where he and Taralyn had first come in: a long hallway with rooms off to the left and right, dark red carpet and dingy white walls. Harp wondered if the carpet was dark red to conceal all the blood that had probably been spilled on it. He started walking down the corridor to the front of the house. The doors to all the rooms were open, so he stuck his head into each one to look around. Knowing what had gone on in these rooms gave him a shiver.

These poor kids. He had only been here a little less than two hours, and he already could not wait to get out. He could not even comprehend how the abused tenants that lived here must have felt.

He finally got to the room where the boy was.

"*Ahoj*," he waved to the boy and introduced himself, "*jmenuji se Harper Rowe*."

The boy smiled weakly. "*Jmenuji se Ladislav Novak.*"

"*Rád vás poznávám, Ladislave. Jste připraveni se odsud dostat?*" Harper asked Ladislav if he was ready to get going.

The boy nodded and pointed to an already-packed bag that was sitting just inside the door. Harper bent over and picked it up. It was much lighter than he expected it to be. Harper checked with the boy. "*Jsi v pořádku?*"

The boy nodded and asked Harper where the others were.

Rowe explained to him that most of the children had already been taken to safety and that there were only three other kids still in the home because – much like Ladislav – they needed some medical attention before they could be moved.

"*Jsou v pořádku?*" the boy asked if they were okay.

"*Ano.*"

He gingerly stood up from his bed and started making his way toward Harper. Harp took a step toward him, but Ladislav waved him off. He looked at Harper and patted his chest as he hobbled by, as if to say, "I've got this."

The boy walked out into the hallway just in time to see Kinley headed his way. Ladislav stopped and turned around with a worried look on his face.

"*To je v pořádku. Je to přítel.*" Harper told Lad that it was okay, that Kinley was a friend.

"Does he need any help?" Kinley asked.

"He says he's fine. We'll get him set up downstairs and then go down and get the boy and the girl from the basement. Sound good?"

Kinley did not answer. He seemed not to hear anything that Harper had just said.

Instead, his attention was on the window at the end of the hallway. The window that faced out into the street. Kinley walked past Ladislav and then past Harper.

"What's going on, buddy? You see something?"

"I think we've got problems. Take the boy down into the basement. The doctors, too. That woman, Lu, is down there in the room where I've got all the pervs tied up. Get her. I think we're going to need her."

"The people from Dubai? They're here?"

"Somebody's here."

TITO'S SHOCKING CONFESSION

Her finger was on the trigger. They appeared at the top of the stairs – two men.

And as soon as she saw them...she took her finger off of the trigger.

"Don't shoot!" Chase held her gun up for the two men to see, then put it away in her hip holster as she walked up the steps toward them.

"How did you two get in here?" she asked in a loud whisper.

"Well, we waited around outside for more guys to come out and shoot at us," Baldwin explained, "but after that didn't happen, we decided to walk up front. We heard some gunshots come from inside, so we circumvented the security panel on the front gate and let ourselves in."

"Is that your pile of dead guys over there?" Crool asked, pointing to the four men that Diego had put down.

Laurie looked over, arched her brow at the sight, and shook her head. "Not my handiwork, but since it was done by one of the members of my team, and I am the honorary team captain...I'll take credit for it."

"So? Are you about wrapped up in here?" Jeb looked at her. "Remember, we had a deal now."

"I do remember, and, no, I am not *quite* wrapped up in here. As a matter of fact, you two got here just in time," Chase flashed a grin. "You guys wanna help me have a little fun at the expense of an evil drug lord?"

"Well, normally we would say no to such childish hijinks, but since it's at the expense of an evil drug lord...what do we have to do?"

"Nothing, really. Just play along." Laurie turned and walked back down to the landing. "James? How are you and Diego doing down there?"

"Fine. What's going on up there? You okay?"

"I just want you two to be cool, is all."

"Okay. We're cool."

"Because I've got some bad news…"

"How bad?" James asked a bit anxious.

"Two of Tito's men – the two we saw out back by the fence before we came in – they've got the drop on me."

"The two we saw out back by the fence?" James ran with it.

"That's right."

"And they have you at gunpoint?"

"They sure do."

"Well...crap." James looked at Diego. "Just be cool, Diego."

Diego looked skeptically at Big James, and James gave him a quick wink and repeated, "Just be cool."

"I am cool."

"Ha!" Tito was all smiles again, bloody ear and all. "I knew my men would come, and now, you will all pay dearly."

Hearing this, Laurie did a double fist pump and smiled at Jeb and Dave.

"They're going to walk me down now. You two just be cool. It's all going to be okay." She motioned for the two NSA agents to follow her down, but to stay out of sight on the steps.

"So, Mitra, now that your husband has thee upper hand, and

eet looks like I weell surely die," said a sullen Diego, "you can tell me thee truth...deed you know that Tito was going to keell my Mary and my boys?"

Mitra looked at Tito, and they both started laughing maniacally. "*Claro, eu sabia.*" Of course, she knew.

Laurie stepped off the stairs and back toward Tito and Mitra.

Tito looked at her and laughed. "Not feeling so tough now, are you, *puta*? Miss American DEA agent?" He yelled over to the steps, "*Onde estão meus homens?*"

"Hey," Chase turned toward the steps, "he wants to know where his men are."

Awkward silence.

Finally, Jeb said, "Oh. Are we supposed to come out now?"

"Well, yeah."

"Hey, I didn't know," Jeb protested. "It's not like we rehearsed this or anything."

Laurie turned back to Tito. She did not want to miss the look on his face.

"Que diabos está acontecendo aqui?" Tito's face lost all expression – except fear.

"What's going on here is...you just got punked, nerf dick."

Now it was Big James' turn to laugh. "Oh, man. I gotta say... this is awesome. I am *so* glad that I am here right now because it won't matter how many times I tell this story to my grandkids... whew...it will *never* get old."

Crool and Baldwin walked over to the group.

"So, now what, Ms. Chase?"

"Well, Agent Crool, I'm glad you asked. See, just before you and Agent Baldwin came walking in on the festivities, Tito here was getting ready to tell me the names of two U.S. government members that had made an arrangement with him about a year and a half ago to wipe out my DEA team in Mexico City. In exchange, he was given certain liberties with some drug shipments coming out of North America and into Brazil."

"Is that right?" Jeb asked.

"I think that's where we were. Right, Tito?"

The Brazilian did not answer.

"Here's how it's going to go, Tito. You give me those names, and me and the big guy and these two gentlemen here, we'll get out of your hair and be on our way. We'll leave you and the missus with Diego to sort out whatever family quarrels you might have amongst yourselves. I never really was one to get caught up in other people's domestic squabbles anyway."

Chase paused for a moment and became very serious.

"Or...you can choose to not give me those names, in which case these two gentlemen will step outside while I make you watch me torture and kill your wife and children right in front of you." She leaned in close to him and whispered. "The choice is yours."

Tito began to grow restless as he pondered his decision. When it took him too long to answer, Mitra slapped him in the head and called him several vulgar names in her native dialect.

"Oh, it sounds like Mrs. Tito doesn't want to die today," Laurie mused. "And I don't feel like standing around here all day either, so let's get it together, Moe. Decision time. Now."

"Fine," he growled. "I'll give you the names."

"There, there," Chase patted him on the head, "that wasn't so hard was it? Now spill."

"There were two government members. One was a politician and the other one was what I believe is called a *cabinet member*?"

"Yes, that's right, a cabinet member."

"One was a man and one was a woman. The man – he was the cabinet member. And the woman – she was the politician."

"The man, what's his name?"

"It will not matter at this point what the man's name was. He is dead."

Laurie Chase turned to Jeb. "I have a feeling that you might want to pay close attention to this." She turned back to Tito. "It's okay that the man's dead. We just need you to tell us his name."

"His name was Paul Michaels. He was the U.S. Secretary of Defense."

"Aww, Judas Priest," Jeb sighed. "Are you absolutely sure that was the man's name? Paul Michaels?"

"When someone from the American government makes a deal with you like that, you do not soon forget his name."

"Come on, Agent Crool," Chase said, "you can't tell me that this one comes as a total shock to you. In the last however long you've been assigned to find out what happened to the former Secretary of Defense, you must have come across more than a few indicators that he was into some pretty shady stuff."

"What I may or may not have come across in the last several months doesn't even begin to hold a light to hearing someone come right out and confess to me that Secretary Michaels was dealing dirty."

"Sounds like you're just getting confirmation on what I have known for the last year and a half. What I'm more interested in is... who's the woman in all of this? Any ideas?"

"Maybe. I have names that I have come across, but none of them that ever jumped off the page and screamed complicity at me."

The three of them looked at Tito. "So who's the woman, Tito?" Jeb asked.

"She was a U.S. senator. I only spoke with her once. It was a three-way phone conversation with me and Michaels and her. The woman's name was Senator Brenda Cobb-Schmidt."

"Brenda Cobb-Schmidt? Are you sure?" Laurie asked with sudden consternation.

"Yes, the woman's name was Senator Brenda Cobb-Schmidt."

Chase's heart suddenly jumped into her throat. She reached down into her pants to get her cell phone, but it was not to be found. She looked over at Big James as if he might have it for some reason. "I can't find my phone. I need a phone."

"Okay, things have taken a serious turn here," Jeb said. "All bets are off the table—"

"I need a phone!" she screamed.

"Miss Chase, we'll get you a phone, but you have to realize the impact of—"

Laurie heard nothing that Jeb Crool was saying. All she could think about was the last conversation that she had with Kinley Devereaux. The conversation where he told her that he and Harper Rowe were flying back to the United States to meet with someone that was going to be helping them clear their names in the assassination of U.S. Secretary of Defense Paul Michaels. The conversation where Kinley had told her that they would be meeting up with *Senator Brenda Cobb-Schmidt.*

James Gray walked over to her and handed him his cell phone. "What happened to yours?" he asked her.

"If I knew that I wouldn't be needing yours," she snapped. "I must've lost it on my way in."

Her hands trembled as she attempted to dial Devereaux's number. She dialed the first three numbers and then stopped. Her mind was in such mental distress that she could not remember his cell phone number.

"Come on. Come on," she yelled at herself.

The sounds of police sirens could be heard in the distance.

"We're going to need to take this guy back to the States with us," Agent Baldwin said.

"What?" Chase asked. "What guy?"

"Tito del Fuento. You may have missed this in your grand plan of revenge and justification, but he's a witness to some major, *major* crimes against the United States. Maybe you don't know this, but not only is Brenda Cobb-Schmidt a sitting U.S. senator, but she also happens to be one of the leading candidates to be the next American president," Jeb disclosed. "Not to mention what he just told us about the deal Paul Michaels made with him. That's another can of worms all unto itself. Besides, the police are on their way here. If we don't take del Fuento, they will. Plus, they'll probably want to talk to your friend there, too," Jeb pointed to Big James.

"You won't need Tito to bring down Brenda Cobb-Schmidt," Laurie Chase sighed.

"Oh? Really? Explain this one to me, if you don't mind."

"What if I told you that I could get you Harper Rowe, Kinley Devereaux, *and* Senator Brenda Cobb-Schmidt all on one, big, shiny, silver platter?"

"Then I'd say you got my attention. Now what are you going to do with it?"

Lu Lets the Dogs In

Harper quickly explained the situation to young Ladislav and told him to go to the lower level as fast as he could. Then Harper raced to the girl's room where the three doctors were still tending to her wounds.

"Okay, gang, you need to wrap it up and get downstairs. The company that we've been trying to beat the clock against has apparently shown up."

"We are almost finished with—"

"I'm sorry, but there is no more time. The three of you need to get downstairs."

Mary Clements looked at her two colleagues. "You two go. I will stay here and finish."

Riddle and McCoy balked at the idea.

Harper was not crazy about it either. He spoke through the com to Kinley, "Are we sure it's them, partner?"

"I'm not a hundred percent sure, but there's about seven men of Middle Eastern descent standing out in the road where the vans used to be, and they're looking around as if they're trying to figure out why the vans aren't there. Granted, those aren't smoking guns, but they're pretty good circumstantial clues."

"Yeah, I'm in agreement with you." Harper turned his attention back to the doctors, and Dr. Mary Clements in particular. "We were trying to get this place cleared out before these people showed up here. The situation is almost certainly about to get volatile. My partner and I will do our best to keep things as under control as possible, but your chances of coming through this unharmed are a lot better down in the lower level than they are up here."

"I still do not have this last wound stitched up. If I leave her like this, this girl will bleed to death in just a few minutes. I'm staying."

"Fine," Harper said, "if that's how it's going to be, I don't have time to stand around and bicker. Gentlemen, if you will follow me?"

Riddle gave one more crack at getting Dr. Clements to come with them. "Mary, this is one girl. We are all very well aware of the oath we took as doctors, but the amount—"

"I'm staying. Now, go."

"Let's go, fellas," Harper ushered the two doctors out of the room and downstairs to the basement. "Get the three children in one room and you guys stay with them." Rowe reached into one of the deep pockets of his snowsuit and pulled out two handguns. "Take these. Anybody tries coming into the room where you are, you shoot 'em. Understood?"

Each doctor took a gun and nodded in understanding.

Harper went in search of the room where Lu was.

"What's going on now, Kin?" Harper inquired to his partner on lookout duty upstairs. He saw that the doors to all the rooms on the lower level were open with the exception of one. He headed straight for it.

"One of the men just took out a cell phone and is making a call. My money says that he's probably calling one of his boys on the police force."

"That sounds about right."

Harper had gotten to the closed door, turned the knob, and carefully pushed it open. Along the back wall he saw eight men and women bound and gagged. Rowe walked over and gave a quick check of their restraints to make sure none of them were going anywhere. Next he turned his attention to the woman and two men that were sitting along the wall to his left.

"Are you Lu?" he asked the woman.

"Yes. Who are you?"

"Harper Rowe. Who are they?" he pointed to the two men.

"They work here."

"Why aren't you tied up?"

"The other man said that if we tried to leave he would kill us."

"I did tell them that," Devereaux confirmed through the com.

"Get up," Rowe said to Lu. "I need you to come with me."

"Why?"

"Because if you don't, the other man will come in here and kill you."

"Okay."

Lu stood up and walked out of the room.

Harper looked at the other occupants of the room, waved his gun at them and said, "Stay."

He closed the door behind him and walked with Luckinka Dvorsky up the stairs to the main level of the orphanage.

"All right, Kin. I've got her up here. What now?"

"Call Taralyn. Tell her what's going on. Tell her that she or Derek needs to bring one of those vans back here right now. We're going to get Lu to draw the seven men into the house. Then you and I are going to try to get the drop on them as best we can.

"While we're doing that, the doctors can take the other kids out through the back door where you and Tara came in. They can come up the side of the house, across the front yard area, and, hopefully, right into the van. Whoever's driving the van can get the rest of the kids and the doctors off to safety. Best case scenario, we all meet back at Miss Ondracek's place for cookies and hot cocoa."

"Given the wall our collective backs are up against, I'd say that plan has more promise than anything I could've come up with. Point of fact, though, we still have one doctor and one girl here on the ground floor."

"Call Taralyn. I'm coming down."

Kinley took one last look out the window. The seven men were still standing out in the street near where the two vans had been parked, although now it appeared that the one that had been on his cell phone earlier was finished with the call.

Dev made his way down the upper level corridor to the stairs. Through his com, he could hear Harper relaying the crucial information to Taralyn. Part one of the plan was now in motion.

Kinley came off the stairs and darted to the room with Dr. Mary Clements and the ailing girl.

"How are we doing, Doc?"

"I have her stitched back up, but I don't think we can move her. If any of these wounds were to re-open, there's a good chance that she would bleed out before I could get them closed back up again."

"You're the doctor, and you make whatever decision you deem necessary. All I can do is tell you the facts. And here they are: There are seven men that are getting ready to come into this house. My partner and I are going to try to put them down. One of the passenger vans that took the kids to your people at the *Hostel Svehlova* is on its way back here now. Once the men are inside this house and engaged, we're sending your cohorts and the other three children out the back. They're going to come around and get in the van, and the van is going to be taking all of them back to your people. If you and the girl are not on it, I can't say that there's much of a chance that she's going to make it anyway. You, either."

A look of despair slid over the doctor's face.

"Look," Kinley said. "I can carry her downstairs now, and I'm sure that one of your doctor friends can carry her through the snow and to the van. But if we're doing it, we need to do it now."

Clements thought as fast as she could, weighing the pros and cons of each scenario.

"Please, Doc."

"Okay," she said, "please, be careful."

Kinley moved over to the girl and gently lifted her slight frame. He did not expect her to weigh much, but even so, he was surprised at how light she was. Had she been a twenty-pound bag of feathers, she would have only weighed twelve pounds. He carefully brought her down to the lower level, instructing Harper on the way.

"Harp, you need to get Lu out there and get those guys' attention and get them in here. I have a feeling they are waiting for reinforcements or something. I don't think that they're going to come in here on their own."

"You got it." Harper looked at Lu and gave her the news. "You need to get them to come in here."

Luckinka sneaked over to the front door and peeked through its small window. "How do you expect me to do that?"

"Do they always stand out there like that when they come here?"

"No. Usually when they come here they are with the police."

"Oh, the police," Harper shook his head. "I guess that's probably who they're out there waiting for now. Of course, I'm guessing most of the police are probably already being used to look for that mother and daughter, and the police that aren't doing that are probably on snow patrol."

"I do not know," Lu said dismissively. "They probably will wait."

"Nope. They won't wait because you're going to get them to come in here now."

"And again, I ask you how do you expect me to do that?"

Harper tried to think. In his com, he could hear Kin describing the plan to the doctors and the kids. How the van was on its way, how they were going to draw the men from outside into the house, how to be ready and when they heard the first gunshot to head for the back door and get out and around to the van as quickly as possible.

"Well?" Lu smacked Harper's arm.

"Now do I understand it right that these men are here to pick up three girls and take them out of here?"

"Yes."

"Okay...here's what you say..." Harper took a deep breath. "Tell them that the kids got sick – food poisoning, so that they know it's nothing contagious – and most of them had to be taken to the hospital, but that the three girls, they are still inside, but that they are sick, too...and they – those seven men – need to come help you...because you are here alone. Sound good?"

"It sounds like you are just making it up as you go along."

Harper just stared at her blankly. "Do you understand what you're supposed to say or not?"

"Yes."

"Do you speak to them in Czech or Arabic?"

"Czech. I do not speak Arabic."

"I speak Czech, too," Harper informed her, "and I'll be listening, so don't go trying to change things halfway through thinking you'll sneak one by me."

"They will probably think I am lying." Lu objected.

"I don't think so. I know men like this. They are dogs. All they want is what they came here for, and if they think those girls are in here, they'll come in to get them."

"So, I have one last question: If they come in —"

"Not if. When."

"When they come in, where do you want me to send them?"

"I want you to bring them through those two front rooms and send them down this hallway toward the back of the house, okay?"

"I understand."

"And, Lu, when you do"— Harp put his hand on the diminutive

woman's shoulder and looked her right in the eyes—"get outta the way."

Luckinka Dvorsky took a deep breath and stepped out the front door.

"Okay, Harper, we're all good to go down here. I'm coming back up. Where do you want me?"

"Um...ya know what? Come up here to the video surveillance room. You can keep an eye on our Dubai guests from in there, and I can stay here and listen to what this kooky little woman is saying."

"Good idea. I'm headed there now," Devereaux responded. "By the way, good job by you coming up with what to tell her to say to those guys to get them to come in here."

Kinley hustled up the hallway toward the front of the house. The hidden surveillance room was inside the wall on his left. He slid past the removable panel and into the small room, then quickly scanned the monitors until he found the one that he wanted.

"Okay, I can see them. How's our Lu doing?"

"Pretty well, actually," Rowe admitted. "Quite the convincing performance. She's got them talking back to her. Any movement to go along with this chitter-chatter?"

"No, not yet. They seem to be...whoops...hold on. Hold on," he said slowly. "Looks like we've got some fish on the line, Harp. We have...one, two, three, four, five...five of them coming this way. The other two are staying out in the street," Kinley confirmed. "You should probably get on back here, brother. Looks like it's getting ready to go down."

Harper hurried into the hallway, where Kinley was waiting for him.

"Back of the hallway," Harp said. "She's going to be leading them right down through here. Lock every one of the bedroom doors that are on your side of the hallway. I don't want them to be able to duck into one of these rooms. I want them to be bottlenecked right here."

Kinley made quick work of locking all the bedroom doors on his side of the hall – four in all. At the fifth and final doorway at the end of the corridor, he stepped just inside and waited.

Harper did the same thing along his side of the hallway. However, when he stepped inside his doorway, he pulled out his cell phone and began composing a text to Taralyn:

Expect 2 bogeys n street on arrival. Kill. Have coms on + make contact thru them asap. Stay near van + b ready 2 asst dr.s + kids coming from side o house.

Send.

He put his phone away and pulled out two handguns: a Glock 17 and the Kimber 1911 that he had picked up earlier in the morning from the cab driver. He and Kinley both double-checked the silencers on their weapons.

Harper looked across the hall at his partner and nodded. They both ducked back inside the thresholds of their respective rooms and listened.

The voices of the men from the United Arab Emirates carried throughout the ground level of the domicile. Lu was bringing them closer to where Kin and Harp needed them to be.

The two men made eye contact once again.

It was just about that time.

STRANGE BEDFELLOWS

"You've been on the trail of Harper Rowe for well over a year now, Agent Crool, because you knew he held the key as to why the S.O.D. was assassinated, who pulled the trigger, and what the circumstances were leading up to it. Right?"

"Yes, that is what my team and I have been endeavoring to do."

"And now that you know the S.O.D. was a corrupt P.O.S., I'm sure you want those answers even more than ever."

"Stop screwing around with telling me things that anybody with half a brain already knows. You said you could get me Harper Rowe, Kinley Devereaux, and Brenda Cobb-Schmidt on a silver platter. Just get to how you plan on doing that, will ya?"

"Right now, Kinley and Harper are in the Czech Republic busting up an international sex trafficking operation that is being run out of an orphanage in Prague. I don't know all the details, but what I do know for a fact is this: Once they finish their business there, Kinley and Harper are headed back to the U.S. because their former handler has found someone that can back up their story as to the events leading up to the assassination of Paul Michaels. The two of them are going back so that they can finally clear their names. The person that supposedly has the information to do that?" Laurie paused for dramatic effect. "Senator Brenda Cobb-Schmidt."

"Okay. Okay." Jeb tried to process what Laurie Chase had just said. "I gotta tell ya, Miss Chase, for as far-fetched as your story seems to be, I'm inclined to believe you. Which means that the real question is this: Do you believe that the senator has what she says she has?"

"Based on what Tito just told us – that she and Michaels were in on this from the get-go – then yes, it makes perfect sense that she would. And now she is luring Kinley and Harper back to the States with it."

"Then what do you think her endgame is? It seems to me that if she does have it, what will clear your friends' names will most likely implicate her in all of this. And I don't think that she is about to do that, ya know?"

"No, she's not. And that brings us to the most likely and dreadful of conclusions," Laurie fretted. "Kinley Devereaux and Harper Rowe are walking right into a trap...and I can't even remember my own boyfriend's freaking telephone number to call him and warn him about it."

"Alright. Let's just relax a minute," Crool said. "Now's not the time to be losing our heads over lost cell phones and forgotten phone numbers. We've got ways around that."

"I know you do. I just need to know how long this is going to take."

"We'll get to that in due time, Miss Chase. Our bigger problem is this: The police are outside, and they are led by a fiery spark plug of a woman named Aline Rapido, and she is going to want her pound of flesh. Inside here, we have a major drug lord: you"—he pointed at Tito—"and a big time arms dealer: you"—Jeb pointed at Big James.

"So, here's what we're going to do," he continued. "Now pay close attention because I'm gonna go fast. Rapido wants you, Big James, but we're going to give her the drug lord and his wife instead. No offense, Mr. Gray, but Tito's the bigger fish in this pond."

"No offense taken," Big James put up his hands. "None at all."

"Good, because I'm going to tell her that I need you to come to the States with us. After all, you're a witness to all this craziness.

"Number two, you and her"—he pointed to Laurie—"make a great team. You two had the stones to break into a drug dealer's safe house and take him and his family hostage and put down all of his armed guards in the process." Crool looked over at Baldwin. "Let's face it, Dave, you and I were here to help, but we were never anything more than a well-armed distraction. But you two"—he looked back to Laurie and Big James—"I don't know if I should be impressed or sorely afraid."

"I helped a leetle beet," Diego spoke up.

Jeb looked at him and nodded. "Good for you, chum."

"Okay, let me make sure I've got this straight," Laurie said. "We're going to give Tito and his wife over to the cops. Big James and I are with you, headed back to the States." She looked at the three children that were still sitting on the floor. "What do we do with them?"

"I weell take them," Diego volunteered.

"No." Tito and Mitra objected loudly.

"Uh, you two don't get a say in any of this," Jeb let them know. "Just sit there and be quiet and let the people who aren't about to go to jail for seventy years figure this out."

Crool looked at Diego and asked him, "Why should you get the children?"

"They are my cousins. Family should be weeth family."

"Is this true?" Jeb asked Laurie. "Is he really their cousin?"

"God's honest truth, Agent Crool. He *is* their cousin."

"Great. I mean, I don't really know how all this works down here in South America, but if he's family, ain't no reason why the kids can't stay with him until all this gets sorted out."

Tito looked at Diego with resentment and outrage.

Diego just smiled and said, "Don't worry, Tito. I weell take care of them like they are my very own."

"All right, then, let's get 'em up and move 'em out, people," Jeb ordered. "And, Miss Chase, all of this is probably going to take a little bit of time to get ironed out. So in the interim I'll see if we can't find a computer, and Dave can help you pull up your cell phone bill online so you can get your boyfriend's phone number off of it. Give him a call. Let him know what he and his buddy are getting ready to walk into."

"Thank you, Agent Crool. Thank you."

Agent Baldwin walked Tito and Mitra out.

Agent Crool took Laurie and Big James into his custody.

Diego del Fuento got down on the floor next to his three cousins and began the long road of building a relationship with them.

"Oh, Agent Crool, I almost forgot," snickered James Gray. "We tied up about four or five of Tito's goons and put them in the utility room back there."

Jeb shrugged. "I'm sure the police will find them at some point."

61

PUTTING THE DOGS DOWN

Harper and Kinley peeked into the hallway long enough to see the first of the men step foot into the target zone, then the two wetwork agents backed out of sight. Devereaux held up four fingers...then three...then two...then one.

The two assassins fell to their knees out into the hallway and began firing. Kinley put a bullet through the forehead of the first man. The second and third men were walking side-by-side behind him. Kin took out the one on the right, and Harper riddled the man on the left with four or five kill shots. The last two men had enough time draw their weapons and get off one shot each before their final curtain call. The five bodies laid lifeless on the floor.

Harper stood to his feet, adrenaline pumping, screaming at the top of his lungs as he ran up to the quintet of corpses and emptied what bullets he had left into their worthless bodies and threw down his guns on top of them for good measure.

"I wish I had some gasoline and matches because I'd set these cretins on fire and just let this whole place burn to the ground."

"Harp," Devereaux called out from behind him.

"Yeah?"

"I'm hit."

Harper spun on his heels to see his friend laying in the fetal position on the floor. He had been shot, and he was bleeding badly.

Taralyn Tharp made a left turn onto the road that ran in front of the orphanage. She had a little over two blocks to go. Derek Cooke was in the passenger's seat.

"Hey, if you two can hear me," he said, "we'll be pulling up to the house in about ten seconds. We see the two bogeys. Getting ready to take them out." Cooke looked over at Taralyn. "Just pull up next to them, okay?"

"Okay."

"I'm going to get out and start talking to them. I want you to come around the front of the van and take them out. I'll have them so distracted, they'll never see you coming."

"Okay."

Cooke scrambled out of the passenger's seat and into the back of the van.

Taralyn slowed the ride down carefully on the snow-covered street, but even using the utmost caution, she was unable to keep the van from sliding sideways and almost clipping the two men standing alongside the roadway.

It was the perfect opening for Cooke.

Derek came out of the van's side door and began apologizing profusely. "Oh my goodness, are you okay? Are you guys all right? I am so sorry about that. These streets are something else, aren't they? You two guys might not want to stand so close to the road..."

Taralyn came around the front of the van and felled both men with two head shots each.

"...because you could very easily get hurt, or even worse...killed."

"Nice work," Tara slapped Cooke on the back. "Now let's clear these bodies out of sight before the doctors show up with the rest of the kids."

The two dragged the bodies across the street and tossed them into a snow drift.

"Somebody's in for a real treat when the spring thaw comes."

As if on cue, the doctors and the children appeared the minute Tara and Derek returned to the van.

Dr. Riddle carried the unconscious girl, while Dr. McCoy and Dr. Clements did their best to bring the other three children through the hip-deep snow. Taralyn and Derek quickly joined them to lend a hand.

"Kin? Harp? Are you guys reading us?" Taralyn asked.

"I'm reading you. Kinley's down."

"What? His com is down, or he's down?"

"He's been shot."

"I'm fine," Kinley argued.

"What happened?" Taralyn asked, continuing to shepherd the children into the van.

"He got shot, but it looks like a through and through," Harper said. "Actually, check that. It's a through and through, through and through. It went through his cell phone, and then it went through his hip. There's a lot of blood, but I think he'll be alright. I'm performing some Time Life home surgery on him now."

"You better be careful. If there are parts of his cell phone in his leg, it could get infected."

"Or it could be a good hotspot."

"I'm serious," Taralyn warned.

"And I'm serious, too, when I say get those kids and those doctors out of here. I didn't want to bring this up before, but if anything would have happened to any of those docs, Constance would have killed me herself."

"Okay, we're loaded up and ready. Do you want us to swing back by here and pick you up?"

"No, we expect more not-so-friendlies to be showing up before too long. I'm gonna finish cleaning this wound and take Hopalong here back to Constance's place. Just meet us back there when you're through."

"We'll see ya there."

Leniency

Luckinka Dvorsky and Harper Rowe finished cleaning and bandaging Kinley's gunshot wound and got him up on his feet. Harper went and grabbed their two snowsuits.

"So you will leave now?" Lu asked.

"Yeah, we're outta here," Harper said.

"You are not going to kill me, too?" she asked.

Harper looked at Lu with a great deal of concern. "I want to thank you. You came through when we needed you to. So, here's a thimbleful of advice for you. These men we put down here today, they're not the bosses. They're the runners. Eventually, someone's going to come looking for answers. When they do, if you're still around, I can't imagine a happy ending for you.

"Let someone else answer for this. You and your co-workers need to get whatever money you have and go. Don't look back, because I assure you that there is truly nothing to see here. You've allowed monstrous crimes to be committed in this place. I'm sure your penance will be remembering the faces of those you've wronged for the rest of your days, and in many ways, that is a punishment worse than death. Normally, I would say 'See ya 'round downtown, Lu', but in this particular instance, I'm really hoping that I don't."

Harper put Kinley's arm around his shoulder, and the two men walked out the front door of the orphanage and headed back toward the modeling agency.

"I gotta tell you," Kinley said, "being in there made me feel like I was in the belly of Satan's sewer. There was just nothing of good in that entire place."

"Well, there was some good in that place," Harper amended, "but we got it out. We did what we came here to do. I feel good about that."

"Me, too, I guess. I just know that most or all of those kids are going to be scarred for life. They'll never feel safe again."

"At least we got them to someplace safer. What healing there is that can be done...it can start now."

"Speaking of healing," Kinley said, "I say we get back to Constance's place, get cleaned up, say our goodbyes, and see if we can't find a ride back to the plane. I'm ready to head for home."

"Then let's head for home."

GOODBYES

By the time Derek Cooke and Taralyn Tharp came rolling back into the modeling agency, Kinley and Harper had already turned in their snowsuits, gotten cleaned up, and had Constance do a much better job of cleaning and re-bandaging Kinley's wound.

"How ya feeling, buddy?" Derek asked him.

"Eh," Kin groaned.

"I think he feels worse about his cell phone getting shot than he does about his leg getting shot. He was supposed to call his girl once we were free and clear of here and let her know that we were okay."

"You don't know your girlfriend's number?" Taralyn asked.

"No, I'm afraid that I have turned into yet another victim on technology's long list of casualties."

"What happened to the illegal papers guy? Did he leave already?" asked Harper.

"Yes, make good IDs then take cab home. Very nice man," Coni smiled.

"Did my guy from Interpol get here?" Derek asked.

"Yes, he is in other room with mother and daughter. Taking statements now," Constance answered.

"What's the prospects of you and your models and the Buceks making it to St. Thomas tonight?"

"I will let Buceks stay here tonight. In morning, I will make them up even better than already are. Will leave out after that. Will be fine."

"I can't thank you enough, Constance. You came through for me – for all of us – in a big way."

"And you return snowsuits in good condition. Get children safe. Is very good, Harper Rowe," Ondracek smiled.

Taralyn came over and extended her hand to Constance. "Thank you for all your help. For helping us and for helping my friends."

"Welcome."

"Tara, were you planning on flying back to the States via commercial lines?"

"Well, I do have to return the rental car."

"Those cameras probably picked up your face at the orphanage," Kinley said, "and who knows who will have had a look at them by the time you're able to fly out of here. Why don't you just hop a ride with us."

"What about the rental car?"

"Did you get the insurance on it?"

"Of course."

"Then just call them when we land and report it stolen. Tell them the last place you parked it. They'll find it."

"Okay, then I guess I'm with you guys."

"Well, Derek Cooke," Harper sighed, "I'm guessing it's time for us to be hitting the road."

"Can I give you a ride somewhere?"

"Well, we might be a bit off the beaten path. The plane we flew in on isn't exactly at a local airport."

"Wait," Cooke squinted his eyes and smiled. "Let me guess: private plane? Landed on an airstrip about 30-35 minutes from here?"

"It's been a long day, but, yeah, that does sound about right," Harper answered. "I'm going to go out on a limb and figure you know something about it because you're not *that* good of a guesser. I remember our days together when you *weren't* Derek Cooke, and you could barely guess which one was Cherry Coke and which one was Vanilla Coke."

"To be fair," objected Cooke, "where I grew up in the former Soviet Union, those two tasted very similar. As far as where your plane is, let's just say that I have been slowly shifting out of the hired gun business and shifting into the real estate business. Just so happens that the airstrip you guys landed on is one of my holdings. One of my people called me and reported the plane. I was actually planning on taking a run out there today and see what was going on, but...I guess I got sidetracked."

"Well, it is just about dark out."

"I'll run you on out there. My car's got all-wheel drive. We should be fine."

"Well, cool. Offer accepted."

"Coni, I'm gonna run these three on outta here," Cooke told Ondracek. "Don't let my boy from Interpol leave till I get back. I want to make sure that he's got everything he needs before he heads out."

Eliska Lukasik threw her arms around Taralyn and hugged her tightly. "Thank you, my best friend. Thank you for helping my friends get new life. I am sad to see you go."

"Once things get settled, Ellie, I will come back. I miss you already."

One last round of hugs, handshakes, and goodbyes with Constance, and the gang was on their way to the plane that would be taking them home.

"I cannot even begin to tell you how ready I am to be back in the contiguous, Kin."

"I am with you a hundred percent on that, my good man. Let's head back to America: land of the free and the home of the perpetually offended."

A WORD FROM DOC

Thank you for reading *Chasing Liberation*.
I hope you enjoyed it.

Please read on, because I've included an excerpt
from *Chasing Redemption,* the final installment in the
Boom!!...Killers. series.

I occasionally send newsletters with details on new
releases, special offers, and other bits of news relating to
my characters. If you would like to sign up to the mailing
list, please go to:

www.docephraimbates.com or
www.goldenalleypress.com/boom-killers-series

You can make a difference . . .

Reviews are the most powerful weapon I have when it
comes to getting my books noticed. Honest reviews help
bring them to the attention of other readers.

If you've enjoyed this book, please consider leaving a
review on Amazon.com.

Doc

ABOUT THE AUTHOR

Doc Ephraim Bates is the author of the popular *Boom!!...Killers.* series.

He has been writing comedic action thrillers since age fourteen. The youngest of seven sons, Doc mastered the three skills most valuable to his assassin characters: maintaining a sense of humor, learning how to take a beating, and the art of not getting caught.

Doc makes his online home at www.docephraimbates.com.

You can connect with him on Facebook at www.facebook.com/DocEphraimBates.

If the mood strikes you, send him an email at doc@docephraimbates.com.

If you enjoyed *Chasing Liberation*,
please keep reading for an exciting preview of

CHASING REDEMPTION

Boom!!...Killers.
SERIES BOOK #4

Doc Ephraim Bates

Available in print and ebook
from Golden Alley Press

Coming 2019

Worst Morning Ever

With a Beemer like hers, all she had to do was press a button on her key fob to start the car and melt off the snow and ice.

But, of course, of all days for the thing to not work...it just had to be today.

She hit the button over and over again only to get the same result: nothing.

"Ugh, you stupid piece of crap," she said out loud to no one. Still in her pajamas, she pulled on her puffer coat and trudged through the swirling snow to her vehicle.

She stuck the key in the lock to manually unlock the door, then slid in and shut the door behind her. Shivering, she pressed the ignition button. The engine made a horrible sound.

Erica was about to panic when she noticed that all of the auxiliaries were working. The gauges were reading properly, the fan was blowing, even the radio was playing a promo for Senator Brenda Cobb-Schmidt.

"Good Lord, it's only January, and they are already playing campaign ads," she shook her head in disgust. "I just recovered from Christmas carols 24 hours a day...and now this nonsense. Come on, November." She raised her eyebrows and said, "Although you've got my vote for president, Senator Cobb-Schmidt."

And that thought...was the last thought...Erica Bradley ever had.

With twenty inches expected on the ground, most people were being urged to stay home. But some people *had* to go to work.

Erica Bradley was one of those people. She was not a doctor. She was not an officer of the law. She was not a snow plow driver. She was, in fact, an astrophysics engineer.

Erica was paid millions to do the kind of work that she did, but on a day like today, she would have gladly given half a million back just to have someone send a car to drive her to work.

She was the head of a team of experimental theorists at an organization called OMGlobal, which was nothing more than a front for one of the many secret government test labs all across the United States of America.

Just a few years ago, Erica had been a mid-level lackey for NASA at Kennedy Space Center in Orlando, Florida. Little did they recognize the genius they had in their midst. Little did they know that when Erica Bradley went home after work, she was configuring a spacecraft that could set the human race ahead by light years. Little did they know that one day Erica Bradley's name would go down in the annals of history alongside the likes of Benjamin Franklin, Thomas Alva Edison, and Percy Spencer.

At least, that's how it should have been.

What someone did know was that Erica Bradley was a great mother to her two kids. Kids that her ex-husband gave not two craps about when he walked out on them, leaving her on her own to raise a son, Brady, and a daughter, Johnica, who was the spitting image of her mother when she was that age.

Some three years ago, Erica had showed her off-time project to her superiors. Instead of public recognition, they cloaked her idea in secrecy. To keep her on the hook, they rewarded her with her own team at a secure state-of-the-art facility in Minneapolis, where she was to produce a working model of her space shuttle idea. Plus $1.3M annual salary, twelve weeks' vacation, free college tuition for her kids, a luxury condo, and a company car of her choosing.

Erica knew she could have become famous for all time if she had pressed the point, but what good would that have done her and her kids? Getting a patent would probably have taken longer than she had left to live, given she was already in her mid-thirties. Best to give it to NASA, the people that could do the most good with it. Their offer was everything she needed. So she took the deal, and never regretted it.

Although on snowy Minneapolis mornings, she considered regretting it.

HEADED HOME

Bairre Dolan did what he said he would do.

He kept the snow from building up around the plane's wheels, kept the plane's wings de-iced, and had the bird ready for take-off once Kinley and Harper returned. He did not even mind that they had brought their friend, Taralyn Tharp.

Once the trio boarded, the pilot had the plane rolling through the snow and headed back to the States. He flew low enough to stay off the radar until he got it out over the ocean.

In the back of the plane, Kinley, Harper, and Taralyn were talking about what they had just been through. Tara was letting the two assassins know how much she appreciated their help.

"I don't think I will ever get those images out of my head," she said.

"Me either," Kin lamented.

"You guys," she said. "You guys were amazing. The things you did...I knew I came to the right guys to get this job done."

"I'll probably see those kids in my dreams for a while, but, for what it's worth, I know those boys and girls are so much better off now. Constance will make sure of that."

Tara was lost in thought for a few seconds. "If ever there is anything that the two of you need, I will do it. I owe you both big time. I know that you are headed back to the States to get some clarity about Mexico City and the fallout from that. So if there is anything I can do to help further that along, please, let me know."

"Tara, you're golden, baby," Kinley said. He was feeling the effects of the pain meds that Constance Ondracek had administered to him to help with his utter discomfort from being shot while liberating the children from the orphanage back in Prague.

"Yeah, Tara, you're golden...like a properly cooked waffle. Can't believe I got shot," Kin laughed. "The stupid guys got two shots off before we put them down, and one of them happened its way right in and out of me."

"How ya feelin' right about now?" Harper asked.

"Kinda feelin' a little higher than the plane. Kinda feelin' like I can look down on the plane and guide it safely home," Dev said, a glazed look coming over his eyes.

"I think you need to lay down on that couch you're sitting on," Harper recommended.

Kin did not put up a fight. He laid down and closed his eyes. "Wake me up once we're home...and try not to kill anybody, Harper...I need to call Laurie. I miss her," and Kinley was out.

Harper looked at Taralyn. "We need to call Kelly Campbell."

"Why is that?"

"She's the only one that knows what's going on. We're supposed to meet some senator who has an idea about how to clear our names. Kelly is our only contact to her."

"Do you have her number?"

"I sure do. I'll wait for Kin to wake up, and he can call her. She likes him better anyway." Harper picked up his cell phone and began flipping through his contacts. "It's a long flight. You must be tired, too. We'll figure out the finer points of this plan once we've all gotten some sleep."

"What are you going to do?" Tharp asked as she pulled up her footrest and leaned the recliner back.

"I've got someone else that I need to call first. Then I'll join you guys in Slumberland."

After only one ring, Harper heard her answer.

"Harper Rowe, please, tell me that it's you, and you're okay!"

"It's good to hear your voice, Mercedes."

FRUSTRATION

Tenente Aline Rapido was there, waiting for her catch.

Laurie Chase, Big James Gray, Jeb Crool, David Baldwin, Tito del Fuento and his wife had all been brought up from the basement of Tito del Fuento's safe house.

NSA Agent Jeb Crool gave her Tito del Fuento and his wife, and promised her that if she needed anything at all, he would be more than happy to oblige.

For himself, he kept the larger catch of former DEA Agent Laurie Chase, big time gun runner James Gray, and their knowledge of where Kinley Devereaux, Harper Rowe, and Senator Brenda Cobb-Schmidt might be showing up.

Agent David Baldwin, for his part, did what Jeb had promised he would do. He brought Laurie Chase over to a laptop, and the two of them were able to find her boyfriend Kinley Devereaux's cell phone number.

Using a spare burner phone from Agent Baldwin, Laurie tried Kinley's number over and over again only to get the same result: the call went directly to voicemail.

"Unbelievable," Chase finally gave up. "How can he have his phone turned off at a time like this?"

"Could be a lot of reasons," Baldwin tried to encourage. "He's coming out of a huge adventure. I mean, give me a chance to save orphans from becoming sex slaves, and I would definitely want some down time."

"Do you think that's it?" Chase asked. "He's just spent, and he will call me later?"

"Absolutely," Baldwin smiled. "I can't imagine any other reason why a guy wouldn't call you."

"All I know is that until I can talk to him, my stomach is going to be in knots."

Agent Jeb Crool had been talking to Tenente Aline Rapido, getting everything squared away with her as far as James Gray and Laurie Chase were concerned. It was easy to do, as Tito del Fuento and his wife, Mitra, were the biggest arrests of Rapido's career. In trade, she willingly allowed Crool to take James Gray into custody.

Crool and Gray finally made their way from the center of the busy scene and over to Laurie Chase and Agent David Baldwin.

"How's things going over there?" Dave asked.

"As far as we're concerned, everything's great. I signed off on a few things to get you and Mr. Gray here free and clear of all this. I told Tenente Rapido that we would make ourselves available in the future in regards to del Fuego's case. She was good with that."

"What about Diego and his being able to keep Tito's kids for now?"

Crool let out a little laugh and looked at Laurie. "I'm going to go out on a limb here and guess that you knew that your little friend has been 'dead' for a couple of years now?"

"I did. Tito killed Diego's wife and children, and he thought he had killed Diego, too."

"So, how did you end up with him?"

"It's a long story," Chase said.

"It's a long plane ride," Jeb countered. "Still, being able to put away the man who killed your entire family and get *his* kids in the process...not the worst ending to a story that I've ever heard."

"Are they going to let him keep Tito's kids?" Baldwin asked.

"Rapido is working on it. She's got some people in the child services division that can pull a few strings. According to Diego, he has a lot of money. Apparently, being dead is a pretty lucrative undertaking," Crool punned. "He says he can get a house for the four of them within the next week or two."

"He'll be fine," Chase commented. "He's just what those kids need."

Aline Rapido came over to the quartet. "Give you and your people a ride somewhere, Agent Crool?"

"Oddly enough, we are both parked about a half mile over that way," Jeb pointed in the appropriate direction. "If you can give us a lift to there, we'll be on our way and out of your hair."

"Right this way then," the *tenente* began walking. "I will say this, Agent Crool. Things certainly have gotten a lot more interesting for me since you got into town."

"It's been a pretty wild ride, some of it a bit more wild than I would have liked," Crool said, alluding to the car wreck that he and Baldwin had been in the night before, compliments of Laurie Chase and Big James Gray. Chase and Gray looked at each other, then back to Jeb.

"Well," Big Time smiled, "the important thing is that we're all okay so we can laugh about it now."

THE SENATOR AND KENT McCLEARY

When his burner phone rang, the caller ID displayed, "Unavailable." Normally, Kent McCleary would have disregarded the call altogether. But since only one person had the number, he answered.

"Hello, Senator," he said. "Are you calling me with an update about Harper Rowe and Kinley Devereaux?"

"No update. Just calling to see how our package is doing."

"The package is fine," assured McCleary. "It's downstairs in the basement all tied up."

"How many men do you have there at the house?"

"Seven, counting me."

"And how many men will you have at the exchange?"

"I could have seven there, too, Senator. I mean, it's just two guys, but since I know how important this is to you, I will have fourteen men at the exchange."

"Mr. McCleary, let me make myself perfectly clear. If anything goes wrong at the exchange, it's going to get messy. My political career will be over, and I promise you that if I go down, you go down with me. So, I don't care if it's *just two guys* that you're going to be dealing with, you make good and sure that you have more than enough men to make sure this situation is taken care of properly."

"Senator, please," Kent said. "You don't need to spend even one second worrying. The exchange will go just the way we planned it. You're going to look like a hero *and* a victim. The country will feel your pain but love your power and resolve. What we are getting ready to do is going to get you elected President of the United States, Senator."

"Yes, it will. I know you and your team will be able to pull this off. I just need to make sure that you understand the gravity of the situation," Brenda paused and took a deep breath. "Tell me that you – without the slightest misgivings – understand the gravity of this situation."

"Boss, I – without the slightest misgivings – understand the gravity of this situation."

"And your team?"

"And my team," McCleary affirmed. "We are just waiting for the go from you, Senator, and a few hours later you'll be the number one news topic all around the globe. You'll shine like the leader that you are, and your poll numbers will jump through the roof."

"One last thing, Kent."

"What's that, Senator?

"Other than you and your men...no survivors at the exchange."

.

ACKNOWLEDGEMENTS

I would like to thank the following people for their help and input on this project: Derek Cooke, Alene Fast, Michael J. Hoffman, Dr. Cyril Jenkins, Sandy Kirkendall, Susan Lincoln, Loren Marsters, Michael Riddle, Laurie Shen, Donna Somerville, PJ Steelman, and Misty VanArsdale.

I would also like to thank you, the reader. Knowing that you take time out of your life to give me the opportunity to entertain you is truly humbling. I hope that I have held up my end of the deal by bringing you some smiles and enjoyment.

To my brother, Bobby, who passed away unexpectedly on August 29, 2017. I have six older brothers, and he was the youngest of those six. After dealing with the initial storm of sorrow of his passing, I learned a sobering but valuable lesson—that when you have a chance to spend time with a loved one or close friends, don't put it off. I loved my brother, but I missed out on way too many opportunities to spend time with him. Bobby was a wonderful husband and a fantastic father, but, most of all, he loved the Lord Jesus Christ and was a faithful servant to Him. He fought the good fight, he finished the course, and he kept the faith. I know that might not be a popular stance nowadays, but where I come from that is a very big deal. Thank you, brother, for a lifetime of great memories and loving your little brother with the kind of unconditional love that all families should know. You are missed. You are loved.

And I would be remiss if I did not thank my amazing friend. I can never be thankful enough for all that you have contributed to this book. I am so sad for what you had to endure. Still, now more than ever, the world needs your light that shines through the darkness as a beacon to us all. You are an inspiration to everyone that knows you. I hope I've done you justice with this story.

www.ingramcontent.com/pod-product-compliance
Lightning Source LLC
Chambersburg PA
CBHW071158100726
47908CB00002B/424